Sleep

Sleeping Partner

Mariah Greene

LIBRIS

An *X Libris* Book

First published by X Libris in 1996

A CIP catalogue record for this book
is available from the British Library.

ISBN 0 7515 1727 5

Photoset in North Wales by
Derek Doyle & Associates, Mold, Clwyd
Printed and bound in Great Britain by
Clays Ltd, St Ives plc

UK companies, institutions and other organisations wishing
to make bulk purchases of this or any other book published
by Little, Brown should contact their local bookshop or the
special sales department at the address below.
Tel: 0171 911 8000.   Fax: 0171 911 8100

X Libris
A Division of
Little, Brown and Company (UK)
Brettenham House
Lancaster Place
London WC2E 7EN

Sleeping Partner

Chapter One

EMMA FOX LOOKED up, distracted from the task at hand, when she heard the deep voice of Roger Metz, head of Mergers and Acquisitions at Morse Callahan, broadcasting itself over the small speaker system installed at various points around the office.

'I know she doesn't want me to make a scene on her last day here,' his detached voice hummed, 'but we can't let our favourite investment banker just walk away without making a little fuss.'

Emma sighed, glanced momentarily at the familiar skyline of downtown Manhattan and turned her attention back to Knox Turner, the young star of arbitrage, who had just licked his lips and pushed his trousers and underwear to the floor and was standing with his erect penis poking rather improbably through the front of his shirt. Knox, she knew, had been waiting for this moment for almost two years and she was not going to let Roger Metz spoil it for both of them. They would just have to live with Roger serenely continuing his monologue.

'. . . and when she joined us from Goldman, Sachs, I remember how fresh she appeared and what a killer she turned out to be. I know plenty of clients and targets who've found out the same – to their cost.'

It being her last day, Emma had vamped herself up a touch more than was normal for a work day, looking more ready for a party. Early that morning she had zipped her curvaceous body into an expensive Dior dress, and that same dress was currently around her hips, as she sat on the edge of her desk with her legs open, waiting for Knox to make the next move. She hoped he wasn't going to lose his nerve after waiting so long, although it would not have surprised her. Emma had come across lots of men on Wall Street who had more to say than to do. Her pussy was pleasantly wet and the promise of Knox and his cock was rather impressive, peeking out as it was from under a striped shirt – Brooks Brothers, most likely. The prospect of sex in the sanctity of Morse Callahan's hallowed offices to the monotone of its figurehead Roger Metz suddenly seemed very attractive.

'. . . and her work on the Colworth takeover generated the most significant amount of fee-income this firm had seen. Until, that is, she completed the Contrelle bid. All of which Morse Callahan rewarded by sharing those profits with the people who generated them. In fact, we've paid her so much in the past that there's nothing we can offer her in the future. Let that be a lesson – for you and for us, I think.'

When Emma told Roger she had decided to quit, he was not as surprised as she had hoped he would be. At first, he seemed more shell-shocked than surprised and later he went through a period of taking it personally. Roger believed in the game and for someone like Emma to go and tell him that she did not – and was ready to get out – was tantamount to tugging the rug from under him. Roger told her that thirty-two was not the age to get out, but Emma could tell that even he knew the argument held little sway. Morse Callahan had made her rich. Period. Emma would not have to work again for the rest of her life. It

2

was that simple. The bank had given her a bright future, just not with them. Roger had upped the stakes by offering increasingly ridiculous sums of money for her to stay and for a few moments she had considered it, then she remembered why she wanted to leave in the first place and politely declined all his offers.

Knox held himself, looking as though he were reassuring himself it wasn't a dream by pinching his cock. His body was work-out lean, his hair brushed back, and he had the kind of smile that opened doors as well as legs. He licked his lips again and moved closer to her, and Emma smiled warmly by way of an invitation for him to do his worst, although she hoped it would be his best. The tip of his cock was less than an inch from her pussy and Emma could feel heat jumping across the small gap between them, drawing them together. She wanted him to plunder her, hoping it would obliterate Roger's voice; and the whole of Morse Callahan, for that matter. The final part of the wind-down.

Over the course of the previous week, one by one, people had stopped calling. Her phone became quiet and she did exit-interviews with the people she was handing over her work to. It satisfied her that she needed to pass over to three people, indicating the magnitude of her effort while at Morse Callahan. Slowly, she withdrew. She had told Roger of her intention to leave six weeks earlier and, following a week of fruitless persuasion, Emma had spent the last five weeks leaving the game. There were only two pieces of unfinished business at Morse Callahan: to accept her leaving gift gracefully and to fuck Knox Turner.

'Do you have to wear that?' she barked at Knox, who had stopped again and was fumbling.

'Everyone needs a little protection, baby,' he said, fiddling with the remote telephone headset, the one that made him look like a telephonist. 'Someone could need to get in touch with me.'

'And I thought you were going to phone your mother,' she said, gripping his hips and guiding his cock into her.

They quickly fell into a powerful jerking rhythm, her position on the edge of the large oak desk making her pussy tight and ultrasensitive.

He leaned into her ear, nibbled on the lobe and breathed hotly into it before speaking.

'Is it true that Lasch is about to go in play? I hear you were teeing them up for Ikon. Is that true?'

She pushed him away and looked at him.

'Knox, tell me this isn't the only reason you're fucking me,' she said, a mix of amusement and irritation in her voice.

His rhythm unabated, being the sort of guy who wouldn't miss a stroke, he said, 'Of course not. But it would be good information to have.'

'It would be inside information, Knox. Just settle for being inside, huh? Besides, you couldn't trade on it for Morse anyway. The SEC aren't that stupid. Unless you've got a little trading account of your own somewhere in the Caymans?'

'You still haven't answered my question.'

Emma ground herself more firmly onto Knox's cock which had hardened noticeably at the talk of hostile takeovers.

'What about Chinese walls, Knox? We're not meant to talk about things like that.'

'In arbitrage, we call you the Great Wall of China.'

'Really. I'd say what we call you in M&A, but then I don't recall ever hearing your name mentioned in our department.'

'You really are a . . .'

Knox's headset bleeped and he paused, his cock in mid-thrust. Emma clutched at him, tugging him closer to her.

4

'Hi,' Knox was saying. 'No, we went short on that one. You're kidding. It did what? Jesus, that's fucking amazing.'

His thrusting had begun again, somewhere in the middle of the obviously good news, and Emma felt his cock swell inside her, the onset of an orgasm. She wasn't prepared to let him have all the fun and she ground herself against him, moving urgently up and down.

Off in the background, now at an almost subliminal level, she was conscious of Roger Metz finishing up his impromptu speech over the speakers. Roger had nothing if not impeccable timing. There would be just enough time to finish off Knox and make herself look good for the presentation.

If Knox had been pushed over the edge by some piece of stock news, what it did for Emma was completely the opposite. Emma had thought many times about what it would be like to be free of Morse Callahan and the world of M&A, but it was at that moment, as her orgasm bloomed, that it really touched her for the first time. She was out of the game and she loved it. Her future would be whatever she decided to make it. As she came, she gripped onto Knox, her pussy pulsing round his spurting cock. She called out wildly, making him groan helplessly in time like they were animals. She rode him and her orgasm expertly, the feel of it more intense than any she could recently remember. And then she realised why that feeling was so intense and fresh. Literally, she did not have a care in the world.

Emma dispatched Knox quickly, not wanting to linger with him and knowing he was most likely keen to go and parade for everyone. She did not mind this, but drew the line when he asked for her knickers as a trophy. Those arbitrage boys, she thought. With Knox gone, there was only the leaving speech and gift-giving to get through and she pulled her knickers back on and went into her private bathroom.

At Morse Callahan, her power had been such that she had been able to have the bathroom remodelled in a soft gold marble, giving it a look both sumptuous and feminine. She put on the light over the mirror and looked at herself for what would be the last time in this setting. It was a flattering light, but she did not need flattering and she knew it.

Leaning into the mirror she studied her face, imagining it not at Morse Callahan. Out of the game. How would she translate to another context? she wondered, savouring the prospect. She rubbed a finger over one of her carefully shaped eyebrows and blinked several times. A grey blue, her eyes were darker at the edge of the iris, the colour of corn near the centre. Emma applied the gentlest dusting of powder and then freshened her lipstick, pouting her already full lips at her reflection.

Emma enjoyed the self-confidence that casual beauty gave her, the way she could lean her head towards someone and collude empathically with them, making them feel comfortable with her. Her computer-like mind assimilated and processed data at an incredible speed and when she needed or chose to, she could also be hard. In her looks, there was the faintest hint of this, a clue as to what lay beneath, but she was confident and controlled to the extent that she alone chose when and where to use it.

Teasing at her hair, she wondered if she would find a hairdresser back in London who would be able to lighten her dark brown hair in the same way and use the scissors to give the short, centre-parted effect that swept behind her ear, only the wispiest side curls visible at the front. As soon as she arrived, she would seek out a recommendation and go to a salon, telling the stylist that this is how she wanted it cut when she came back in five weeks. She was ready and gathered the last of her things into the make-up bag and went to the door.

Before she turned off the bathroom light, she turned, taking one last look at it, the gold seeming to oscillate at a frequency that was so attuned to her. She pulled her shoulders a touch, her breasts part of the graceful line of her whole body. She smoothed the black Dior dress around herself, her stomach tight under her palms. She turned side-on to the mirror and admired the firm behind and the musculature of her upper legs, just visible in the mirror.

'One more time,' she said to herself, flicking off the light and making her way out into the main office.

Despite requesting minimal fuss, Emma was pleased to see she had drawn such a big crowd, so big that some faces were barely familiar. In the midst of it was Roger Metz. A few whistles went up and mild applause broke out when she appeared from her office. Business over for the day, people were starting to relax, many vicariously enjoying Emma's leaving and using it as a way to play out their own fantasies. She made her way to the front where Roger Metz awaited, beaming through a coarse forest of beard. He raised his hand to call the murmuring to order. Just a year off fifty, he had the sort of stature that could silence a room with the simple move of an arm.

'I'm aware,' he began, 'that I stand between you guys and the cocktail hour and you've heard it all already, so I'll be as brief as I can. I'm sorry to see Emma go and I really wish I'd persuaded her to stay.'

Roger Metz paused. He did not seem lost for words but, on the contrary, too full of them. For a moment, he appeared to be considering whether or not to say something and then his face showed that he had thought better of it.

'Emma, because she's Emma, has a plane to catch, so

I'll cut right to it. Thank you. Good luck. I'll miss you and I know I speak for almost everyone.'

This time, he paused for the laughter. Emma surveyed the crowd of about forty people and she looked at the expectant faces, feeling their eyes on her. She knew that, in the most part, she would not miss any of them.

'We, Morse Callahan, your friends here, have bought you a gift as a way of saying thanks and think of us from time to time – every pun intended.' He handed her a box perfectly wrapped in tight silver foil.

Emma unwrapped it and opened the box. It was a watch by Patek Philippe. One she had mentioned to another woman colleague what seemed like ages ago. She found the face of the woman and smiled at her knowingly, impressed that she had taken such notice of a small comment. Her colleague was one of very few women in the wash of faces. She took a breath and launched into her pre-prepared words.

'This must be the longest goodbye in history,' she said. 'I feel like we've been partying every night for the last ten days and I'm too old for it. A special thank you to Frank for taking me to a little-known Midtown bar – it's so nice to know what teenagers are wearing these days. All parties stop somewhere and I suppose this is it for this particular one. I will miss you all. Almost all. My time at Morse Callahan has been one of the great learning experiences of my life. I'll think of you and I'll let you know when I've found my next great learning experience. As you know, I'm horribly unsentimental about these things and I've already said individual goodbyes to you all, so now I can say a communal goodbye. Thank you.'

There was more polite applause and Roger touched her arm.

'Do you have all your things?' he asked.

'Yes. Just a briefcase and one big overnight bag. The

rest is being shipped.'

'I'll walk you upstairs if you don't mind?'

'Of course I don't mind.'

As they made their way through the crowd, one or two people said goodbye or patted her on the shoulder. She gathered her coat and the two bags while Roger waited discreetly at the door. In the lift, on the way up to the roof, he said little. She knew he was still wishing she had stayed. Even big bear Roger with his beard and smile hadn't been able to persuade her.

'This feels like when I gave my daughter away,' he said finally, breaking the low whirring semi-silence of the elevator.

'You can throw confetti or rice if you want, Roger.'

'Just before we left the house to go to the church, I said to her, "you can still change your mind. Even now. I won't mind or even be angry". The same applies for you, Emma.'

'Roger, tell me you didn't ride with me just to do this?'

He smiled and said nothing. The elevator gently thudded to a halt.

Out on the roof, the Manhattan skyline glowing in the dusk like the embers of a dying fire, the wind was high and the noise of the helicopter made it difficult to say very much.

'Thank you for arranging this,' she said to him. 'I could have gone in a limo.'

'Oh please,' he said, waving an arm dismissively. 'I even called to see if they'd hold the afternoon Concorde for you, but they wouldn't. You'll have to make do with first class.' His smile became a laugh.

'Thanks for everything, Roger. I'll be in touch.'

She leaned over and planted a kiss on his hairy cheek. Then she darted across the short piece of tarmac, the black Chanel coat flapping in the wind of the helicopter's rotors, and jumped in.

9

As it took off and she was lifted vertically into the darkening sky, she saw Roger squinting up and was unable to tell if he was smiling or grimacing. She looked at the Patek Philippe watch and read the inscription on the back: 'From your friends at MC.' Carefully, she slipped it into its box and then into a compartment in her briefcase, wondering if she would ever look at it again.

Chapter Two

ON A COOL Thursday morning in the Kings Road, Wall Street might as well have been a million miles away rather than just several thousand. Only two days after arriving back for good, Emma Fox had moved into a new flat, bought different clothes and made contact with no one at all. She paced decisively towards her destination, remembering the Lomax Property Agency from her only visit to it four months earlier. That had been a fleeting and secretive sojourn, over from Wall Street and back again in just three days, all courtesy of Concorde. The last time, she had been in London for longer than the total time she had now been back and she missed that transitory feeling. The Patek Phillipe watch from Morse Callahan was still in a box somewhere and she had even replaced her normal Raymond Weil with an older, more kitsch watch that was a lot more expensive than it looked. Just like I need to be, she had thought when donning it that morning: more expensive than I look. Coming to the heavy glass door of the Lomax Property Agency, she pushed it open and crossed the threshold, exchanging the noise of the street for the burr of the small office.

The reception area was large and comfortable, like a small living room in a well furnished flat. Three sofas, a glass-topped table with neatly folded unread magazines and several rented plants divided the space into restful chunks. A large low desk marked the boundary of the reception and the office beyond, but there was no one sitting at it. Emma stood and waited, looking at the open-plan office and its strategic partitions giving a modicum of privacy to each desk. Ten desks in all, five down each side. This she remembered. Her last visit had been late at night and the place had felt empty and lifeless, lacking the buzz it now had.

'Can I help you?'

Not having seen the owner of the voice, Emma had formulated the accent and manner of it into an instant vision of a stuffy man in his late forties with a ruddy face and an angry moustache. Instead, she saw a blustering man in his twenties, longish black hair brushed back and held to his head with a touch too much gel. He had the gangling awkwardness, clumsy dress sense and supreme self-confidence that Emma could only associate with good schooling and breeding too close to one's own gene pool. All of that, Emma had established before he reached the reception area. This one must be Ed Shields, she thought.

'I'm Emma Fox. I'm here to see Catherine Lomax.'

'The new girl,' he said, more to himself than her.

It seemed as though this revelation, of being a new girl, had removed her from the public domain and placed her as fair game in his territory. She was not a potential customer so that made her just a potential. Seeing this predator in pin-striped trousers with braces and a striped shirt, Emma was haunted by the familiarity of a hundred Wall Street brokers, all able to eat this boy before breakfast but still no match for her. Making no attempt to move or speak, he stood and stared at her, looking her over as though she were a car he might want to buy. Emma could almost feel his attempts to exude charm and squeeze magnetism from himself, as though constipated with lust. The stare seemed to say, 'I saw you first and now you're mine.' Immediately, Emma was gripped by the urge to inform him just how far out of his league he was, but she realised she could not. The fact that he had just accepted her as the new girl and up for grabs was a pleasing confirmation that she would be able to pass herself off as plain Emma Fox. She would be able to fit in naturally, arousing no suspicion. Another part of her knew, however, that this boy thought no mountain too high and that she could have been Elizabeth Taylor and been given the same once-over.

'I'm Ed Shields,' he said to her, smiling and extending a hand, which was clammy. 'Why don't you come through?'

Several people raised their eyes to look at her. Her arrival had been anticipated, she sensed. Phones rang politely and keyboards were tapped with the irregular metre of those who could not really type. The backbeat of office life was the same everywhere, though this office was more plush than many Emma had seen, designed to convey the correct image for the Lomax Property Agency and its clients.

'Far to come?' Ed was asking.

'No, not really. This is a nice office,' she said, deflecting his question.

'Hmm,' he responded, seeming more distracted by the front of her dress. 'Here we are.'

The door to Catherine Lomax's office was ajar and she sat behind her desk, looking at some papers that were placed neatly on its surface.

'Catherine, this is Emma Fox. The new girl,' Ed said, more politely than when he had used the phrase to Emma.

'Come in, please do,' Catherine said, a tone of formality in her voice. 'Close the door on your way

13

out, Ed. Thank you.' She gave him a benevolent smile as he left.

After a few seconds Emma broke the silence.

'The new girl?'

They both laughed and then Catherine was out from behind her desk and beside Emma, giving her a quick embrace and kissing her on the cheek.

'I would have called you this morning,' Catherine was saying, 'but I thought you'd like a chance to settle in. I wasn't sure if you would definitely be here today, but I told people you would. I wasn't sure if you'd even come at all.'

'Don't be silly, Catherine. I don't back out, you know me.'

'Well, you've met Ed at least. Your new workmate, but don't let that put you off,' Catherine smiled, not the merely benign one she had given Ed, but one with a genuine warmth and depth.

'You look great,' Emma said.

It was no idle comment on Emma's part. At thirty-six Catherine was four years older than Emma, but she was gently on the way to a maturity that seemed almost unexpected to her, and which would be all her own, shaping and extending her beauty into the future. Catherine's hair cascaded in long curls that fell to below her shoulders, touching her face at the sides and framing it so that it would not have looked out of place staring into the lens of a camera. Catherine's face was beautiful in a classic sense, rendering Emma's mental image of her into black and white photographs of Hollywood stars of the thirties and forties. The femme fatale, ready to stir up a little trouble if necessary.

For ten years, on and off, they had kept in touch with each other. They had met at a wedding. A distant cousin of Emma's was marrying a friend of Catherine's then husband, Victor Lomax. That was how tenuous their connection had been – as random as a seating plan, but they had engaged in conversation and both Victor and Emma's date at the wedding were forgotten. They promised to stay in touch and it was something of a surprise to them both when they actually did, exchanging one or two letters a year, having the odd phone call and the less frequent meeting. Emma enjoyed hearing about the charmed circles that Catherine and Victor moved in, the blasé elegance of their lifestyle and the ease and comfort with which they accepted it. It was a good long-distance friendship that did not place demands on either of them.

Then, nearly six years ago, Emma received a call from Catherine telling her that Victor had died. The light aircraft he so loved to pilot had crashed in the South of England. For a while afterwards, nearly two years, their contact was less frequent. Emma made every offer of help she could but sensed that Catherine needed room and time to set things right. She understood and knew she would have been the same. Emma waited and did not rush things, ready to help if Catherine needed it. The various Lomax interests were wound up, a mixture of good and bad companies that seemed to cancel each other out. At the end of it, Catherine was left, mostly by her own choice, with one of Victor's first businesses, the Lomax Property Agency. Dealing in property in the centre of London for an élite client base built up through contacts of Victor's, the agency made enough money to augment what was left over from Victor's estate.

To Emma, it was as though she and Catherine had passed each other, one ascending and the other descending. Emma knew she was on the path to a successful career and had always thought of Catherine as something of a role model, an object lesson in how to handle success. Then, just as Emma felt herself on

15

the way up, Catherine seemed to tumble down after Victor's death. She was far from poor, but her life changed without Victor, and the winding up of his interests, the selling off, seemed to Emma to be Catherine's way of throwing off the ghosts. Emma's and Catherine's lives had different trajectories and directions and other than their own willingness to stay in contact with each other, there would have been no reason for them to know each other.

The suggestion that Emma become a silent partner in the agency, providing it with a cash injection, had started as a throwaway line in a phone call. They could not even remember which one of them had suggested it first. But it had played on Emma's mind for days afterwards, all kinds of scenarios running through her brain. Another phone conversation followed quickly in the wake of the first and suddenly they were talking details, both of them fired up and feeding off the other's energy. It was Catherine who had put the final twist into things, suggesting that if Emma really were giving up Morse Callahan and the life of an investment banker, why didn't she come dirty her hands at Lomax before parting with any money? Emma thought about it, liked the idea, but added just one caveat. 'I will,' Emma told her, 'but it has to be our secret.' In her years at Morse Callahan, where she had been involved in numerous takeovers, the opportunity to be so close to a company had never presented itself.

'You settled into the flat fine, then? I would have greeted you personally, but I thought it better to let you get on with things.'

'I've not been here long enough to feel settled,' Emma said. 'It's been like a secret-agent movie – the flat keys in the envelope, the notes on the agency. I was waiting for the self-destructing tape. I'm a girl with a mission. Thank you for stocking with groceries – I'd forgotten what half of them are called after all this time.'

'Oh, just the basics for you to survive. I hope you'll be happy there for a little while. I've passed the bank details onto Sonia, so you are officially on the payroll as short-term temporary, renewable month on month. Where do you want to start earning some of this princely amount?'

Emma thought about the question and reached to her briefcase to retrieve the information file Catherine had sent to her. She opened it and flicked her eyes across the page, the bulk of the information, and certainly all the important data, already stored in her memory.

'What have you told the people here?'

'What we agreed. You're Emma Fox, a bank clerk made redundant and a very distant family friend of Victor's. You are working here in the rental section, temporarily until a proper job comes along, learning about the estate agency business.'

'Nobody has any suspicions?'

'No. A few eyebrows were raised when I mentioned Victor, as though nepotism was at work from beyond the grave. Did the notes I sent you help at all?' Catherine asked. 'It felt like writing my auto-biography.'

'They were useful. I need to get into the middle of it all to see how it really works. Your little notes on the people were very politic. I wouldn't have expected Ed to be quite as priapic, for instance, but the clues were there.'

'Ed deals with the rental side, along with Malcolm. To be frank, it's the easiest part of the agency to drop you into like this.'

'Are they comfortable with it?'

'Malcolm is careful. He won't upset the order, although his feathers were somewhat ruffled because he wasn't able to interview you. Ed likes to think of himself as the ungovernable force, the thrusting young

17

blade. A lot of the time, that works to everyone's advantage. He might try and rile you or be a little obstructive.'

'I can handle that,' Emma said.

The agency was split into three sections: UK business, foreign business and the administration section. UK business was both sales and rentals while the foreign section dealt only in sales, mainly in the USA but also in Europe. Underpinning this was the finance and administration function that looked after contracts and fee-billing. In the UK section, three people, including Ed Shields, worked for Malcolm Dean. Jane Bennett was in charge of foreign properties and Sonia Morgan looked after administration for the agency. Each had one person working for them. Eight people in total. Nine including Emma and ten counting Catherine Lomax.

'How long would you like to . . .' Catherine reached for a word – 'observe?'

'Only a few weeks, Catherine. It'll put some blood into the numbers. The data I've seen from you looks fine but I'd like to delve deeper.'

Catherine frowned. 'That's really as deep as I get into the numbers. The sheets I sent you were photocopies of the exact ones I get from Sonia each month. You know as much as I do.'

'You have an accountant?'

'Oh no. We went full circle on that. Before Victor diversified his business interests, Sonia looked after them. Then, there was a group accountant – all that talk of expanding the share capital. It was one long fight between the accountant and Sonia. When the group dissolved, Sonia took over again.'

'Is she a qualified accountant?'

'Oh yes.'

Emma was surprised: she had assumed that the Lomax Property Agency would have an independent accountant, someone she would be able to talk to or have Catherine talk to. It had simply not occurred to her that Sonia would do it. All big companies have accountants, she thought. Then another thought came. Lomax was not a big company. From Emma's perspective, someone as entrenched in the business as Sonia Morgan was not a favourable person to hold such financial information. Any attempt to retrieve it could arouse suspicion. Everyone in the agency would ultimately know if she did become an investor in it, but in Emma's experience, she was in a much stronger position while the possibility of a takeover was still secret. It may have been quite a difference, the Wall Street politics of mergers and acquisitions, putting companies into play and asset-stripping, but Emma believed that in the case of a modest investment in the Lomax Property Agency, the basic philosophy and tactics were no different.

'Is there going to be any way I can get more detailed financial information?'

'No.'

Emma would have to get the information some other way, she knew. When the possibility of her investing in Lomax had first become serious, Catherine had been very free and trusting with the information she had provided. But Emma was not comfortable with what she knew about Lomax: there was a troubling downward trend, almost indiscernible, that was hard to pin down based on the financial information she had. Emma hoped that working in the agency would give some substance to the figures. It was imprudent to say it, so Emma did not, but it was alarming to think that so much of Catherine's destiny rested in the hands of Sonia Morgan. From the file, Emma knew that Sonia was well compensated in terms of pay, but there were no other benefits, no partnership status or stake in the agency. Emma speculated as to how that might make her or the other two senior managers feel.

'We'll arrange a sort of welcome dinner for one night next week, introduce you to the agency. This morning, I thought I could introduce you to Malcolm and let him look after you. If I spirit you around too much, people will think it's odd.'

'That sounds good. I'm assuming I have a desk?'

'Oh yes. There's a desk, phone and a computer with the things you asked for.'

'Can we have lunch today, to go over a few things? I won't mention it to anyone here.'

'Of course. I'll have Ian book somewhere.'

Ian Cameron, Emma knew, worked on the front desk and also for Sonia Morgan, a receptionist-cum-administrative assistant. Actually going to work in the agency after speaking with Catherine about it and reading the file was like going to see the movie of a book she had read. Would all the characters be the way she imagined them? Ed had not disappointed her.

'Malcolm, this is Emma Fox.'

'Oh yes,' he said, rising from behind his desk and shaking her hand. 'Malcolm, Malcolm Dean. I head up the UK section.'

'Pleased to meet you,' Emma said, gripping his hand firmly.

They kept eye contact for a moment longer. He was forty or so, she recalled. Well-dressed in a frayed-around-the-edges way, he did not have a particularly strong presence, seeming more eager to please and ready to go with the flow. Again, Emma was making instinctual guesses based only on a handshake and a few lines penned by Catherine. Malcolm's hair was a soft brown and styled like Melvyn Bragg, the school-teacher-from-the-early-eighties look. He was married with two young children and looked every bit the fledgling father, ready to grab a football and encourage his son to kick it around. Emma checked herself for making too many snap judgements, even though she tended to be right more often than not.

Catherine withdrew and left her with Malcolm to do introductions. Malcolm introduced her to Ed, Emma informing him she had already had the pleasure. The other two men who worked for him were Tony Wilson and Dominic Lester. Tony and Dominic looked after sales while Ed was responsible for rentals, along with some paternalistic support from Malcolm. Emma picked up on a father–son camaraderie between Malcolm and Ed. Tony and Dominic were polite and seemed at a loss as to what to say to her beyond a welcome.

'Is the agency split boy–girl as well as UK–Foreign?' she asked Malcolm lightly.

They were in the small kitchen area, he pouring her some coffee from a large glass filter jug, half-empty, condensation clinging in droplets to the empty part.

'Sort of,' he said, nodding vigorously in what Emma could already tell would become an irritating habit to her. 'Tony and Dominic are very capable on the sales side and Ed brings a certain flair to the rentals. Rentals are a different market for us and we have clients who expect a maximum of flexibility. With the sales of some of these houses, the cycle can often take months of coordination and cajoling. It takes a lot of patience and nerve. Has Catherine given you an overview?'

'Yes, she has. Very impressive. I'm looking forward to helping out.'

'What made you want to work at an estate agent's?'

'I used to work for a bank in a clerical job and I was there for nearly ten years. It got to the point that when they offered me redundancy, it was too good not to turn down. But I didn't want to fritter it away or end up never leaving the house, so I was determined to get back to work quickly.'

'It's something of a jump, though,' he said to her.

'I've had enough of banks and big companies,' she said. 'I want to work somewhere smaller. This part of the property market seemed interesting and I knew Catherine's husband.'

'And strings were pulled?' he asked tentatively, as though wandering into dangerous ground.

'I don't think of it as quite that sinister. I gather you could use an extra pair of hands and I fit that bill. I've no preconceptions, Malcolm, and I'm happy to pitch in when and where necessary.'

'Malcolm, sorry to interrupt, the Rayners are here.' It was a young man, dressed smartly in a blue Oxford shirt with a red tie and dark blue canvas trousers. Ian Cameron, twenty-two. Sonia's boy, Emma thought. The superior knowledge was pleasant.

'Okay. Ian, this is Emma Fox who'll be joining us. Can you take her to meet Jane and then Sonia?'

'Of course. I've put the Rayners in Room Two and I'll bring coffee through in a minute,' he said to Malcolm, nodding acknowledgement to Emma at the same time.

'The Rayners,' Malcolm said to Emma in a tone of mild exasperation as if their surname was meant to say it all. 'They want us to find a flat for their son. He graduated two years ago and now he's decided it's finally time to leave the family home. They want him to have a bijou mews flat but the son's obsessed with New York loft living. I'm in the middle.'

While they spoke, Ian busied himself with cups and saucers, oblivious to them. His hair was in a close buzz cut revealing the pleasing shape of his head. Emma found herself staring at him as she listened to Malcolm, memories of English boys flooding back to her.

'The parents are paying, presumably?' she asked Malcolm.

'Very definitely.'

'Do Lomax have any New York-style loft apartments on their rental portfolio?'

'We've got a couple, unusually. One on the borders of the city and the other in Soho. The parents still can't see beyond Kensington though, and I'm inclined to agree. We don't really know enough about lofts here. They're a bit too modern for us.'

Without thinking about it, Emma was involved. She had plunged herself into the situation and was trying to work an angle on it.

'How strong-willed are the parents?' she asked.

'They're not really. More interfering than anything else.'

'Let me know if I can help. I don't want to get in the way, but I spent a few months living in New York once and I stayed in a loft. I could either talk the parents into the idea or the son out of it.'

While Malcolm considered it, Emma let memories of a summer spent in a New York loft flow over her.

'That might be helpful,' he said. 'I'll suggest it to them this morning and see what they think.'

'Do Lomax have a preference as to where the son lives?' she asked.

'No, we just have a preference for the client to be happy. In this case, the clients are the parents, but the son might be too, in the future. He'll end up more than just a trust-fund baby. In terms of fee income, there wouldn't be much in it if he went bijou in Kensington or for the loft.'

'I'll just pop this coffee in for the Rayners and I'll come back and get you,' Ian said, carefully inserting his words between hers and Malcolm's, as though practised in the art of not getting in the way.

Ian took her to meet Jane Bennett, head of Foreign. On the way, she glimpsed the Rayner family in Room Two, the door slightly open. The parents sat either side of their son, both leaning almost imperceptibly, but protectively nonetheless, towards him. She could only see the back of the son's head, his hair almost down to his shoulders, the shoulders themselves strong and square inside the pale denim shirt. He quickly turned to say something to his mother and she caught the briefest flash of the side of his face, unable to tell exactly what he looked like but struck by the golden skin, a definite smile and the vigour of his movements. Malcolm closed the door and the view was gone. In her mind it stayed for several long seconds, the parents' postures and the son's movements composing themselves in her mind into something she could not quite label but which pleasantly troubled her nonetheless.

The warm fuzzy feeling left her the moment she saw Jane Bennett rise from her desk. Emma almost leaned and whispered to Ian, 'What's her problem?' but caught herself in time.

'Jane, Emma Fox. Emma, Jane Bennett. Emma is going to be working with Malcolm and Ed.'

Jane Bennett stretched her hand reluctantly, as though Emma might be wearing a joke buzzer concealed in her palm. I wish I was, Emma thought, it might liven her up. Jane's chin came to a kind of severe point that looked lethal on the thin sagging neck. Her mouth was a wounded smudge of orange lipstick and her eyes a metallic grey set into the corrugated bags under her eyes. Emma found it hard not to stare. Thin hair was brushed, blown and lacquered wildly, a streaked auburn fire hazard adrift on her head. She looked like the reconstructed First Lady of an even more reconstructed American president. Emma waited for the thin smile to evaporate and then realised this was Jane Bennett's natural demeanour, all the charm of a contract killer dressed by Laura Ashley – furniture department.

It got worse.

'I'm Jane Bennett,' she whistled in a telephone voice,

24

'and I am in charge of the Foreign section at the Lomax Property Agency.'

It was as if someone had pressed play on a tape as Jane went into a monotone monologue about what the Foreign section did, the importance of it to the agency and the unsung heroics of herself and her junior, Nicola Morris. 'Welcome home,' said a voice in Emma's head as she listened and nodded in time with Jane Bennett. Ian stood beside Emma with a glazed look on his face, no doubt having heard this all before. For Emma, it was horribly compulsive, like the need to stare at a road accident.

'Unless you have any questions, I really must get on. It has been nice to meet you. I hope you enjoy it here. Nicola is not here at the moment, but I will introduce you when she is.'

It was as though Jane were vocalising self-affirming thoughts rather than actually speaking to her. Emma said she was looking forward to working at Lomax.

Out of earshot, Ian spoke. 'Sonia's with Catherine now, but I'll introduce you to her later. I'll show you your desk, give you a chance to recuperate after Jane. She's the same with everyone.' He grinned slyly.

Emma opened and closed the drawers on the desk, their noise hollow from emptiness. She moved the phone to the opposite side of the work surface and switched on the PC. A folded piece of the agency's headed paper had a note, typed in an unusual script font that looked like handwriting, telling her that her password had been set as *good morning*. The swirling brush script text was signed in an equally swirly signature by Ian. Emma sighed at the lack of security. The PC booted and she looked at the icons, her eyes falling on the familiar name of her favourite spreadsheet package. For the next half an hour, she tinkered, customising the package to her liking. She was so engrossed, she did not see Malcolm approach her.

'The Rayners just left. They're warming to the loft idea, I think. Sometimes our job is more like social work,' he said.

'Is there anything I can do to help?' she said.

'I mentioned that you were here and familiar with these sorts of properties.'

'Were they interested?'

'Yes. Once we have details drawn up on the properties, they'd like to meet you. I didn't want to drop it on you today, so I said you would visit them,' Malcolm said.

'Can't they just come and look at the flats?'

'It's not that simple for many of our clients. They want to feel we provide more than just a set of keys.'

'I guess,' Emma said, uncertain.

'We do that a lot here,' he continued. 'We go to see the client. We see Lomas as a consultative resource for the client.'

'Did you schedule a time?'

'I assumed your diary would be free, but I told them I'd have to check with you, to find an opening in your schedule.'

'That makes me sound terribly glamorous,' she replied.

He paused for a moment. 'Get Ian to call and make the appointment. When we set meetings, we use him rather than calling direct. There's a file on the Rayners that I'll let you have. I can come to the meeting if you want me to.'

'I'll look at the file and you can fill me in on them. If you want to come, that's fine.'

Emma left it open, not wanting to alienate him.

Finished, he ambled off and Emma turned her attention back to the PC. She waited until she was sure no one was going to disturb her and then she looked through the file cabinet section. The computers were networked. Emma clicked the mouse and moved from her personal drive onto the network. On the network, there were a number of different areas. She went into a general data area and found directories for each person in Lomax. Returning to the top level of the directory, she searched downwards for any sub-directories that were protected. She smiled. There did not seem to be. When the time came, she thought, there could be more than one way to get information.

Chapter Three

ON HER BED, Emma's clothes from her first day at the Lomax Property Agency lay discarded. They had fallen in such a way that the creases and folds still suggested some ghost might be occupying them. Emma looked at them and saw her other identity. Plain Emma Fox. She felt like a comic-book heroine, about to change into an alter ego.

In the mirror, another image had taken shape as she made herself up, concentrating on making her eyes more catlike and her mouth sharper, making it look as though a kiss could cut. Her earrings were small, close to the lobe and stylish. This was far removed from plain Emma, but it was also a long way from the normal Emma. It was the first time she had decided to go out in London since she had been back. Casting her mind back over her most recent jaunts from New York, she realised that she had not really been out in London for almost two years. Leaning closer into the mirror, Emma twisted a tendril of hair between her fingers and pouted at herself. Turning, she surveyed herself in the full-length mirror, the short black Lacroix dress clinging to her tight buttocks and accenting her breasts, revealing shoulders and just the right amount of cleavage to hint at sex. It was an unequivocal outfit and Emma liked it.

The doorbell rang.

'I'm Jackson,' said the woman.

Standing very straight on the step, the evening light framing her, she was dressed in a black suit with a white blouse buttoned up to the top. The outfit could have passed as a uniform. She was of average height, with green eyes, pale skin and very little make-up.

Behind her, double-parked and with the engine purring quietly, was a large black limousine with dark windows. It looked diplomatic and heavy with armour-plate, the windows giving off a sheen that betrayed bullet-proofing.

'I'll be right there,' Emma said.

Jackson was standing by an open rear door when Emma emerged. When she had closed it for Emma and taken her place in the driver's seat, she spoke.

'Do you have a specific destination in mind?'

'I've been out of town. Could we just cruise around for a while?' Emma said.

'Fine,' Jackson replied, talking over her shoulder, projecting her voice so that it carried to where Emma was seated. 'Like a tour.'

'Exactly,' Emma said.

'Just let me run through the car. There's a phone, a bar and a television set. It's like a hotel – the company will bill you for what you use. On the control panel, there's a button that raises the glass screen between the front and back of the car, in case you want privacy. It's one way, like the windows. You can see me, I can't see or hear you, so if you want to make phone calls or whatever, go ahead. Are you familiar with this kind of travel?'

Emma smiled in the dim light of the car. 'Yes.'

'Okay. I can talk or I can be quiet, whichever you want.'

'Thank you,' Emma said, not certain if she wanted to

29

talk or enjoy a silent ride and view London through the blackened one-way glass of the car's windows.

The lavish leather upholstery was the colour of biscuits and the walnut trim was preserved like a fossil in a deep casing of lacquer. All the fittings were highly polished silver. Just like every limousine she had ridden in, in fact. Apart from trips to the airport, all her other business travel in chauffeured cars had been in the company of bankers or board members, invariably men, and it had always been very brisk and business-like, papers spread out about the cabin, a multitude of portable phones trilling continuously. It was good to have the car to herself and to have the freedom to go where she wanted.

Jackson drove calmly and with the arrogant confidence of someone driving a car that weighed as much as a tank and was as secure. Up the Kings Road, around Sloane Square and on up Sloane Street until they passed Harvey Nichols and headed towards Hyde Park Corner. The underpass was closed and the car swung around the Corner and headed up Piccadilly, towards the perpetual fluorescent daytime of the Circus.

It was her first candid look at London since arriving back. There were buildings and shops she did not recognise. The arrangement of lights, the decoration and garnish of London had changed, but underneath it all, it remained the same. She could feel the pulse of the city beating almost unnoticed beneath the surface. At Coventry Street, they pulled past the line at Planet Hollywood and up a side street onto Shaftesbury Avenue, a tight concentration of half-familiar shows that seemed mere echoes of their former Broadway selves.

'Do you know if Franklins is still open?' Emma asked the back of Jackson's head.

Jackson looked up in the mirror and glanced at

Emma knowingly.

'Yes,' she replied.

Some things had not changed then, Emma thought.

'Is it as exclusive as ever?' Emma asked.

'Sure. I can get you in. Want me to make a call?'

Emma was impressed. 'If you could.'

'No problem.'

Jackson had her own phone in the front of the car. She spoke on first-name terms with someone, her tone suggesting she knew them well. She put the phone away.

'No problem,' Jackson repeated, turning her head slightly to Emma, a smile visible.

The car turned onto Charing Cross Road and headed along the convoluted one-way route via Trafalgar Square to take them back towards Piccadilly.

As they pulled up at Franklins, the image through the window of the car came into focus as clearly as seeing an old photograph. A piece of London that looked the same on the surface. Exclusive. Chic. Glamorous. Emma had been only a few times, but it had stuck in her memory enough to make her want to return.

'Ask the cloakroom to send for me when you want to leave. They can call me on this number.'

Jackson handed Emma a small white card just as a doorman stepped up and opened the car door. Emma placed the toe of her Prada shoe onto the plush red deepness that covered the kerb.

'Miss Fox,' the doorman said as though he was her oldest friend. 'Good evening.'

Emma walked the stretch of carpet and was ushered past the line and in through the heavy door which opened and closed as quickly as she was through it. Down carpeted steps and past the cloakroom, Emma stepped into the club.

A large rectangular room with a low ceiling, it was

an intimate space, not a cavernous and anonymous disco, but more of a drinking club. At either end were large well-stocked bars manned by actor-pretty barmen in waistcoats and bow ties. There were just enough people to make the place thrum but not so many for it to be overcrowded. It was one of the few places she had been to in London that she liked to enter on her own. Emma felt eyes coming out of the subdued lighting and finding her, homing in on her as if she were a target. Brushing one hand lazily over the side of her dress she approached the bar and sat on a stool. A waiter was instantly in front of her, his expression a question in itself.

'Champagne,' she said.

Emma sipped from the flute and wondered how long it would take. Music hung in the air like a perfume, lingering prudently at just the right volume. It did not take long at all.

'Hi,' a voice said.

Emma turned and looked at him. He'd do.

'Hi,' she said back.

'I haven't seen you here before.'

Emma was about to say something sharp but resisted, remembering that she was not there to engage in an interesting or original conversation.

'I don't go out much,' she said.

'I find that hard to believe. My name's Kim,' he said.

'Hello Kim. I'm Emma.'

'There, that's the introductions. Can I get you a drink?'

Emma held up her three-quarters-full glass to indicate the obvious and he faltered for a second. Not wanting to put him off, she took a deliberately slow and sensual sip from the glass, letting her lips linger around the edges and her tongue flick out for a second.

'Champagne,' she said to him.

He signalled for a waiter, and she saw a gold bracelet

hanging down onto the cuff of his lightweight jacket. Probably early forties trying to pass himself off as late thirties, his tan was manufactured and his smile a victory for his dentist. His hair was coloured, very well, but coloured nonetheless. Carefully layered and conditioned, the long strands were styled in a flick-back around the sides and over the top of his head, the victory being his hairdresser's on that score. Still, he was good-looking, his skin seamless and bone structure solid. Emma did not want to speculate on the level of manufacture any of that had. Even sitting on the stool, he had the vanity of movement that Emma associated with dancers or magicians. A heterosexual man with more hair products than her. A rare and precious commodity in its own strange way. Why should she expect anything else from him? She had, to an extent, manufactured her own image tonight. She had dressed and made herself up for the sole reason she was now sitting on the barstool, pointing her bare leg at him and sipping her second glass of champagne.

'What do you do?' he asked.

'Is it important?'

'Only if you want it to be.'

'It's not important.'

'That's fine. I work for a television company. I earn too much fucking money.'

He said it in a way that was meant to impress. Emma made the requisite facial gestures and looked into his eyes, egging him on. This was the sort of man who should be able to read a signal, she thought. He reached out and gripped her thigh. She did not miss a beat and continued to look at him as he squeezed and manipulated the muscle and flesh. His hand went higher, touching the hem of the skirt. Her legs were freshly waxed and the follicles were sensitive to his touch, a tingle spreading where his palm made contact.

'Would you like to dance?' he asked her.

33

'No,' she said. She leaned over, rested a hand on his leg and whispered into his ear, 'I'd like to fuck.'

Emma let her breath linger on his ear and she pulled away slowly, enjoying the slightly dismayed expression on his face. Obviously, Kim thought this was a suggestion *he* should have been making.

'Where?' was all he managed.

'I have a car.'

'You do?' He seemed surprised.

'I'll have it sent round front. Come on.'

She stood and gripped his hand, leading him out of the club to the cloakroom at the bottom of the stairs, handing the card to the attendant and asking him to call for the car.

It was waiting for them as they exited into the night, the lights on the awning bright, a queue of expectant faces before them. He seemed flustered by it all. Jackson was at her post by the open door and she was impassive as he got into the car. Emma shot her a smile before she got in and Jackson returned it.

'I've already put the screen up, Miss Fox,' she said.

'Very good,' she replied wryly.

They sat side by side in the car. Emma was quiet and confident, poised on the seat. Kim seemed shifty and uncertain but desperate not to appear that way.

'Can I fix you a drink?' he asked, his voice worldly and attempting to sound not at all out of place.

'Maybe later.'

Emma flicked a switch on the control pad and the central locking system tumbled dozens of levers into place, the lubricated sound an audible indication of the fortress in which they were now ensconced. Kim's eyes darted from door to door as they locked in sequence. Emma looked at him. This area belonged to her. She had not spent very long in the car, but it was her territory. This whole experience belonged to her alone.

She turned to him and knelt up on the seat,

throwing one leg over him so she straddled him. Sitting in his lap, her skirt riding up, she undid the buttons on his shirt as she gave him a hot and deep kiss. Their bodies rocked with the motion of the car and the leather of the seats made a squeaking sound as her knees pressed into it.

Already she could feel his hardness pressing into her behind as she bared his chest and pushed his jacket off. She tugged his shirt from the trousers and let it fly free about him. Her temperature was rising, oblivious to the air-conditioning of the car, and her movements grew more frantic. Out of the back window, she saw the car behind, driver and passenger impassive and unaware of what was going on. They were back on Piccadilly Circus, Eros visible.

'Take my knickers off,' she instructed him.

His hands were on her immediately, finding the skimpy fabric that stretched across her behind and down between her legs, pulling at her crotch. With one tug he had them down as far as they would go, exposing her behind and her pussy, his hands readily exploring the newly available flesh of her rear.

'Finger my pussy.'

Obediently, he did. A hand pushed down between their bodies, his arm at an awkward angle, and he found her. Her pussy was wet, and eager for his touch. Kim found her clitoris and rubbed it, soon finding a direction that was pleasurable for her. She sighed and dug her nails into his shoulders, clinging to him as he used his hand on her.

'Harder,' she said.

Breathing heavily, a mix of passion and exertion, he pressed harder. It gave her a straining feeling in her pussy as he fingered her clitoris. He was sweating. Emma looked at his body, what she could see of it. His torso was pleasing, solid and sculpted, his stomach flat and his cock pushing the front of his trousers high.

35

Roughly, he pushed a finger into her and she bit her lip, her hips gyrating. It was pleasurable, mostly because of the small hint it gave as to what she really desired.

Unable to wait, she pulled his hand away and slipped from his lap to the floor of the car, removing her knickers completely. Still on her knees, she unzipped and unbuttoned his trousers, pulling them to his knees along with his underwear. From the dark thatch of pubic hair, his tumescent member rose. Emma pulled the trousers all the way to the ankles and Kim lifted his rear, pushing his cock closer to her face.

'You wish,' was all she said.

Abruptly, she was on him again and she quickly and remorselessly sat on his erect cock. With no pomp or ceremony, she gripped it in her hand and pushed down on it, pushing it between her labia, letting it open her vagina and find its way along the passage. Juices ran from her as the penetration opened her. Emma was fully on his lap, as much of his cock as he had to offer rudely stuck in her as she straddled him, riding smoothly through the London night in a limousine.

Emma held onto the back of the seat where it rose several inches above the back window ledge. She pulled herself up off his cock, levering with her knees, letting inches of him out of her and then falling back into his lap, her vagina already accommodating him. The seat moved with her, pushing him into it as she bounced on him furiously, using him like a trampoline, his cock a hard, blunt intrusion into her. Like a piece of rounded marble, his cock fed her hunger as she pushed back and forth onto it, riding it roughly.

'Who are you?' he asked, sounding like a particularly melodramatic soap-opera scene.

'Shut up,' she told him firmly. 'And fuck me.'

She leaned her head forward and ground herself

onto him, letting his cock push against her, the depth not as important as the sheer sensation of him. Around his shaft, her pussy gripped hard, holding him and then letting him go, the sensations building in intensity.

Emma reached behind herself, her hand brushing the smooth leather upholstery, and gripped his balls, letting her thumb trace the base of his shaft where he was joined to her. She took hold of him, a hand on each shoulder, and continued to writhe on his cock. She let the movements of the car, of the seat, of his body, all gather momentum in her. To all of these movements she was readying one single effort of her own.

Kim cupped her buttocks in his hands and then pushed a finger into the cleft of her cheeks. He carefully stroked the skin around her anus, tickling it and coyly pressing at the dry and sensitive skin.

'You're a little too free with those hands,' she told him.

She took his right hand and stretched it to the seat-belt, pulling the black nylon fabric from its holder, putting his wrist behind it and turning his hand several times until he was bound by it. Ignoring the indignant protest of his expression, she did the same to his left hand on the other side of the car. The width of the limousine strung him out like an athlete performing on the rings. As she resettled herself more comfortably on him, he simply stared at her, no words to say. She liked it like that. His outstretched arms pulled the shirt open and she raked the sides of his torso with her nails, leaving long trails on the soft hairless skin. She repeated the dragging of her nails several times, until he cried out for her to stop. She did. And started to do the same to the sides of his buttocks, reaching round her own legs to get to him.

With Kim's hands anchoring him firmly against the

seat, Emma leaned back with her arms behind her and rested her hands on his knees, changing the angle at which he penetrated her. She squeezed him tight with her legs and her pussy, and he groaned at the tightness of her clinch. The top of his shaft pressed hard against the front of her pussy, pushing directly upwards whilst she was at an angle. Sweat ran from his chest, over his stomach and into his pubic hair. Her breasts bounced in front of him but he was powerless to touch them.

The car had left the centre of town and was speeding out on the elevated road towards Heathrow Airport, swinging from lane to lane to cut through the steady evening flow of traffic. Outside, the scenery and the cars went past like a television with the sound off, no noises to indicate they were even a part of the world. Inside the car, their noises were furious. Kim grunted and spat his passion whilst Emma was making loud exhaling noises in time with his entering her.

His head thrashed from side to side and his arms strained on the belt. Inside her, Emma felt his cock throb, the head of it swelling outwards. She rode him hard and fast, speeding his orgasm along as surely as the car. Eventually his orgasm burst from him and he jerked about on the seat in grateful spasm, his semen inside her. Now he threw his head back and let it rest on the seat, arching his back and tensing his stomach muscles as he let the final come tremor from him.

Emma could fight it no longer and she relinquished herself. Just as she came, her hand flailed for the switch and she opened one of the side windows of the car. Instantly, the cabin was filled with noise and cold air. She did not care if anyone saw her. She cried out, her noise becoming one with that of the city. The cool wind bathed her sweating face and her pussy gave in to exquisite spasms around Kim's still hard cock. She threw herself forward and held him again, letting her orgasm course through her, her pussy full of his come and of his cock, grinding helplessly on him until she was reduced to a flickering of the energy that had forced her on.

An hour later, Kim stood on a kerb in Knightsbridge looking into the open window of the limousine where Emma sat.

'When will I see you again?' he asked her.

As the one-way glass of the window rose to put a partition between them, she spoke.

'You won't.'

Chapter Four

EMMA STOOD AT the door of her old house in Islington, letting the strange sense of being a visitor there sweep over her. When she had called to arrange meeting its current occupants for dinner, she had had to pause and remember what her old phone number was, though her brain had stored it away like most numbers she needed to know. Letting the house to friends had been ideal for Emma. She was not put off by stories she had heard of other people who rented to friends and was comfortable that her house was in good hands.

The house was a picture of Victorian double-fronted largesse that she had purchased at the down-swing of a cycle. Like many of her investments, it would yield a good return in the long run. Light came over the fanlight of the large front door and she heard the heavy footfalls of Neil.

'Hello, darling,' he said to her as he always did.

She responded as she always did, 'Darling?' Like it was a question.

They hugged tightly.

'Come to evict us then, evil landlady?'

'Just dinner will suffice. It smells good. Only you in at the moment?' Emma asked.

'Yes, but not for long, so let's talk.'

Emma and Neil had worked at a bank together just after Emma left Harvard and returned to England. Worked in the same building, as Neil would remind her, but not really worked together. Emma was speeding along the MBA fast-track and Neil, six years younger, was a postroom boy. Quickly realising that the oracle for the bank resided in the postroom generally and Neil specifically, she had cultivated a friendship with him. It was only several months later, after they had done a lot of drinking and partying together that she realised she enjoyed him as a friend. She had made, very early on, one slightly clumsy pass that he had gracefully corrected and she had chalked up to experience.

'We would have met you at the airport,' Neil said, pouring wine and setting a glass down on the table for her.

'Morse arranged a limo at Heathrow and they laid on a helicopter to JFK. Glamour all the way.'

'Last thing you would have wanted was us screeching at you as you came through arrivals then. Are you going to tell me why you really left? None of that technical jargon you use with Tom. The real reason.'

She sat at the dinner table, set off to one side in the huge kitchen, and remembered how much she had liked the room the first time she saw it. In New York, you didn't need a kitchen. It felt as though in four years she had only ordered food, never made any. Emma couldn't remember the last time she had cooked.

'I'll tell you, but only if you let me chop something.'

Neil looked at her, all brown eyes as usual. He was twenty-six now, she thought, and still looked as boyish as when she had first met him. Tall and rangy, he was broad-shouldered and handsome in a typically English

41

way. And his hair was the one thing in life that could be relied on never to change. He had shown Emma a photograph of him aged nine and the saucer-eyed boy had the same carefully cut fringe and clean-around-the-back-and-ears haircut he still wore.

'It's all yours,' he said and handed her a sharp-looking knife. He poured some more wine into both their glasses and sat at the table.

For a while she chopped away silently, observing Neil from the corner of her eye and familiarising herself with the work surface, fighting a sense of déjà vu.

'So?' Neil asked.

'So why did I leave? You'll be disappointed, darling. There's no great scandal or conspiracy. Did you know I studied art in my first year at university?'

'You never mentioned it.'

'I think I'd almost forgotten until recently. Actually, I had a meeting with a Spanish bank last year and they had two Mirós in their foyer and I started babbling on about them. It was like speaking in tongues. I forgot why I was even at the bank, I was so taken with them and that I had things to say about them. I did a year of art and then I switched to economics.'

'So, you've had a religious experience in a Spanish bank and you've come home to paint?' he asked her sarcastically.

'All the boys I worked with at Morse Callahan would go on and on about the game. Being in the game. Playing the game. I used to think it was such a cliché until I realised that if you were in the game, you could also be out of it.'

'Did you hate it that much then?'

She gave a small nod and paused. 'Eventually, I did. It stopped being fun and then stopped even being interesting. I didn't understand the rules or the point of the game any more. Now, I'm out of the game.'

'I'm not prying – well I am – but can you *afford* to be out of the game?'

She smiled at him. So few people realised the kind of stakes she had played for in her old world.

'Without being specific,' she said, 'let's just say I'm a bit better set up than your average lottery winner. I don't imagine I'll have to work for the next two or three hundred years.'

'You could paint horrible pictures and sell them to yourself. I could do a horrible picture and you could buy it. Tom said you had plans but he didn't know what they were.'

She had reduced the vegetables on the counter to a pile of slices and dices. Feeling she had got something out of her system, she sat at the table and faced Neil.

'I might buy part of a property agency that has a very élite client base.'

'How did that come about?'

'The woman who owns it is a friend – more of an acquaintance,' she said.

'Someone I don't know about?' he interrupted, a strain of jealousy in his voice.

'We've had an on-off friendship for nearly ten years. I knew her before I even met you.'

'Hmm . . .' was all he said in response.

'Neil, you've got friends that aren't my friends. It's all overlap. Don't get queeny about it.'

'All right,' he said, leaning forward in his chair to show interest.

'She needs some money and some business sense. I've got both. I'm working there at the moment.'

'Is it a bit, you know, of a come-down?' he frowned.

'Quite a bit. The staff think I've been employed as a junior agent. Hence . . .' she said tugging at her clothes.

'I would have been too polite to mention it, but you do look a tad dowdier than usual. I thought perhaps you were dressing down for us. Why all the cloak and dagger?'

'I just want to make sure I'm making a sound investment. This gives me a chance to sniff around and make sure I don't commit to something that's not viable. Ultimately, I just want to be a silent partner, but I want to be sure my investment is solid. Besides, it's fun.'

'I'm sure. All those braying stuck-up customers and boy estate agents.'

The front door opened and closed and almost instantly, Tom filled the doorway of the kitchen, dressed in a smart striped business suit.

'Darling,' he said.

'Darling?' she responded.

'My cupid,' he said.

Tom crossed the room, stopping to peck at Neil's cheekbone before hauling Emma from her chair and bear-hugging her.

'Group hug,' Neil called.

'What's happened to our glamour-puss?' Tom asked, holding her away from him and surveying her.

'She's in disguise,' Neil told him.

'What's the Nikkei and the Dow doing?' he asked her.

'Tom,' was all Neil said, slapping at him.

'That's okay,' she replied. 'Do you know what, Tom? I don't know and I don't even care.'

'Wonderful. Been waiting long?' he asked, releasing her from the hug.

'Tom, what makes you think everyone had been waiting for you?' Neil asked.

For several minutes, Emma watched as they bantered on in the language of two people who had lived together for a significant amount of time. In their bantering couple-speak they referred to her theatrically, as if she weren't there.

Tom's hair was much shorter than when she had seen him last, almost a year earlier, but his bushy moustache was still intact on his top lip. At forty-three, he was still fit, showing no thickening in the waist or any loss of his cheekbones. Emma had introduced Neil and Tom and was pleased that things had turned out so well. Initially, she had been reluctant to push them together as she had only met Tom a few times. Twice in a work context when he had been a client and once when her firm organised a theatre outing for clients and their partners. Tom called her the week before and told her that he did not currently have a partner and that he would rather duck the evening. Emma told him she herself was currently without a partner and that they should go together. They went, had a good time and a long talk, at which point Emma's instincts had kicked in and told her to introduce Tom to Neil. Nearly five and a half years later, here they were living in her house and talking in code to each other. Sometimes, they referred to her as Mother.

'So what are you telling these people at the agency?' Tom asked, now fully apprised of the situation.

'That I was a bank clerk made redundant. A few of them seem troubled by my presence, like I might be promoted before them – the usual office crap. I don't want to set off any alarm bells if I don't have to.'

'What about when they find out who you really are?' Tom asked her.

'Then they'll probably wish they'd been nicer to me,' she smiled.

'Why property, of all things, Emma?' Tom asked, his tie loosened and Neil off fiddling with pots on the stove.

'Catherine, the woman who owns it, needs help. I only want to be a silent partner, collecting a reasonable return, not a hands-on person. At the moment, I'm just researching. Not unlike I would have done in any takeover situation.'

'Always your strong suit, I recall.'

'You flatter. How's the retail banking world?'

'Wearing. Very wearing. With your brains, and your balls, I'd jump at the chance to work in M&A. Of course, you go and give it up to become an estate agent.'

'It's just a stepping stone. I believe in springboards. Use one thing as a way of jumping into another,' she told him.

'Yes, yes, but much more importantly,' Neil said, returning, 'are you getting laid?'

'I've only been back just over a week,' she replied.

'Quite a few times then,' Neil responded.

'Just the once. To make sure I haven't lost it with English men.'

'And have you?' they asked almost in unison.

'As if.'

'There was no one special in the States?' Tom asked, a genuinely pained and concerned expression on his face.

Emma shook her head and snorted quietly.

'Would you boys be on for a shopping trip next week sometime? I need to get some new clothes for the agency and some nicer ones too.'

She watched Neil's face illuminate with the suggestion and Tom's drop into an even more pained frown.

'Of course we would, Mother,' Neil said.

'You don't have to come, Tom, really,' she said.

'Don't be silly, he'd love to, wouldn't you, Tom? We could set out really early, just when they open so we get a good run at it.'

Emma and Neil burst into simultaneous laughter as Tom rose to his feet and left the room, mumbling to himself.

'You two seem quite the couple. More every time I

see you,' she said to Neil in a subdued voice when Tom was out of earshot.

'He's such an old fuddy, he kills me. I took him dancing last month and you should have seen his face when we walked in, it was a picture.'

'I bet Tom had a wild time in the seventies while you were still playing with whatever it was you played with,' Emma said.

'I can't see it, Emma. I tease him about that but he gets all elusive on me. Where do you want to shop?'

'The usual places. Harvey Nichols, Harrods, Sloane Street. I want to go to that new department at Hamiltons I keep reading about.'

By the time she left and got into a taxi, it was late but it did not worry her. At Morse Callahan, if she went out in the evening, she would be clock-watching by nine, fretting that she would not get enough sleep for the trials of the following day. Now, it did not bother her. Emma did not care how late it was, what the stock market indices were saying or what other people might or might not have been saying about her. It was as though a whole din of background noise had abruptly ceased and she could hear her own thoughts, clear and undistorted, for the first time in a long while. Even the need endlessly to analyse and compute this feeling ebbed slowly away from her as she began to relax into her new rhythm of life. How she felt came down to a simple, single-syllable word.

Free.

Chapter Five

EMMA SETTLED BACK into the sofa and surveyed her current living room. One advantage of having a relationship with a property agency was not worrying about where to live on arriving back in England. Catherine had arranged for her to have the use of an apartment on Wellington Square off the Kings Road. The gentle scramble of people along Kings Road, the number of shops and the convenience of its proximity to Lomax were advantageous. It was vastly different from her last house in England, the one in Islington looked after by Tom and Neil. It was also unlike her New York apartment in many ways, except that that too had been a place that never felt permanent.

The apartment was low-ceilinged and cottage-like, the exterior standing flush with the pavement while the interior radiated the urbane modesty that glowed stylishly in the pages of some of the world's glossiest magazines. Not particularly to her taste, it would do for the time being, serving to enhance the transitory feeling that would eventually spur her on to looking for somewhere permanent. In ten short days, the past life of Wall Street had started to recede into a memory, not yet old enough for her to feel a fondness towards it, not fresh enough to completely bury. That would not be changed by seeing Chris tonight, she thought.

Emma knew there wasn't a saying 'never fuck your broker', but perhaps there should have been. Emma knew Chris at Goldman, Sachs and now he was with a smaller firm and flourishing in it. It occurred to her that she had fucked him before he became her broker. 'Never make a lover a broker' did not have quite the same ring to it.

Unlike many, Emma had never traded on the inside information she was privy to in order to turn a profit. She had been smart enough not to need to and proud enough not to want to. All of the money that now circulated in her various accounts and trusts, looked after by Chris, was there by virtue of her own honest efforts. She didn't actually need a financial adviser, but as brokers went he was good. As brokers went, he was also a pretty good fuck, she thought devilishly.

As with Tom and Neil, it had been almost a year since she had seen him. They kept in touch by phone on a weekly basis, their relationship able to glide between the formal and the sexual with ease. Emma did not spend too much time pondering it, but Chris was like a sexy brother with whom she'd occasionally fuck. She moved her rear around on the sofa and realised she was anxious to see him. She had not bothered to make dinner, assuming they would find something later on. They had waited ten days to meet, speaking on the phone a number of times, the sexual edge always there but never quite spoken. Chris must have known that this was the main reason she had asked him to come and see her.

Emma was ready for him. She wore a tight Bruce Oldfield dress that touched where she wanted it, accentuating the line of her body and showing off her good shoulders. She was bereft of jewellery and had kept her make-up to a minimum. The only other thing that would stand between her and him was a pair of sheer white knickers by Calvin Klein. A dab of Donna Karan perfume had set her to feeling dirty and two glasses of wine had finished the job. In short, she sat waiting for Chris to arrive, calmly pondering her life and feeling horny as hell for him.

The doorbell jolted her and she set the wine glass down, jumping off the sofa and heading down the hall in her bare feet. Before opening the door for him, she surveyed him on the video entryphone. His short dark hair was curly in a boyish way and his eyes were shocking in the way they shone, even on the scratchy picture she was observing. His face was short and quite broad with smallish ears. Emma looked at him for a moment longer, remembering what a taut little ball of sex he was and then opened the door for him.

The smile on his face soaked her. Straight from the City he was wearing a single-breasted four-button suit, white shirt and tie. With the front door still open and no words exchanged, they kissed. She pushed her hands into the back of his hair and plastered herself onto him, enjoying the feel of the wool of his suit around her scantily clad figure. She wanted to climb him, to clamber on his hard-muscled body. She wanted to touch and taste him, to make him cry out and to have him do the same to her. His whole body radiated desire to her, his every movement indicating that shortly he would be making love to her. Emma dragged him into the hall and kicked the door loudly shut.

'I've missed this,' he said to her.

'Me too,' she replied, cracking at the sound of his voice in person after what had seemed ages.

It was no use. There was no sense in making any pretence that they should talk. They had spoken on the phone and they knew each other well enough not to need any small talk. There would be time later for that, Emma thought. What she wanted was simple and did not need to be made complex by a lot of words.

Emma removed his jacket and threw it on the hall table, taking him by the hand and leading him up to the bedroom, swinging her behind provocatively as he followed it at eye-level all the way. He stopped her at the top of the stairs and kissed her again, deeper and more fervently than the first. His hand reached under the short hem of her skirt, brushing against her smooth thighs and tracing the line of the underwear where it bordered on her skin. His hand pushed under it and onto one of the cheeks of her behind, cupping and squeezing it.

Chris positioned her so she was sitting on the top stair and he backed down a few himself, loosening his tie and undoing the top button of the white shirt, gently creased from the day's work. Emma imagined him at work, always popular with the lads and the girls, the latter flirting with him and he with them. She tousled the curls and he smiled at her before efficiently finding the sides of her knickers under her dress and giving them a tug, she raising her bottom as he did so. It was surprising the difference such a small piece of fabric could make to her sense of nudity. With them off, she felt exposed even though she was covered by her dress. But that was not for long. He lifted it and brought it off over her head in a whip-like movement that left her bared before him.

Kneeling on a stair he cupped both buttocks as he buried his face into her. His face reappeared quickly and he arched his back up to kiss her breasts, distributing himself evenly from nipple to nipple, making Emma wetter and wetter down below and fostering an ache for him that was hard to withstand. He nipped at the tips and rolled them in his mouth, tongue flicking at them and then his mouth drawing them tightly in. She sighed and rocked her body, clutching him to her, her legs widely spread and he between them, the wool of his suit brushing her inner

51

thighs. He moved his head away, surveying her, his hands covering the whole of her breasts while his eyes peered into the depths of hers. His gaze sent a deep-seated movement through her.

Her body had been waiting for him, she realised. It had been holding itself in check for this moment which would be so fleeting and yet so profound. They served a purpose for each other and it was without complication because they each chose to make it so. Each of them knew that they existed in this way for the other only in terms of the sex. Outside of the passion they shared, their relationship was normal, mundane almost. It was this which made their sexual time together so acute and sharply focused. Chris was able to set her alight in a way that few men had, with his mix of power, confidence and a willingness to please her. There had been times in the past when they had made love for hours on end, Emma coming effortlessly and easily, and Chris apparently unconcerned about himself. There had also been times when she had done the same for him. Emma and Chris distilled the most vital elements of their individual desires and mingled them in their sex, a compound more potent than anything she had experienced outside of it, but like so many things of that nature, ephemeral. At this instant, that did not matter. This was their moment.

With a gently circling finger, Chris caressed her labia. His breathing was oddly patterned and he was staring down at her as though he had discovered her for the first time. Occasionally, he would look up at her, a pleased expression on his face as he began to gently probe more deeply into her. Emma leaned back, supporting herself by extending her arms behind her. Her legs hung down the stairs and the carpet was pleasantly warm and fleecy on her rear. His finger was a small and welcome intrusion into her, touching the sides of her vagina and then pushing directly into the deep centre of her. Her muscles clenched onto the small part of him that was in her.

Emma gave a sigh of contentment and surrender, relinquishing herself to him. She let her head fall back and she stared at the ceiling while shuffling restlessly on the stair, wanting to have more of him in her. His breath was warm on her pussy and she felt it light on her clitoris, shortly followed by his mouth, the whole of which he used to smother the small craving bud. Below his mouth, and more gently, his finger pressed and teased. Sitting up straight, legs still pointing down the stairs, she looked at the powerful line of his back sheathed in the cotton shirt and the robust backside, tight and rounded.

Removing his mouth and his finger in time with each other, leaving a quivering emptiness in their wake, he knelt upright. Emma watched his hands as he placed one on each of her ankles and lifted her feet up onto the step directly below the top one on which she sat. Her thigh muscles strained from the position of her legs now so close to her rear and Chris gently eased her knees wider. When her legs had been trailing lazily down the stairs, her body had been almost a straight line and her pussy more of a secret from him. Now, she was wide and on display for him and the angle of her body was more urgent and ready. Emma was more alert to the cool of the air about her pussy, the warmth of her juices in the still and silent apartment.

Now he used two fingers. It was rougher and sexier than the teasing way he had dealt first with her breasts and then tentatively with her pussy. It was the Chris she knew and in a certain way loved. His single-mindedness, the almost cruel way he would labour at her until she would come in broken and muffled sobs, sometimes clinging onto his solid body as he moved in her, other times on all fours as he pleasured her. His fingers roamed freely in her, expanding and readying her, making her juices run freely and sleekly. Knowing her well, he was avoiding her clitoris, using the fingering as a prelude to his cock which she was getting more and more desperate to see and, more importantly, feel. Emma could tell from the look on his face, the blaze in his eyes, that he knew she was ready for him. Still fingering her, he frantically used the free hand to undo his trousers. He awkwardly nudged them and his underwear over his hips.

Releasing her from him, Chris stood, perhaps four or five stairs down, his head at eye level with her waist. Emma's feet were still on the final step; she put her feet down and leaned forward, taking his trousers all the way down. She cradled his balls, the waistband of his underwear pushed under them, and he murmured to himself. She slowly pulled the underwear over his legs, his thigh muscles solid, a light smattering of dark hair covering his legs. The tops of his socks were just visible where his trousers bunched at his feet. Emma gave his cock some attention but it did not need much. Looking at Chris, one would have expected him to be large and he did not disappoint. Despite the adage of what you did with it rather than what you had, Chris both had and knew. Emma raked her nails along the shaft of his over-sized cock, the skin tight around it, veins pulsing expectantly. She squeezed the circumcised head and tickled the heavy ridge along the top. Then, she simply sat back and waited.

Chris again took her ankles, but this time he eased her onto her back and raised her legs high in the air until her feet were hooked onto the ends of each bannister. The angle lifted the small of her back from the carpet and displayed both her pussy and most of her behind. Emma made fists of her hands and paced them into the small of her back to support herself and after lifting her head to look through her legs to see him, she dropped back to the floor and looked at the ceiling instead. As she waited, she heard him remove the shirt and tie and saw them fly past her face and land somewhere off to the right of her head.

Two or three stairs down from where Emma was perched, Chris was standing. Emma craned up again to see him. He was on tip-toe on the edge of the stair as though it were a diving board. His cock was held firmly in his hand. Supporting himself with one hand on the stair, he leaned his body in and his cock made contact with her. Emma felt so wet and expectant that she knew if he wanted he could simply sink into the maximum right away and she would accommodate him. As the head of his cock opened the lips of her pussy and then his shaft dilated the walls of her vagina, Emma clenched her fists tighter under the small of her back and drew a half-breath in and held onto it, as though unable to take both air and him into her at the same time. As each inch slid in, so Emma exhaled some air, making room for him almost.

When he had completed his task, his groin resting against the tautly flexed cheeks of her bottom, Chris put a hand on either side of the bannister, just under each of her feet. His legs were straight, as was his back. The whole of his rugged athlete's body was poised over her as though about to start press-ups in and out of her. The position of his arms accentuated the bulk of his biceps and the solid semi-circle of tricep. His chest was the same carefully worked sculpture of sinew that topped off his well-set abdominal muscles. It was like being fucked by an underwear model, she thought.

'Oh my God,' she said loudly.

The first lunge was bewildering. He had pulled virtually the whole of his lengthy cock from her until just the glans of his phallus rested in her inner labia and then he practically fell onto her, repeating in under a second the process of penetration which he

55

had previously spent careful time on. She felt light-headed and slightly giddy, her head suddenly awash with what was happening to her. He did it again, except that as he re-entered her, he twisted his hips very slightly, changing the angle of his huge cock inside her, making new promises to her hungry sex. A few more times he tormented her, inflicting his size on her. It accustomed her to him once more and then he set to work on her properly.

Emma loved to fuck with Chris. His body, his big cock, his face, his smile and his brains. He had too much of everything and sex with him was an overwhelming experience for her, something she restricted to only a few encounters, making each time that bit different and new. It did not do to be selfish or sentimental about it. It was a case of taking it for what it was. A very enjoyable, efficient and ruthless fucking. She settled her head back and let him get to it.

As his body slapped into hers, there was the sound of hot and sweaty skin contact. Hot inside her, Chris's cock seemed almost bigger than he was himself, it was as though it were controlling him, leading him on. He fucked her with an insistent and unforgiving pace that took her some time to get into sequence with. It was a learning experience of sorts and when she found the same note as he, there was harmony. Now, she felt a part of him and that the hardened member was part of her as it filled and refilled her vagina. As it pushed her down onto her fists, and felt like it lifted her whole consciousness out of her body and then back into it again, Emma grunted. Every single time he plunged and his body banged hers, so she let out the grunt, the audible and outward expression of her inner feeling, the feeling he was causing in her.

The walls of her vagina tingled around him, her labia welcoming and pulling with his motion. Emma felt alive with the sensation he was giving her as he flexed his whole body to produce the thrusting movement. Over the sound of her grunts came one of Chris's own. He had more come than anyone she had ever been with and every time they made love, he filled her with it in some way. When he came in her, he would propel himself into her depths, getting closer still to her. Then it would spill from her, run back out and down his shaft, mingled with her own juices. But none of this would be before Emma herself had come.

Emma's grunts became louder and closer together, her clitoris now near screaming point and her body smothered by the weight of sex. It held her bound up. Their fucking was a way of shackling herself to him and using his cock as the key to unlock her orgasm and set her free. With what little room there was for it, the walls of her vagina contracted and held onto Chris's shaft. Emma's cheeks flushed and she gritted her teeth, her orgasm swelling through the confinement and finally bursting out of her. She shifted herself up and down frantically, her passion rampant and disorderly.

Chris was not far behind her. His orgasm seemed to be a more straightforward affair. The force of his drives into her increased and then he howled, the animal sound gravelly in his throat. His semen pumped into her, the first three shots distinct and urgent – after that, she could not tell. Emma removed her hands from under her and reached to jiggle with his balls which were sandwiched between them, pulling tightly into him as they beat a retreat from his orgasm.

He stopped.

Emma sat up, her pussy wet with their juices. He withdrew from her and his shaft glistened with her and was tipped by his own come, gathering on the head of his cock. He leaned in close to her, heat coming off of him, and kissed her. They broke away and he grinned at her.

'Welcome home,' he said.

57

Chapter Six

'I'VE BROUGHT YOU some coffee,' Sonia Morgan was saying, a smile on her face. 'You seem so engrossed.'

Emma looked up, startled. As a matter of reflex, she casually clicked an icon that made the spreadsheet on her screen disappear and then returned Sonia's smile, unflustered.

'Thank you,' said Emma, searching for the coaster to place it on.

'You look very smart today,' Sonia commented.

'I have a meeting. My first.' Emma made a meek-looking face, cradling her coffee cup in both hands.

'I'm sure you'll do wonderfully.'

Sonia Morgan, in charge of administration and finance at Lomax, was the mother of the office. That in itself did not mean much, Emma knew. The first office mother Emma had come across when she started work had been of the Joan Crawford variety and they had nicknamed her *Mommie Dearest*. Sonia Morgan, by contrast, was at the Mother Theresa end of the scale. Sonia had been at Lomax for sixteen years and had seen it through good and bad times. Apart from Catherine, she was the only person who had properly known Victor Lomax. Jane Bennett had arrived after his death and Malcolm was acquainted with him, but Victor had let the reins of the property side go by the time he arrived. Sonia was a familiar character to Emma. Most offices had a Sonia. Someone who had been there longer than the carpet, with the company at a previous building, willing and able to deal with the most important client or to put paper in the printer, someone who could open a photocopier and strip it down with the efficiency of a field soldier.

'How are you settling in?' Sonia was asking. 'I've been so busy, I don't feel as though I've spent any time with you. I hear we are having a welcome dinner next week. Catherine gave me your bank details, so we will be paying you at least.'

Sonia was rolling on. Emma was not quite sure which point to respond to and decided to go for a neutral tack.

'I'm enjoying myself. It's quite different from the bank in some ways, particularly the size, but I like the difference.'

Emma had found that if she volunteered information about her background, fewer questions were asked. It allowed her to set the parameters.

'If there's anything I can do to help, please feel free to ask me.'

'I will. Thank you.'

'I'll leave you to it.'

Emma watched her go. A year from forty, the signs of office life were visible in her gait. Still Sonia was attractive, her hair almost ginger and in loose curls, her skin lightly freckled in a youthful way. Emma would have seen her as a middle sister, not as spoiled or damaged as a youngest nor as confident or put-upon as an eldest. Catherine had made a comment to Emma about Sonia's eternal single life. Emma felt for Sonia.

The meeting with the Rayners was at their house in Kensington. Emma had looked through the file and had a brief conversation with Malcolm. She sensed that sexually, he found her unsettling. On Wall Street, she had fucked a good number of the men she worked with, worked for or who worked for her and it was always chalked up to experience. Hard feelings were rare and time-consuming. Emma realised she was back in a different culture and a different business. One pleasing result of Malcolm's diffident attitude was that it had given her the chance to get involved with the Rayners. Malcolm did not like them, did not like loft apartments and apparently did not want to spend time alone with Emma. The net result was she was being left to deal with the Rayners herself. Ed had made a few clucking noises about it, but had relented.

Ian Cameron approached her desk, carrying papers and looking pleased with himself.

'There we are,' he said, placing the paper on her desk. 'Nick of time as usual.'

The sheets were details of the loft apartments. There were numerous photographs, all of magazine quality, and the descriptions were florid to say the least. The photographs were carefully and tastefully mounted on Lomax headed paper.

'Did you take the pictures?' she asked him.

'No, we have a photographer who does it for us. Lomax wouldn't send me out with a Polaroid to take a few snaps.'

'So, do you write the descriptions?'

'No. I'm just the grunt. I do the typing, the copying and the mounting. Whoever has seen the place will write the descriptions. Sometimes, for a sale, they'll write something specially for one client.'

It was very grand. High quality photography, nicely produced information, so different from her normal experience of estate agents.

'Thank you,' she said. 'This will make things easier.'

'You've got the address of where you're going?'

'Yes.'

'Well. Have fun,' he said jovially.

In her first week at the agency, Emma had been given a few things to do, but most of her time was spent leafing through the catalogues of rental and sale properties. It was useful as it helped her understand the sort of properties Lomax offered, making more tangible the general ideas she had about them and their opulent glamour. Malcolm had been keeping his distance from her and she did not push him too hard for work to do. Photocopying, occasionally word processing a letter and manually typing some rental agreements was fine, but Emma needed to involve herself with the business more. The meeting at the Rayners was a first step towards it. Soon, however, she would have to insist on becoming more involved.

Emma took a taxi to the Rayners' house. It was, as she expected, impressive. The father, John Rayner, was part of a family business dealing in antiques and art on the international market. His wife, Elaine, was a therapist with a successful practice. Catherine had told her that John sold people art at a phenomenal cost and Elaine helped them rationalise it afterwards – the perfect marriage of commerce and therapy. Elaine's family were more wealthy than John's, who had only caught up lately. Strong people, independent in their own right, they could form a strong front when necessary. Emma suspected that would centre around their son, Matthew, an only child, twenty-two and still living at home. He had, Catherine said, gone to university a year early.

At three o'clock precisely, Emma rang the bell. The door was quickly answered by a tall man in a brown tweed suit, just a shade too tight for him. His face was broad and his features pronounced, a strong jaw and square forehead. His hair was greying into late middle

61

age and a small pair of half-frame glasses protruded from the breast pocket of his jacket. Slightly more attractive than an average college don, slightly less than a movie star, and Emma was drawn to him immediately.

'Emma Fox?' he asked.

'Yes,' she replied, 'from Lomax.'

'I'm John Rayner. Come in, do.'

His accent was very Home Counties, lots of solid consonants and drawn-out vowels. He led her through a hall that was like a gallery in a museum and into a large room, with high windows, several mirrors and lots of glass surfaces. The light bounced in various directions so that the whole room felt as though it were made of glass. A woman, equally tall and also in her fifties, was standing to meet her, dressed formally in navy blue and with her hair tied back. Every bit the therapist.

'I'm Elaine Rayner. Hello.'

Introductions and pleasantries were exchanged. The house had been a Lomax find, John Rayner had furnished it. Elaine had a consulting room there and John an office.

'Ah, here he is,' Elaine said, cutting off John Rayner in mid-flow. 'Matthew, this is Emma Fox from the property people.'

'Lomax,' Emma said.

She stood and shook his hand, freezing the moment to allow herself to survey him. He was beautiful. A word thrown around so easily, more often in relation to women than to men. This boy was beautiful in a way that was neither simply masculine or feminine. There were obvious things about him. He was tall, like his parents, and had all the most appealing physical characteristics of each. His eyebrows were thin like his mother's but the forehead was strong like his father's. The broadness of his father's face was stretched into a more exquisite length, leaving a long jaw like his mother's. He was wearing a loosely-fitting pair of grey jeans and a tight T-shirt under a green check overshirt. The few seconds she had held his hand seemed to last longer and when they released the clasp, she was momentarily at a loss for words. His eyes held hers and they narrowed; less than a millimetre, but they certainly narrowed as though trying to communicate something to her.

'The chap at the agency, Malcolm isn't it? He said you know a bit about these warehouses and that you would have some details to show us,' John Rayner said.

Husband and wife were on a sofa with ornamental gold working and heavily stuffed red velour cushions. Emma sat in an armchair, perched on the edge and close to the glass-topped table that separated her from the Rayners. The son sat on a small stool he had pulled up, his elbows resting on his knees, head leaning towards her.

'Matthew, does Ms Fox want coffee?' his mother asked.

He looked at Emma. 'Would you?'

'Please. White, no sugar.'

Emma wondered why his mother felt the need to go through her son as an interpreter. She addressed John Rayner's remarks.

'They're not warehouses as such. There's been a trend of late towards lofts. They're really just pent-houses without dividing walls.'

John Rayner chuckled appreciatively at her irreverence and Emma joined in.

'There's no real need for him to leave,' John Rayner said suddenly.

'My husband doesn't feel Matthew should leave.'

'There's plenty of room here,' her husband said.

'Physically, John, yes, there is a lot of room. We've had this conversation several times.'

John Rayner turned to Emma and spoke as though imparting a secret. 'Elaine calls it a conversation for your benefit. We've argued about it. And more than several times.'

Emma could see there was no real rancour between them. John Rayner produced a small cigarette case from his jacket and lit one with a lighter that looked like a small expensive chunk of gold. He did not ask Emma if she minded, which she did, or if she wanted one.

'The lease we can offer on one of the lofts is short term, three months and renewable ongoing for up to a year. The commitment in that instance is not so great,' Emma said.

Matthew returned with a tray. Emma had been practically holding her breath the whole time he had been gone. The glimpse she had caught of him on her first morning at Lomax had niggled at her for over a week. In the lead-up to the meeting, she had thought about him in a very abstract way, as a pleasing presence, something nice to have around but nothing more. In the search for some excitement, the brief sighting of him had been one very small part. But a significant one, she now understood. His presence changed the whole feeling of the room. Emma was worried that his mother might pick up on it, her analytical radar seeming to scan her with a mixture of therapeutic and maternal interest.

'Do you have the details on the places?' Matt asked.

Emma produced them and set them out on the table. Each one comprised three sheets. Matthew seemed impressed, Elaine pleased and John impassive, smoking.

'The one in Soho might be more suitable for Matthew,' Emma explained. 'It's furnished rather nicely. The other is not. The person who bought it has decided not to live in it now. They want to keep the space but rent it out, leaving the tenant to do what they want. There's a commitment from the owner to quite a long lease in this instance. Of course, there would be a high cost associated with that and I'm not sure we're going to be able to let that property easily. I'd be tempted to go for Soho for cost and practicality.'

'Soho, you say. What do you think to that, Matt?' his father asked him.

'It's very sought-after,' Emma said, knowing what was going through the father's mind but unable to tell if he viewed the seedy connotations of Soho positively or negatively.

'It looks great,' was all Matt said, staring at the pictures on the table.

'I had a friend who lived in a similar space in New York. I spent some time there and it was very different. So much space and light. It depends on your personality, I think, as to whether or not it suits you,' said Emma.

Emma looked to the mother, to see if she had an opinion. Elaine was looking at her son, who was still studying the sheet of paper he had picked up, and then she looked at Emma.

'I still think a place nearer to here, something more practical, would make more sense,' said John Rayner.

Matt looked up and said nothing, glancing at his mother.

'John,' his wife said, 'the practicality of it is not relevant. A move is a move. As long as Matthew is content.'

'I still don't like it,' he said.

'What don't you like about it?' asked his wife in a resigned tone that did not seem to expect an answer.

As the two of them continued, no longer paying Emma or their son any attention, Matthew looked at her over the sheet of paper.

'Thanks for bringing these. Will I be able to look at

the one in Soho?'

As he spoke over the sheet of paper, she could see only his eyes, not his mouth.

'Yes, there are keys,' she said.

'Could I look at it tomorrow?'

'If that will be okay,' she said, looking at his parents and meaning that she thought their permission would be needed.

'They're going to let me live wherever I want, ultimately. They have to argue, rationalise, recriminate and the whole other gamut of therapeutic methods before anything happens,' he whispered to her, not unlike the way his father had turned to her earlier. 'I've been in analysis since I was in the womb. Call me Matt, by the way. I prefer it. Matthew sounds like a choir boy.'

A white-smocked image floated agreeably in her mind.

'Guys,' Matt said. 'Emma said they have keys for this one in Soho. I'd like to look at it and then I'll tell you what I think. We can talk about it. Anyone have a problem with that?'

Both parents stopped their cross-talking. His words seemed to soothe them. Emma watched him skilfully play them, appealing to mother the therapist and father the knowing philistine.

It was agreed. Emma said she could arrange for him to see the loft in Soho the next day. She asked the parents if they would like to come. Matt interjected before either of them could speak.

'No,' he said, looking at Emma and narrowing his eyes the way he had when they shook hands. 'I'll go alone.'

Chapter Seven

'*IT'S SO BRIGHT* in here,' Matt said as he stepped into the loft apartment in Soho.

It was just after two-fifteen in the afternoon and the sun was glaring through the long rows of high windows that made up the apartment.

'There aren't many of these available for rental at the moment. We're lucky to have two on the books, although I think the one in Clerkenwell will be around for a long time,' Emma said, picking up on his eagerness.

'Why is this one available?' he asked.

'The owner is in Japan. Runs her own consulting business and won't be needing the place for a year. Usually, people buy these as empty shells, with just the basic feeds for gas and electricity.'

Catherine had given her some background, a few things to say about loft-living in London. As Emma looked at Matt, availing herself of the odd sly glance, she wondered if Catherine suspected any ulterior motive on her part for getting herself involved so readily with the Rayners. Emma was not sure herself if she really wanted this. Something nagged at her, and was holding her back just a fraction more than normal.

'Is this what your friend's was like in New York?'

'This is much more modern and clean-looking. His was very bohemian.'

Emma looked around the apartment. In some ways it was predictable, but a nice sort of predictability. Lots of bare brick, tall windows, lofty ceilings and brushed chrome in the kitchen area. The furniture was lots of strong primary colours and the floor light beech strips in wide boards. It was very much like a photo shoot in a home magazine. She could tell Matt was enamoured of it.

'Can my parents afford this?'

'Yes.'

'I'm not sure how that makes me feel.'

He gave her a smile and wandered off towards an open-plan staircase that led up to a gantry with a bed on it. He was wearing a cotton jacket, white and overlong, a silk shirt that was almost Hawaiian and battered brown corduroy trousers. She watched him climb the stairs, catching a glimpse of his behind under the tail of his jacket as he raised his leg to mount a step. Emma gave him some time to look and went over to the dining area, admiring the large maple table, ten chairs easily fitting round it.

Paintings hung here and there, where there was a lack of window and sufficient supply of wall. The notes Emma had in her hand said these could be removed, as could small items of furniture if the tenant wished. The bulky items had to stay as the owner did not want to warehouse them. It's one big warehouse, anyway, Emma thought.

She heard Matt's footfalls on the stairs and turned to see him.

'What do you think?' she asked.

'It's not like I imagined it would be. You see all those pictures of lofts, but now, it seems so big. I don't know if I could sleep with all this space around me. I'd get agoraphobia. What do you think of it?' he asked.

'I like it. I could see myself living here. It's different as far as the rest of London goes.'

'The view's not that brilliant,' he said.

'Just a lot of building tops. But then what view would you have in a chintzy mews flat?' she asked him.

'I know. Tell my mum and dad that, though. Is this more expensive than renting a flat in Kensington?'

'Not really,' she replied. 'It's a question of supply, that's all. This has only been on with us for the last few days and we're exclusive on it, like most of our properties. No one's seen it except for you.' Emma amazed herself at how easily she slipped into the role of property agent.

'My parents were really charmed by you, you know,' he said to her, looking out of the window.

Emma looked at his profile, the light behind his face accentuating it. She wanted to reach out and touch him as he stared out on the urban scene below. Did he know that was what she wanted to do? Did he want her to?

'I'm flattered. They're nice people.'

He turned to look at her and sat on the large sill of the window. His body was now lower and he needed to look up slightly to talk to her. The sun was in his face and he scrunched his features as he spoke.

'Do you like working at Lomax?' he asked.

'Yes. I've only been there a short while, but I'm having a good time. I worked in a bank before, for a long time, and this is quite different.'

Matt was looking at her, a question on the brink of being asked. She said nothing and simply stood looking down at him, taking him in. There was a clear and obvious tension in the air, a tension of the pleasurable sort. Emma was not a person to hesitate, but nor was she one to rush in until she was certain the moment was right.

69

'I'm going to have another look round,' Matt said, breaking the silence and jumping up off the window ledge.

For the next six or seven minutes, they managed to avoid each other in the expanse of an apartment that felt increasingly small around them, as though the walls were closing in and drawing them together. Emma could sense him in the space wherever he was, her instincts acting like a radar. He made nervous shuffling noises as he continued to look around. Emma looked out of the window, at London, and knew that she was home. This was her city, whatever she had told herself those last years in New York. She had missed the city and now she was glad to be back. She thought of Matt, conscious of his movements, and realised that she had been missing something else. She went to find him.

Matt was investigating the fridge, squatting down on his haunches, the right leg dipping lower towards the ground than the left, which was pushing upwards. The loose white jacket hung over his rear, almost touching the floor, and his elbows rested on his knees. Emma stood and looked at him from the doorway of the kitchen. He closed the fridge door but did not stand up. He returned her look, the fingers of his left hand carefully gripping those of his right. His wrists were visible where he had rolled the soft white cotton of the jacket sleeves back several times. In a similar way, he had made makeshift turn-ups with the bottoms of the brown cords, revealing fluffy socks that were practically stuffed into a pair of old moccasins. There, a small band of bronze skin was again visible at the top of the sock. The roundness of his calf made an outline in the back of his trouser leg. Apart from his face, the only other piece of skin Emma could see was his neck and Adam's apple. The elaborately printed shirt was opened two buttons down and the top of his collarbone made a line across his frame.

70

It was hard not to stare. Emma simply looked at him and he did not seem troubled by her gaze, remaining crouched by the fridge as though afraid to break the intensity of the moment. Emma looked at his face. She was seven or eight feet away from him yet she bridged the distance with a yearning gaze that moulded her features into a simple and single signal. He was picking it up, she could tell. His mouth was partially open, his top teeth revealed in the small gap between his lips. His hair arced from his crown and made a wave on the top that flowed out and did not quite touch his ear. Behind his ear lobes, down the back of his neck, the longer mane was apparent, brushing the collar of the jacket. He blinked several times, the lashes fine, and bent his knees further, allowing Emma to look between them and make out the shape of his behind. It was this view which rendered the image so erotic for her.

Emma was rooted, as if she had been set to the floor with concrete. Despite this, in a few seconds she would make the journey across the short distance that separated them. Once she did, she would never again stand that far from him and look at him in the way she had been. The separation of their bodies, the interval between them, was made up entirely of possibilities, of things that might be. It should have been simple to just turn and walk into the other room, brush him off and carry on. The moment would be gone. Matt's eyes narrowed as though he could hear her thoughts. She gave several long blinks, depriving herself of the sight of him for fractions of seconds and realising in those instants that she did not want to walk away from him. She took the first tiny step across the divide of the possible and the actual, wondering exactly what she would find at the end.

Matt stood as she reached him and Emma stretched out to take his hand, holding his fingers to her face, kissing them and rubbing them on her cheek. He looked at her and at his hand like someone watching himself in a dream. Emma touched his trousers, the corduroy making wide ridges under her fingers. The material excited her because it contained the warm flesh beneath. She imagined the soft interior of the corduroy trousers against the skin of his legs, his underwear next to his crotch and his behind, the soft silk of the shirt on his chest. His body felt precious in her hands; fragile but not frail. Something to be cherished and looked after. Emma circled a thumb over one of his knuckles, the skin covering it slightly wrinkled and the bone tactile beneath it. Turning the hand over, she caressed his palm, the soft lines in the centre breaking into many small tributaries near the base of his fingers. Slowly and precisely, he closed his hand over hers and held it.

There was one gap still to be crossed. Emma looked up from her hand and met his eyes. Matt shook his head a fraction, still appearing as a character in his own dream. Her free hand on the back of his neck caressing his hair and rubbing the collar of the jacket, Emma leaned over and kissed Matt, bridging the gap. The kiss went on for longer than either of them had breath for and soon they were both gasping air in the small points of separation they allowed each other. Emma's hands were roving over Matt, the silk of the shirt, the light cotton of the jacket and the gentle corduroy of the trousers. He kept his eyes closed while they were kissing, but Emma, not wanting him out of her sight, kept hers open the whole time, watching his eyes and his forehead and any other piece of him she could see.

Emma broke the kiss but not the embrace and they both panted, more like they had just made love rather than were about to. She reached behind him and cupped one of his buttocks in her hand, squeezing it and fitting it into her grasp. It was pleasingly solid and she moved the hand to slip it into the back pocket.

'The bed?' he asked softly.

She put a finger to his lips, brushed them and gave an ironic laugh. 'There's plenty of floor, some of it's even carpeted.'

'That doesn't seem very special,' he replied.

Emma touched the front of the brown corduroy trousers, weighing him up and feeling the surge.

'Special we can arrange some other time.'

She moved her fingertips over the bulge in his trousers.

'Right now, I want you,' she said.

As they continued their kiss, Emma's hands started to unwrap him, moving almost unconsciously about his body, pulling at fabric and undoing buttons. The white jacket was the first to go, falling off his back and floating to the floor, the light cotton shimmering through the air as it did. The silk shirt surprised her because it had short sleeves, but she enjoyed seeing his arms with their compact musculature. Emma undid the next two buttons at the top of the shirt and her hand made a dive for his chest, a narrow ridge down the centre separating his pectoral muscles. A further button and she was able to touch his stomach, the skin like rubber sheathing a lead core. She moved the layer of skin over the solid group of muscles, dipping her fingers into the warm elasticity of him. With the final button open and the shirt pulled away to the sides of his waistband, Emma saw the sprouting of hair below his navel that would run all the way down into his pubic hair and she let it tickle the backs of her fingers, aware of how, lower down, his cock was straining against the fabric of his trousers.

Emma took him by the hand and led him through into the living area. Squeezing his fingers, she led him up the stairs and into the area with the bed. He smiled at her.

'Can I undress you?' he asked.

'Please,' she replied.

The process fascinated him. Emma followed his every move. First, she stood while he unzipped the skirt and took her out of it along with her shoes and her tights. He kissed her as he removed the blouse, taking his time with her and holding himself back. Once during his stripping of her, she reached and squeezed at his cock through his trousers, making both of them groan. When she was in only her bra and knickers, she went to the bed and waited for him, wanting to watch him undress himself, to be privy to it. He looked at her and seemed uncertain what she wanted.

'Take off all your clothes, Matt,' she said gently, encouraging him with the look on her face.

Emma lay on the bed, leaning up on an elbow and watching as he pulled the shirt fully out of the trousers, listening to the noise the silk made against the waistband. His back was to her when he removed it and she watched the way the shoulder blades moved easily and freely. He stood one foot on the other to remove the moccasins and the socks quickly followed. Still with his back to her, almost shy, she saw his elbows poke out from his sides as he unfastened his trousers, lifting a leg at a time to remove them. She studied him from behind, his long back and narrow hips, the buttocks covered by boxer shorts which were tantalisingly loose, not revealing what the trousers had accentuated so well. He turned to face her and with his eyes fixed on hers, he pushed his underwear off. Emma continued to look in his eyes for a moment longer before averting her gaze to his crotch.

Matt stood, the blaze of the afternoon sun burnishing his skin with light and making him honey-coloured. His hands were awkwardly hanging by his side, yet his cock stood hard and proud from the

74

bulk of light brown pubic hair. His balls were scrunched and hiding in his scrotum and the cock was longer than she expected, the skin not as dark as she anticipated. There was a length and a heaviness to it that was arousing simply to look at. Emma's pussy buzzed from this straightforward act of observation and from contemplating the things she could do to him and the things he could do to her. It was like the breach between them earlier, resplendent with promise but also much more tangible and sexual. He was twenty-two years old and stood before her displaying himself, conveying with his body what he felt for her and what he wanted from her. Beneath the shyness, Emma suspected that he was alight. She reached out her hand and he approached the bed.

'Oh Matt,' she whispered before their mouths connected.

The first thing she did as they kissed, he leaning over her, was to reach down and fondle his shaft, moving the rigid member about and stroking the slightly rough flesh. The roughness of it reminded her of the contrasting slickness of her pussy and the liquid feeling between her legs. His hands were tugging at the side of her knickers and, after he removed them, her behind felt rudely bare. She sat up and he knelt, reaching behind her to unclasp the bra, her breasts springing gloriously free. Matt leaned down and suckled on the tip of her right nipple. It was hard in his mouth and she gasped as he nipped at it and placed pressure on it by closing his lips around it. Emma remained sitting up, her arms out behind her and her legs open. Matt was kneeling between them and quietly feeding himself on her breasts, his hair tickling her mounds as he shifted from one to the other. His fingers daintily massaged her, squeezing her breasts and then feathering over them, heightening their sensitivity. Matt's own nipples were like small hard bullets on his hairless chest and Emma reached to tweak one of them, flicking the tip with her thumb. Touching him there sent a quiver between her legs, a throb of desire for him.

Kissing her between her breasts, and then moving lower, Matt's tongue left a deliciously wet trail along her stomach. Emma lay back on the bed and he crouched over her, pecking at her stomach with tiny kisses and alternately rubbing her skin with the slightly rough tip of his tongue. On her, Matt's tongue was like a highly flexible instrument with a pointed tip, able to mould itself and to probe and then, having found its target, to delve into it with a rough passion. Emma trembled as he flicked at her navel and then started in on the pliant flesh that lay below it and which ultimately led into her.

He used his whole mouth on her pubic hair, opening wide and closing it over her as though trying to fit her all into his mouth at once. In the midst of the coverage, the tongue still bobbed and darted about over her, tickling at her hair. Matt was so desperately close to her clitoris and the opening of her vagina that she could hardly wait for him to travel the inch or so that was necessary for him to connect with her. Emma felt greedy, wanting to take Matt and to use him for her own pleasure and only then to give him something back in return. She placed her hands on the side of his head, his hair between her fingers, and gently she pushed his head downwards.

Emma shifted the position of her legs, feeling his shoulders resting on the underside of her thighs, her calves over the back of his arms. Her feet firmly on the bed, she allowed her knees to open. Matt rested his hand on her leg and she reached down to make contact with it. The position of her legs opened her labia to him and she enjoyed being on display, so close up. Although she could not see his face, she liked to imagine the look on his pretty features as he hovered so close to the centre of her passion. Carefully, she touched the lips of her pussy and held herself open for him, showing herself to him, the moist labia and the engorged clitoris.

Matt's breath was warm on her pussy, enhancing the tingling sensation that had been building since they had arrived at the apartment; since she had seen him and his parents the day before; since she had seen him that first morning in the agency. In the space of only a few days, she had managed to spot this boy and to end up lying on a bed in an apartment in Soho, baring her innermost self to him. There was nothing about it that seemed incorrect in any way. To him either, she thought. There had been a tension brought about by desire that had streaked through the few interactions between them, a silent knowledge that they were drawn to each other. Neither of them had sought to make it vocal but had been content to fly quickly towards where they were at that moment.

Emma gave a long and contented breath when his tongue licked at the inside of her pussy. She continued to hold herself in such a way that allowed him to lick at her inner and outer lips and to snap his tongue at her clitoris. Her breasts, where his tongue had earlier laboured so skilfully, still throbbed from the encounter, her nipples tight and distended. After concentrating on her clitoris for several moments, using his tongue and his lips around it, he suddenly pushed a short way into her. This first penetrative act, coming at the end of his slow and meticulous stimulation of her, seemed to flow naturally from it, as though this was what he had been preparing her for. For long minutes, he worked at her clitoris, licking and sucking at it and then nuzzling her labia. She had long since stopped holding herself, abandoning herself to him. Her clitoris literally felt as though it was floating on his tongue, that he had lifted it and scooped it up, making it weightless under his touch. Gradually, the whole of her body felt suspended on the wave that he generated around her.

It had not been her intention to come, but she did. It almost took her by surprise, again following naturally from what he was doing to her. One moment she was floating on the swell of her desire, content to let it carry her along and then, all at once, she had reached a different level. It was now a wave she rode on top of, rather than one she simply drifted with. Her pussy moved tightly, the muscles clenching themselves, eager for release. Emma's frame lifted itself from the bed, perhaps half an inch or even less. Her shoulders strained and she felt the orgasm erupt inside her. Almost oblivious to Matt, her face was hot and flushed and suddenly she was no longer even riding the wave. Rather, the wave was all through her, making her a part of it and she quivered and rolled, thrashing about on the bed, her arms thrown carelessly on the pillows.

Matt was sitting up and looking at her, as she lay, eyes half-open, totally washed up by the experience. Matt moved himself up so that he was leaning over her. His cock was long and stiff, as ready for her as she felt for him. He knelt between her open legs and supported himself with his hands. She gripped the hard muscles of his forearms and felt the tip of his cock gently brush her labia as he positioned himself over her. He looked at her, his expression serious and alert, as though trying to read her mind. He looked down to where they were about to be joined and his hair hung forward. Emma let her head fall back, no longer able to see him and ready only to feel him.

When he pushed with his groin, the head of his cock delving into her, she looked up, wanting to see the expression on his face. But he was not looking at her. His head was down and he was staring intently at his cock, watching it as it slowly became a part of her. It took him several attempts to guide himself in using his hips alone, but they both knew at exactly the same moment when they had found the right move. In one second, they had crossed a threshold and the muscles of her vagina accommodated him and made welcoming ripples around the shaft.

Matt's cock was perhaps only slightly longer than Emma had anticipated, but it made a delightful difference as he used it on her like a well-honed instrument. His body moved closer to her with the same fractions of an inch that he entered her by. His body came to rest on hers, the bones of his hips resting against hers, his upper frame raised so his chest lighted on hers only occasionally. Matt met her eyes and his face had a happy look. They kissed and held each other, neither ready to move just yet, but rather content to enjoy their posture.

For the next ten or fifteen minutes, in the diminishing light of London's afternoon sun, Matt made love to her. There was an intensity to the act but also a sense that he did not want it to be over too quickly, despite the heated nature of a first encounter. The cavern of the open-plan room swallowed up their steadily increasing volume level. It had started as the hardly audible body against body, then the sound of the fabric of the mattress, the sound of the bed itself and finally, their own sounds.

With his arms wide on the bed and his cock deeply inside her, Matt whispered, 'I'm coming.'

The whole of his lower body movement became exaggerated, his groin making long and elaborate thrusts into her, planting his cock deep into her. Emma felt his cock throb against the walls of her vagina and touched his hair as he yelped in submission to his orgasm. His whole body stiffened into a spasm that appeared similar to the one his cock was having. Emma held him and the shift in his movements inside her helped to bring her closer to her own climax. Warm discharges of semen burst into her and she clenched herself around him, encouraging him to continue pressing into her as she was so close herself. He nodded helplessly and continued to grind away at her, desperate to help her over the edge.

It brought quick reward. Her come-filled pussy let itself go for him a second time, hot and damp as it tensed and untensed around his still firm cock. It was an agreeable sensation, to orgasm while he was in her and his semen was deeper in her, moving about in her. Feeling suddenly close to him, she pulled him to her and squeezed his frame tightly, stopping his cock moving and letting her pussy move of its own accord, her orgasm subsiding and dwindling into a pleasurable flush over her whole body.

Time passed easily as they lay and held each other. Matt kissed and felt her, more carefully and with a greater tenderness than the frank and sexual touch he had used earlier. Emma's mind drifted but was unable to do so for long. Her thoughts turned to Matt and she questioned her judgement, the way she had engineered the situation. There had been no explicit thought in her mind that she would end up in bed with him, but the small details of the situation, the very fact that she had involved herself with his family in the first instance, were all part of where it had led.

There was something striking about him, something that seemed good in itself. Normally, Emma was happy with a simple lack of negatives: no bad past relationships, no domineering mother, no lingering crushes on old flames. Despite knowing nothing about Matt beyond the obvious, her instinct told her that he was not burdened with any of the baggage she so frequently encountered.

The only question that lingered in her mind, which was not unpleasant, was where it would lead.

Chapter Eight

'*COPY THIS,*' ED said, throwing a sheaf of papers onto Emma's desk, not even breaking his stride as he tossed them sidelong.

Emma looked up, her blood pressure instantly at danger level, and clenched her teeth, ready to shout at him.

'Ed!' It was Malcolm, speaking sharply. 'Room One. Now.'

Nicola Morris and Tony Wilson both looked up from their work, distracted and brought to attention by the sudden change in atmosphere brought about in the space of only six words. Sonia Morgan was on the phone and had not noticed Malcolm's sudden outburst.

After several minutes, during which Tony and Nicola shuffled papers and tried to look busy, Malcolm reappeared, minus Ed.

'Emma, could I have a word?' Malcolm asked.

'Of course,' she said, rising.

Ed was waiting for them in the meeting room, sitting on the edge of a table. Malcolm closed the door and leaned against it. Emma stood with her hands on her hips and looked at Ed. The scene was reminiscent of a police interrogation on a television programme.

'I'm sorry,' Ed mumbled under Malcolm's glare.

'Sorry? Ed, what the hell is your problem with me?' she asked, stopping before she lost control of herself.

He neither responded nor looked at her, but she could see his chest rising and falling inside his striped shirt. His adrenalin was flowing. Emma's was coursing through her veins, the only physical effect being the sharpness of her posture and the steely expression on her face. Emma thrived on the rush of energy, whereas Ed seemed to be drowning in his.

'I've been polite and helpful,' she continued. 'All you do is treat me like an idiot. Can I tell you something? I think I am smarter than you. But do you know what? I don't want your job, okay? Believe me.'

'I'm sorry. All right? It won't happen again.'

Ed appeared chided by whatever Malcolm had said to him. Their paternalistic relationship obviously extended to the occasional fatherly telling-off by Malcolm. To an extent, Emma could sympathise with Ed's position. Had she been in the same spot, she would have questioned the sudden presence of an outsider, brought in by a proprietor and landed on her team, virtually imposed. Emma, however, would have acted to neutralise the threat of that person, whether that meant befriending them or making them a bitter enemy. The point was, Emma would have played the situation, not acted in the childish way Ed had carried on. If he was too immature to understand the game, she thought, that was his problem.

Soon, when the purpose of her presence at the agency was revealed, Ed would regret his current behaviour. In the past two weeks he had been deliberately obstructive. Getting more information was the whole purpose of her posting at the agency and Ed had infuriated her by refusing to answer even the most straightforward questions. Any explanations he deigned to give were in the most pointless and swaggering jargon. Emma was not going to be drawn into this one.

'Let's just forget it. I'll do that copying before we leave for the pub,' Emma said.

'You don't have to. I can do it,' said Ed.

'Don't worry about it.'

Malcolm had been a silent presence throughout, nodding profusely in time with any positive statement, like a kite ready to be taken whichever way the wind blew. Perhaps his piece had been said before her arrival. Keep it in the family, she thought.

She left the room.

At the copier, she watched the feeder suck the papers through and she let go of the situation. Putting it into the larger context showed how small and insignificant it was. Ian Cameron tapped her on the shoulder.

'Matthew Rayner is on the phone. He said it's important.'

Ian gave her a look suggesting he knew what was implied by the word important.

'I'll look after this for you,' he said, nodding at the copier.

'Hello,' she said into the receiver.

'Hi, it's Matt.'

There was a pause. Emma thought she heard him swallow. He was nervous. The silence, broken only by the electricity of the phone line, seemed like days. For a second, it was as though they had missed a gear. A cog had failed to connect and there was not a way to move the conversation forwards.

'So, I'm important now?' she asked brightly.

The relief in his voice was palpable. He seized her words like a drowning man after a log.

'Naturally. I just called to say hello.'

'Hello,' she said. 'I called the private line at your parents' house but the machine was on. I called the

83

mobile number given by the message on the machine and got another message. I gave up.'

'You called me?' He sounded surprised and pleased. 'What for?'

'Just to say hi.'

Emma was struck by the faltering, teenaged nature of the conversation. Since viewing the loft apartment in Soho, the memories of late afternoon lovemaking still warm in her, they had not spoken. He had given her his number at home, his private line no less, and she had taken it. He had had to prompt her before she gave him her own. It was then, when he remarked that it was a Chelsea number, that she realised it was not going to be easy to deceive Matt. Not if she felt serious about him. Normally, Emma would not consider the issue of seriousness based on a single encounter, not so early on. But the discomfort she felt, explaining herself away to Matt, was the obvious indication that her feelings for him were strong. Of course, he shared similar feelings towards her, but she did not want him to get attached to a woman – plain Emma Fox – who was, in effect, fictional.

'I have a welcoming drink tonight,' she said. 'It was put back from last week and scaled down from a dinner to just drinks. That's better really. I know most of the people well enough.'

'Can we meet up sometime?'

'Of course. What's happening with the loft?'

'My mother is at a conference at the moment for a couple of days. When she gets back, we have to have a conference of our own. Then the ballot, the postal votes, the recount. It's always like this,' he said.

'Did your father warm to the idea?'

Matt laughed.

'What?' she demanded.

'He warmed to you. He'd be so jealous if he knew.'

Neither of them tried to label what exactly there was to know.

84

'Call me at the weekend,' she said.

'Okay.'

Disappointment in his voice.

The local pub served as the venue for the belated and scaled-down welcome for Emma. It was loosely themed on an American bar, and Emma wondered if Catherine had chosen it with any irony. It would be like her. Malcolm and Tony, the family men, would only be able to stay briefly. Dominic Lester had not been able to make it at all. Jane Bennett was perched on an oversized mahogany barstool, her legs dangling off it as she sucked gin and tonic through a straw like it was a milk shake. Catherine was in conversation with Jane and Sonia Morgan, the three of them looking out of place at a bar, large overhead speakers pumping out album tracks from bands with too many guitarists. Malcolm and Ed had fallen into laddish banter while Ian and Nicola were in deep conversation, nodding at each other like drinking birds in a water glass. At the opposite end of the bar, a group of young men were indulging in a noisy round of liar's poker with twenty-pound notes, trying to guess digits from the serial numbers. Emma had not seen that game played in a while. She sighed and felt nothing like the centre of anyone's attention.

'Welcome, then.'

It was Tony Wilson, the only other spare person apart from herself. At the agency, he spoke very little but it did not affect his ability to work in the team. On the UK side, they had the range of personalities from Ed's arrogance through Malcolm's general lack of certainty to Dominic's brisk and down-to-business approach. Tony Wilson was the quiet and diligent type and Emma did not have a strong opinion, other than that he was a touch Dickensian, a little of the Bob Cratchit about him. She had heard Ed refer to Tony as the undertaker. His skin was permanently five o'clock shadowed and his hair in need of less grease and more conditioner. He was not unpleasant, but the line he ran was thin. 'It's his bloody wife's fault,' Ed had said to her. 'Should look after him better.' Emma's bottom lip was developing a callus from biting it in Ed's presence.

'Sorry I can't stay for longer. Family things,' Tony Wilson said.

'How long have you been married?' she asked.

'Not quite four years. You seem to be fitting in all right. Do you like it here?'

'I'd have to say yes, even if I didn't. Wouldn't I?' She smiled.

'Maybe not,' he said, dolefully.

'Do you like it?' she asked, turning his question around on itself.

'You do what you have to do,' he replied.

'Tony,' she admonished, 'you sound like a grand-father with five dependent children and thirty dependent grandchildren. Do you have any children?'

'Don't listen to this bloody misery,' Ed broke in, throwing an arm around Tony and squeezing him.

Ed's tie was loose and his face had the flush of a couple of quick drinks.

'Tony's Mr Pipe and Slippers, aren't you?' Ed said.

Tony was unflustered.

'Are you going to Waterloo, Tony?' Malcolm asked.

He nodded.

'Want to share a cab?'

Another nod.

Malcolm and Tony said their goodbyes in a disorganised group fashion, Ed making sarcastic remarks about people who commuted to London.

'Right,' said Ed when Malcolm and Tony had left. 'Straw poll.'

He paused until he had their attention and surveyed them all like a security camera, lapping up their gaze.

'Who's ever seen Tony's wife?' he asked them all.

'Ed, not that again, please,' said Nicola, a tone of quiet irritation in her voice.

'I never have,' Ian piped in innocently.

Sonia stepped up to explain for Emma's benefit, shooting a pointed glance at Ed prior to speaking. 'Edward thinks it is funny because Tony's wife is somewhat stand-offish. She has not attended Christmas parties for the last two years. I don't think we should pry. I speak to her from time to time, last month in fact, but I think she has problems.'

'You're her favourite,' Ed said. 'She only ever speaks to you. I reckon he killed her. It's always the quiet types.'

'No danger of Ed ever killing anyone then,' Ian murmured in Emma's ear, so close that she could feel his voice vibrating on her earlobe.

'It's something about Lomax,' Ed went on. 'Look at us. All single.'

'Don't forget our Nicola. She may be a baby, but she's a married woman,' wheezed Jane Bennett with her broken megaphone of a voice.

'She's certainly a baby,' whispered Ian.

'Thank you,' Nicola said to no one in particular.

Ed looked at Nicola and it was then that Emma knew. Ed and Nicola. It made sense. The two of them were having an affair. Even if Nicola was a stroppy cow, Emma wouldn't have wished Ed on her.

'No. I'm serious,' persisted Ed. 'Jane's a gay divorcee, Dominic's, well, not divorced certainly.'

People groaned at the innuendo.

'We're all single,' he concluded.

'Some of us would rather not be, Ed.'

It was Catherine.

Nicola Morris seemed embarrassed and looked at her shoes, Jane was somewhat oblivious and Ian made a face at Emma.

'Of course, we're all assuming Emma's single,' Ed said.

It was an unusual comment from Ed, the only one she could recall him uttering which had taken attention away from him and placed it on someone else. Emma felt she was the centre of attention.

'If I were single, Ed, I don't know if you'd be the first or the last person I'd tell.'

Laughter broke out but Ed was confused and had lost interest in the conversation now he no longer formed its centrepiece. He offered to buy another round of drinks by way of compensation.

'Ed's such a prick,' Ian said to her quietly when they had split back down into smaller conversations.

'I know. But is he shagging Nicola?' Emma asked with equal quiet, aware of the danger of having the conversation in such close proximity to its subjects.

'You're sharp. It's meant to be the best kept secret at the agency. They go for lunch ten minutes apart and rendezvous around the corner. If you see them together, they pretend they don't know you. It's sad.'

'So how does a well kept secret get out?' she asked, wondering if hers was safe.

'Well, Ed's a prick, as I said, and Nicola's insanely possessive and very obvious when she's drunk. After a few more drinks, she'll be on Ed's knee. Watch.'

'I didn't realise you were the office gossip,' she said. 'So you have all the scandal at Lomax?'

He raised his eyebrows several times in quick succession. Ian's hair was short and he was good-looking. His looks had grown on her over the last two weeks. He was cheeky, cocksure, but not too much so. He was the sort of boy she liked to have around the office to flirt with or to look at his behind when he was unaware of it. It was the sort of thing that brightened the office.

Emma joined Catherine, Sonia and Jane at the bar.

They appeared very stately, like a Lomax royal family. Nicola and Ian were laughing at something Ed was saying. Emma did not feel she belonged to either group. The ladies at the bar or the raucous youths giggling at Ed. Her age placed her between the two and her experience miles away from each. None of them, except Catherine, had very much in common with her.

'I was just saying we don't get together like this very often,' Catherine said.

'It's because we're ageing,' Sonia said. 'Do you remember ten years ago? We had some times.'

'Our clients were more fun then,' Catherine said. 'They enjoyed spending their money. Now they worry, they fret, they feel guilty.'

'Or get found guilty,' Sonia added, laughing.

'We don't do Spanish business any more,' Jane piped up, 'and I didn't know he was a criminal when I dealt with him.'

'Jane has connections with the criminal fraternity,' Sonia said. 'We got into a difficult deal with a man we later discovered opened security vans with a chain-saw.'

'I just worry that Lomax is not a fun place to work any more,' Catherine said. 'It lacks Victor's verve. I lack his verve.'

'Oh, dear,' Sonia said, 'of course it's fun. No one expects you to be Victor.'

'What does our newest recruit think?' Jane tooted through her nose.

Emma hardly saw her lips move. A career in ventriloquism beckons, she thought. Emma looked at Catherine and then spoke.

'I'm having fun. I'd like to spread my wings a bit, learn as much as I can without being over-ambitious.'

'I don't believe people can be good generalists,' opined Jane, the straw from the gin and tonic still in the side of her mouth, rendering her voice like Popeye's.

Emma ignored her and the urge to suggest they just connect the straw to the gin optic so that she could continue her bilge-pump-like drawing up of the liquid.

'I did some accountancy training at the bank. Very basic, but if you wanted any help for instance, Sonia, I'd be more than willing.'

Sonia smiled and said nothing.

'Even on the foreign side,' Emma added, addressing Jane. 'I might be of some use. We used a lot of documentation in one section I worked and I'm strong on detail. Those are the sort of skills that make for a good generalist.'

Again, there was silence. Emma received the message. They were not interested in her help. They would smile and be helpful, but they were glad she was working with Malcolm and was not their problem, did not impinge on their worlds.

'What do you think, Catherine?' Emma asked, in seek of support.

'It's good for all of us to spread our wings at times,' she said.

'Yes, but not if you're a penguin. Or if you're Icarus,' wheezed Jane, the laugh rattling in her chest like a lost button in a washing machine.

A joke, thought Emma. And at her expense. How funny. She laughed politely and used the smile to nourish an evil thought: you'll laugh when you find out I own you, you silly bitch.

It was clear she would get no further. Catherine did not want to foist Emma on either Sonia or Jane and that was understandable. Catherine knew how to read them better than Emma could, but she had wanted to try it out, just to be certain. She was closer to Sonia and Jane in age than any of the other junior people. It was expected that she would be more ambitious than them.

This was threatening to anyone who was established somewhere.

'I have to leave,' Ed announced theatrically.

As he did, Ian looked at Emma from behind Nicola and touched his watch, mouthing the words 'ten minutes' to her. Sure enough, ten minutes later, Nicola announced that she too had to leave. Ian smiled and naughtily asked if she needed walking to the station, obviously enjoying her floundering refusal.

The group was breaking up. When Catherine said she too had to leave, it was as though it gave Sonia and Jane permission to leave as well. The three of them trailed out in a string, a little like a wedding procession, led by Catherine.

'Looks like it's just me and you, kid,' Ian said.

'Don't you think that's my line?' she replied.

'Maybe they planned to leave us alone,' he said deviously.

Emma made ready for a sinking feeling in her heart.

'You never answered Ed when he asked you about being single,' he continued.

Gently and with a slow but certain course, like a coin in the ocean, Emma felt her heart make its journey down her chest. Ian was coming on to her. How could she let him down as gently as her heart, she wondered.

'It's not been much of a welcome for you. It's still early. Do you want to get something to eat?'

'Ian. . .'

'I know,' he interrupted, and she knew he did. 'But at least let me pretend for a while.'

'I am seeing someone,' she said, before he pretended too far.

'Fuck,' was all he said, and the word had no venom in it, serving as a simple description of his feelings at that moment. 'So does this mean you don't eat any more?' he asked.

'I'm sorry?'

'I mean, we could still get something to eat. We wouldn't have to get married or anything. Maybe engaged, but only if we don't split the bill.'

She laughed and he dipped his head to look at her eyes.

'Okay,' she said.

'I'll even take you home,' he said, persistent hope in his voice.

'Doubtful,' she said, and then looked at him. He grinned at her and out of nowhere, she found herself wondering what he looked like naked. What would that tight little rump look like unwrapped? Stop, she thought to herself. The stop thought was loud. Then the nude thought whispered through it, almost subliminally.

'Well, maybe a little way there,' she said, hoping she could trust herself.

Chapter Nine

THE SMALL CAR lurched forwards as Ed shifted a gear and it pulled them along the street in Chelsea, towards the house they were going to measure up. For most of the short journey, Ed had made several comments about tape measures and size and Emma had politely ignored them, wondering what effect he thought they were having on her. His arrogant confidence about the business spilled over into the sexual for him. Emma wondered if he had even an inkling that he would be no match for her in either area.

'How long have you been at Lomax, Ed?'

'Two and a half years. It's the strangest market I've ever worked in, so insulated from the real world. I get to meet lots of interesting people, not the usual dross.'

Emma listened to the good school burr of his voice, the accent rounding off the rough edges, melding each word into the other in legato fashion. Like many twenty-four-year-olds with his background, he didn't seem to have a nerve in his body and was able to confront any situation with ease and poise.

'Sorry,' he said, grinning as the outside of his hand brushed against her leg when he shifted gear.

'Don't be silly,' she responded, touching his knee

and squeezing it for a second, the whole time watching his face to gauge his reaction. She saw, for the first time, a flicker of doubt, a small flaw in the casual façade.

'You seem to get on very well with Nicola,' she said to him.

He turned and looked at her quickly, as if to ask exactly what she meant.

'She's a good girl. I like her.'

'Has she been at the agency long?' Emma asked, already knowing what the answer would be.

'Only eight, no, must be nine months.'

'She's married, isn't she?'

'Yes.'

The answer was curt. Emma smiled to herself.

'You're not, are you, Ed?' she said winsomely.

'No.'

The same shortness in his response.

'Tell me about the place we're going to look at,' she said to him, veering him away from the tender subject of Nicola.

'The client is familiar, but I've never seen this place. It's an old apartment of his. I think he used it to keep a mistress and he's been rumbled. Probably using us to dispose of it discreetly. We're good at things like that. We won't go and sell it to someone we shouldn't. Catherine's usually got some hidden agenda.'

'Really? She seems open enough to me.'

'You haven't been here very long, Emma, and you probably wouldn't understand Catherine. She's quite complex emotionally. You really have to know how to play her. Not really part of the business, though.'

'What is it about her then?' Emma asked.

'I don't really think she knows what she's doing. No business sense but a lot of contacts from her husband's life. She needs to recognise our involvement a bit more. Do you think the rental section would run without me?'

'I don't know enough, Ed, like you said.'

'Look at Dominic and Tony in sales. Christ, what a pair of wasters. I could look after them and the rental side,' he sputtered.

'Where would that leave Malcolm?' she asked him.

'Malcolm's past it. He's not interested any more. He wants to spend his life gardening. I could head up the home section. I want to set up a meeting with Catherine and lay it all on the table for her. It's about time she heard where Lomax is going wrong.'

'Where exactly do you see it going wrong?' she asked.

'Where? Everywhere. Look at the old duffers we've got on foreign and admin. Sonia needs to understand that she's there to provide support to us in the client-facing end, not to block us when we want to do things.'

'I see,' she said.

'Here we are,' he said, motioning to the side of the road, and losing his passion for the problems of Lomax as quickly as it had found him.

Ed pulled the car into the ramp of an underground car park and tapped a security code which caused the chain gate to lift. They parked and found the elevator up to the sixth floor, where it opened out onto a plush hallway with only two doors. They stood quietly, their breathing now the only sound. Emma deliberately stood just a little too close to Ed, getting into his space a touch more than she could tell he was comfortable with.

For a few moments, Ed fumbled with the keys, seeming nervous and increasingly so when Emma moved closer still. Now, she was near enough to pick up the aftershave he wore and the lower trace of soap or shower gel. She reached out and put her hand on his, letting it rest and then taking the keys from him. In one slick movement, she inserted the key and opened the door and they were inside the flat.

There was a stillness. Bereft of any furniture, even from the hallway there was a sense of the expanse of the place. Emma recalled from a specification sheet that there were four bedrooms, two with their own bathrooms. Late morning light made squares on the carpet and a refrigerator whirred somewhere in the background. Ed seemed flustered by the empty silence and created some noise with his papers, his face making expressions as though he were poring over them and arriving at important decisions.

'Where shall we start?' Emma asked.

'The bedroom?'

Emma giggled.

For half a second, he had a leering grin on his face and then, when he apparently considered the prospect, it faded and instantly he appeared uncomfortable. This was a first, Emma thought.

'I'm sorry. I didn't mean it to sound like that. I meant we could look and measure in their first,' Ed said.

She looked at him, his long black hair smoothed back with a veneer of grease and his rounded cheeks. Ed was incongruous, like a man from another time and class, standing in the hall of a penthouse in Chelsea in his good sensible shoes, striped trousers and a shirt with a dark blue Barbour over the top. It was hard to remember that he was only twenty-four. Still, the bravado was not in evidence, deserting him in his time of greatest need. She reached out and felt the crotch of his trousers, a warm hardness evident once she had pried the coat away.

'Emma.'

'Yes?' she said, stroking her hand over the fly of his trousers.

'Should we be doing this? I have my position to think about at the agency.'

'I don't know, Ed. Should I be doing this?' She unzipped the fly and slipped her hand in, getting a layer nearer to him.

He leaned back against the door, cowering from her but not resisting and Emma felt the heat of his cock through the material of his underwear. As she looked at him, she saw the faintest trace of sweat on his forehead and a barely discernible reddening of his cheeks. With each movement, his cock grew against her hand and the front of his trousers. Fishing in through the slit in the boxer shorts, she found him and squeezed him, letting her thumb trace the skin on the top of his shaft. With her index finger and thumb, she made a circle and squeezed the base of his shaft, the root that led into his pubic hair. With her free fingers she stroked his balls.

Emma slipped his cock out through his flies and as she sank to her knees, Ed dropped his papers and the sonic tape measure. His cock was long and had a pleasing heft to it. Carefully, she shifted his foreskin back over the glans, revealing a glistening tip. She looked at it and then put the head of it into her mouth, hearing his sharp intake of breath as she did so. The taste was part acid and part sex, the combination delicious on her tongue. Taking more of him into her, her face got closer to the pinstripe of his trousers and the sight of his pubic hair, barely sprouting from the small gap she had opened up to get at him.

Sucking quickly and greedily, Emma did all she could to bring him to the edge as fast as possible, hoping that she would be able to drain off some of his arrogance at the same time. Ed was making a high-pitched whine as though in continuous orgasm and Emma was not sure exactly when he would come, but it would not be a long wait. She used her tongue on the underside of his shaft, nestling it into the knot of skin at the base of his glans. Drawing hard on him, she pulled his cock deeply into her mouth, the insides of her cheeks touching and releasing the outside of his shaft. She moved her head back and forth, her lips rubbing the sensitive head of his cock, and his hands gripped her shoulders as his hips began to judder.

Ed was coming.

He called out, the whine reaching an intense pitch. His cock vibrated several heavy shots of warm semen into her mouth and she took each one down as it came, sucking a little harder each time he released into her. She held him tight with the soft warmth of her mouth, feeling the shaft expand from its core as he relinquished his ejaculation to her, he no longer in control. He whipped and thrashed his body around, abandoned and lost, and Emma pondered where the arrogant little boy had gone.

'That was good,' he said to her, a trace of impudence entering his voice. 'You're a bit of a one, aren't you?'

'I haven't finished yet,' Emma said, standing and leading him by the hand in what she hoped would be the direction of a bedroom, her pussy wetly expectant.

With his cock still protruding from his fly, Emma led him along the corridor to a room. It might or not turn out to be a bedroom, but Emma was unconcerned, more worried about the restless desire that was quickening between her legs. She pulled him through a doorway and into a large empty room with an impressive chandelier and wall lights.

Emma grabbed at Ed's Barbour coat and threw it to one side. Her fingers went to his trousers and she undid the numerous buttons and catches, pushing them to the floor along with his boxer shorts. She pushed down on his shoulders and he sank to the floor in a sheepish, awkward movement, his eyes turned up towards her as he did.

Without a word, she reached under her skirt and removed her knickers, peeling the damp fabric away from herself. Emma held them in her hands and went to sit in Ed's lap, hitching her skirt up as she did so.

His face was still flushed from his recent orgasm and Emma wasn't sure he would be up to another one so soon, not that she intended to leave him with much choice in the matter. She reached down between his legs and found his cock tumescent. Emma was impressed.

One hand to the side of his face, she gave him a slow and intimate kiss, exploring his mouth with her own and enjoying the wet softness of it. Ed's hands fiddled with her rear, a finger running along between her buttocks, grazing the delicate area between her anus and vagina. His finger touched the base of her pussy-lips and her knees weakened, causing her to sag onto his sitting body. She wiped her knickers over his face and he burrowed into them keenly, his breathing heavy.

'You're a naughty one,' she said, breaking the embrace and pushing him until he was lying flat on his back.

Emma moved down his legs, allowing herself better access to his groin. She lifted Ed's shift and fondled his cock with both hands, her behind resting on the fronts of his strong thighs. Impressed by the increasing hardness of his cock, she speculated if Nicola ever put him under this kind of pressure. Back and forth, she smoothed his foreskin over the purple head, her other hand making ready down in her pussy. Soon, they were both ready.

Each of them moaned. Emma lowered herself onto Ed, letting the width of his cock pry open her pussy-lips and enter her. Her clitoris was compacted by her desire, poised like a trigger that would fire her off at any moment. She sank lower, feeling stuffed by him, taking her time and conscious that she would very soon close the small gap that existed between their bodies, waiting for the moment when skin would touch skin. For a short time, she would make him a part of her, as though sharing a secret with him. The contact came. Emma let her weight rest heavily down on him, embedding him further into her. She closed her eyes.

'Ah,' was all she could manage, feeling awake and tired, tense and relaxed, all at the same time.

Making a circle with her hips, Emma ground herself into him. Her pubic hair was against his, vagina tightening around the base of his shaft as she did. Emma continued the friction, not yet wanting to rear up and sit back down on him, preferring to enjoy the feeling of his cock planted deep in her. Ed had closed his eyes and his hands were raised up by the sides of his head. He looked lost in a private fantasy, which was fine with Emma as long as it kept him hard enough to do his work inside her.

Once she began the rise and fall onto him, it was with a pace that showed only one desire. To achieve her orgasm quickly and to take him along with her. With Ed, it was the destination, not the journey, that mattered. All of Ed's arrogant confidence had vanished, his face now a mask of concentration as he attempted his second orgasm. In the empty room, the sounds of their coupling echoed around, the high sounds rendered more shrill and every low moan reverberating.

'Fuck me, Ed, that's it,' she encouraged as he added his own upward drive to the fray, hoping a smattering of dirty talk would help him to come again.

Emma rested her hands on his chest and bounced on and off his cock as though he were a trampoline, impaling herself on him with each descent and cruelly depriving herself with every ascent. Inside her there was a part-tingling and part-burning sensation. Some juices had trickled from her and were running over the base of his shaft, matting their pubic hairs together. She changed her angle, giving her clitoris enough stimulation to set off the first tinge of what would follow. It was not something, despite her determination, that she could rush beyond a certain point, her body not willing to surrender itself to pure pleasure without a fight. For Emma, resistance was a part of it, but it was, ultimately, futile.

Their fucking was ruthless, uncompromised and directed to the simple task of climax. Beyond this, Emma did not think, wanting only to use the body below for her own purposes, happy in the knowledge that this was all Ed himself desired. Such a quick and selfish release was what she needed after Matt; something that simply confirmed sex as nothing more than a physical act for her and not something bound up with the very fibre of what she was and what she hoped to be. Where she knew that sex with Matt was an experience that could change her, fucking with Ed was nothing more than that. Fucking.

It must have been the thought of Matt. Thrashing about on top of Ed, she had entered an almost hypnotic state and it was his noise coupled with the first contractions in her pussy that snapped her out of it. Realising that Ed was close to coming, she held onto herself and sharpened her movements, concentrating on making her path over him as inciting as possible. When he groaned approval for the very hard and fast lunges that fed only the head of his cock in and out of her, Emma set to using it as a way of bringing them both off.

The second orgasm seemed to erupt from him, a mix of noise and movement, his shoulders raising off the floor in a fit-like spasm, his breathing short and through an open mouth. Inside her, she felt the warmth of his semen, mixing with fluids of her own. Deeper still in her pussy, she felt her own orgasm emerging.

Oblivious to and unmoved by Ed's cries, Emma

came. Her whole body gave a throb, as though she had completely expanded and then contracted again, but only by the smallest fraction of an inch. She used the cock, letting it despoil her in her rippling pussy, feeling it pushing deep into the source of her pleasure. Long after his own orgasm had subsided, Emma continued to ride him, ignoring the jerking way he was pleading with her to stop. Over his begging, Emma held onto the crest of her own orgasm until, finally, she needed him no more. Abruptly, she stopped and sat back on him, his cock still inside her.

'Jesus,' said Ed, a proud smile spreading over his face. 'You don't know when to give up, do you? That was great, right? Did you ever do that before?'

Puzzling as to exactly what it was going to take to bleed him dry, Emma disengaged herself and scooted down to his feet, removing the sensible shoes and slipping his trousers and underwear off his feet.

Ten minutes later, despite rising protests from Ed, they were in one of the bathrooms. Ed, now naked, was standing where Emma had told him, at the side of the empty tub as though he were about to step into it. Behind him, Emma, still fully clothed, had one hand around his front, harshly masturbating him. She let her left hand roam over his chest and stomach, along his arm and onto his shoulder where it met the collarbone. She squeezed one cheek of his warm behind, giving it a tweak. Ed's cock looked painfully hard, the skin aflame and the feel of it hot.

The dark green marble walls of the bathroom closed in around them, the high windows dripping light into the space. Under Emma's stockinged feet, the hard rubberised tiles became warm. Between the two of them, they had generated a heat that filled the room.

'Let's see what you're made of then, you big swinging dick,' she said to him playfully.

Seeming to realise he had no other choice, Ed leaned

forward and placed his hands against the cold wall, a reflection of him just visible in the darkness of the green marble as his cock aimed at the centre of the bath. He looked as though he had been arrested and been told to assume the position to be searched. That might have been preferable to him, Emma thought, compared to the third painful orgasm she was going to wring from him. On Wall Street, the cockiest young men were described as 'young and full of come'. Emma hoped that by completely emptying him, she might drain off Ed's belligerent and self-assured posturing, like tapping into the source of it.

Certainly, Ed seemed a lot more passive, bent naked over the bath and resigned to his fate as Emma wanked him hard and fast. If she were feeling particularly heartless, she might have insinuated a finger or two from her free hand into the cleft between the meaty cheeks of his behind, but she didn't want to rush his education. Sweat covered him, rolling down his forehead, covering his chest and his back. This was not, however, the fluid she wanted from him and she increased the force of her hand, applying more pressure and feeling the shape of his glans between her thumb and forefinger. Whilst she worked on him with her right hand, she let the left cup his balls and squeeze them, tugging them away from his body.

Ed let out a shout, part-pain and part-ecstasy. Emma pushed her own body against his back as he writhed, his cock throbbing in her hand. Emma kept up the pace and pulled him close to her, peering curiously around his side to watch him ejaculate. Several small shots of come squirted from him and made a splat on the avocado-coloured bath. The fluid was almost clear and ran quickly down the side of the tub. It was a very quick, loud and uncomfortable orgasm for Ed, as far as Emma could gauge. When was the last time Nicola had brought him off three times in half an hour, she thought?

'We should measure up, Emma,' Ed gasped, his breathing erratic and his face flushed.

'If you're sure,' she replied, reaching out and giving his limp member a big squeeze.

She took the look on his face to mean he was quite sure.

Chapter Ten

EMMA WAS FULLY kitted out and ready to embark on a serious shopping trip. Now, she was just waiting for the boys to arrive. There was a natural mediation in the timing since they were already half an hour late but she had only just finished dressing. Over her leather jeans and waistcoat with white piping, she wore a close-fitting black Mark Eisen jacket with shoulder pads. Made up darker than normal around the mouth and eyes, tinges of blue set against a paler foundation, she had an almost gothic look. She checked her Gucci bag to make sure she had everything she needed. She did – her platinum American Express.

The phone rang and Emma glanced at her watch, assuming the boys were about to make some sort of excuse.

'Hello,' she said.

'Hi, it's Matt,' came the voice.

'Hi,' she said breezily, 'how are you?'

'I'm good. I called to say hello. And to say that I think my parents will let me have the place in Soho.'

Emma cast her mind back to the afternoon in the loft apartment. The light and space. The bed. She twiddled the phone cable through her fingers and bent her head to one side.

'That's great.'

'I'd like to have a second viewing, though.'

His voice was flirtatious with a nicely lewd undertow.

'Wouldn't your parents like to see it?' she asked him, deliberately leading him on.

'I don't think they'd like to see what I have in mind.'

Emma was shifting from foot to foot, thinking about Matt, her leather jeans seeming tighter than they had even a few seconds earlier. She was about to make a suggestion to him when the doorbell rang.

'Oh shit,' she said to him, 'there's the door. I'm off out with some friends today.'

'Can we arrange to meet again soon?'

'Of course. Let me call you tomorrow. You can come over here and I'll do dinner or something.'

The door rang again and Emma cursed Neil's impatience.

'Okay, that'd be good. Bye.'

'Sorry we're late, Mother,' Neil said, pecking her on the cheek as he barged past her and into the house.

Tom was more contrite, explaining apologetically about Neil.

'Christ,' Neil was saying from the living room, 'it's like stepping into a virtual-reality *Hello* magazine. Oh my God, look at this kitchen. Do you keep expecting Robert Wagner and Stephanie Powers to walk in?'

And on it went for the next ten minutes while Neil explored the house, Emma following behind and making half-hearted comments about whichever room Neil chose to lead them to next, as though it were his house he were showing them around.

'No water bed. I'm disappointed,' Neil said in the main bedroom. 'Still, you lose leverage on those.'

Tom looked at Emma and raised his eyes indulgently.

'I'm ready,' Neil said when they reached the bottom

106

of the stairs. 'That leather is fabulous on you, by the way. I bet they're an old pair of Tom's, aren't they? When he used to be the Marlboro Man.'

'This is going to be a long day, I can feel it,' said Tom, already beleaguered.

'Nonsense. You'll enjoy it once we get going,' Neil said.

Neil reached into his pocket, took out his wallet and retrieved a credit card. He opened the front door and stood on the step, holding the card aloft, ready to let out his familiar pre-shopping battle cry.

'Charge,' he yelled, striding off the step and into the street.

'Is that the joint account card?' Tom was asking anxiously, following him down the path.

Emma smiled, set the alarm and shut the front door.

Neil, it turned out, was on typically sparkling form. In Gap he fell into a deep discussion with one especially cute assistant about the best way to fold a jumper on the shelf.

'Shall we get coffee somewhere?' Emma suggested.

'Why don't you two do that and I'll see you in Peter Jones, in the lighting section?' Neil replied.

'Fine,' said Tom. 'Don't buy any lamp shades, though.'

'As if,' he replied mischievously.

Ten minutes later, Tom and Emma sat at a small table that was almost taken up by the two cappuccino cups alone.

'You let him off on his own then?' Emma asked Tom, referring to Neil.

'He has these little crushes on shop boys and he can't resist it. Last month he was followed by a store detective because they thought he was shoplifting instead of milling like a doe-eyed teenager to see a Saturday boy.'

'You have to love him,' she said.

'He doesn't give you much choice,' Tom said. 'Are things working out for you back here? It's so brave to just end it all like that.'

'The money's a pretty big safety net, Tom. It's hardly a feat of great courage. More like a whim, really.'

'That's even scarier. You have to motivate yourself more than the rest of us.'

'Well, I'm enjoying the property agency business, what little I've seen of it.'

'The margins must be tight in that business, surely?' he said.

'Not in Lomax's end of the market. The fee income is substantial on the rental side and the sales side is equally profitable.'

'But you couldn't see yourself working there all the time.'

Tom said it not as a question but as though he were vocalising a thought that was in her mind. He looked at her and toyed at his moustache with his fingers, his eyes egging her on to respond.

'No. Just until I'm confident that everything is in order. There are a few oddities.'

'Such as?'

'Without a barrage of detail, a lot of which I don't even have, let's say I think there is something a touch fraudulent about some of the financials, but I can't get close enough to the detail.'

'They want your money but they don't want to give you any information? Sounds like a regular day for me.'

'It's hard for me to talk about it to the woman who owns the agency. It's only a gut feeling on my part, an atmosphere about the place. The numbers might not even back it up when I look at it closely.'

'What sort of information are you looking for?'

'The fine detail, as usual.'

'And you suspect someone?'

Emma sighed. 'Not really.'

'It doesn't sound like you have much to go on, Mother,' Tom said, touching her hand. 'Who could it be?'

'Not Catherine. It's her agency. She would be stealing from herself. It would need to be someone senior – no one else is close enough to it or has the information.'

'How many senior people are there?'

'Only three. A bitch, a dickhead and a Mother Theresa.'

Tom ignored her jibe.

'Do they have any sort of partnership status in the agency?'

'No. Lomax was tight, you can tell that. Catherine is too. They're just employees, well-paid with commission on a quarterly basis, a better pension fund for the senior management, annual Christmas bonus. All the usual stuff.'

'Do any of them have any other outside business interests?' Tom asked her.

Emma thought back to the biographies Catherine had sent her.

'One of them runs a dried flower business with his wife. Nothing was listed for the other two. I'm not totally sure. What are you suggesting, Tom?'

'That you come at the information from a different angle. Stop looking at the agency and look at the people.'

'I'm an investment banker, retired,' she said. 'Not a private detective.'

'I could run personal credit checks on them,' Tom suggested.

'Is that legal?' she asked, knowing the answer.

'I could run personal credit checks on them,' Tom repeated in exactly the same tone.

'What would you need?'

'Name, address and postcode. If you know who they

bank with, all the better, but it's not absolutely necessary.'

'Could you get me the bank statements for the Lomax Property Agency as well?'

'Is it that bad?' he asked. 'They won't even show you the bank account?'

'It's delicate, Tom. I don't want to steamroller over Catherine and I can't just go and ask the admin people for them myself. All the information Catherine gets is processed for her. How many directors do you know who ever see the source data?'

'But she shouldn't be afraid to request it. Nor should you for that matter.'

'If it comes to it, I'll make a scene about it. For now, I think a more covert way of getting the information might be preferable,' she said.

'It'll certainly strengthen your hand – let you stab a few people in the back before they even know you're behind them.'

'You are a very devious man, Tom.'

'I learned it from you, Mother. Send me their details, to the house. Shall we go see if Peter Jones had any lamps left? Neil's been there for nearly half an hour.'

Emma left the boys protesting while she went to The Garden, the women-only department in Hamiltons.

'It's not fair,' Neil pleaded.

'It's only like those bars you and Tom go to that I can't,' she countered quickly.

'You'd probably get in dressed like that anyway,' Neil retorted, pulling at her leather jeans. She agreed to meet them in the menswear department in the basement.

It was nearly an hour later when her heels clicked on the stone steps leading into the menswear department. Neil and Tom had split up. Tom was fingering a Timberland jacket and Neil was in the Donna Karan section.

110

'I'd kill for this,' Neil said as she approached him. 'It's Donna Karan. From the collection, not DKNY. That's important,' he told her. 'Donna herself might have touched this very garment. Imagine.'

Emma looked at it and the price tag.

'Want me to buy it for you?' she asked.

'Don't be stupid,' he said quickly.

Money changed things. It did not matter how much she tried to pretend things were the same, they were not. Life seemed to be a chase for the sort of material comfort she had arrived at so early. As she stood there in the shop, she could easily have given Neil and Tom enough money so neither would have to worry, but she knew they would not take it. They still paid her rent, despite her insistence they should not. She was storing the cheques up in a building society account she had opened. But to give them a whole chunk of money was to break the rules. It pervaded everything, from being able to take care of them for the rest of their lives down to buying an expensive jacket or an argument over a restaurant bill. Emma knew not to push the point.

'So who's the one you fancy in here?' she asked him.

'What's Tom been saying!'

'Nothing I don't already know, you tart. It's Emma you're talking to here. Please. Hello?'

She exaggerated the double syllable nature of the last two words, using each as a sentence in itself and faking a New York accent.

'Don't show off with your New-York phrases to me. Him over there, if you must know.'

'Straight,' Emma said, using the word on Neil like a sword.

'In here?'

'There's always one,' Emma said.

'So who are you fucking?' he asked her from nowhere as they looked at Jean Paul Gaultier shirts.

'Neil. What makes you think there's anyone?'

'Emma. Leather jeans, gothic make-up, that spring in the step. You're getting some. I can always tell. Shall we ask a few of these boys if they agree?'

Emma grabbed his arm, knowing he would happily go up to any of the staff and ask their opinion.

'You're such a cow,' she said to him.

'But I'm right, aren't I?'

His face was an image of certainty.

'You might be.'

'I want to know length and width. Before Tom comes over. You know he can be prudish.'

Emma looked across the other side of the department at Tom, now looking at one then another Timberland jacket.

'I think he'll be there for a while longer,' Emma said. 'Okay, he's a boy I met through the agency. His parents are renting him a flat.'

'A boy? His parents? Emma, you're not dating Macaulay Culkin, are you?'

'He's called Matt and he's twenty-two.'

Neil grabbed her arm and feigned giddiness.

'That's all I need to know. Don't tell me any more, you'll spoil it. Let me guess, he's an absolute doll. He would be if you're chasing him.'

'Who says I'm chasing him?' Emma asked.

'Everything about you says it. Is he good?'

'It doesn't take you long, does it, Neil? Name, age and is he a good fuck?'

'Not necessarily in that order, Mother. Not even name and age, sometimes. Anyway, that's question-dodging.'

'He's more than just a good fuck.'

'Maybe we should get a wedding list from here. Tom can be maid of honour.'

Neil picked up a pair of briefs with a thick waist band and high cut legs. He looked at Emma and poked his tongue out, making flicking motions with it, smiling and raising his eyebrows at the same time.

'Get him some of these, Emma,' he said.

'So you can imagine him wearing them and then get a blow-by-blow from me about it? Doubtful.'

Tom appeared at Neil's side, ignoring his antics with the briefs.

'Neil, come and look at these jackets. I can't decide which I like,' Tom said.

'Mother's in love,' Neil said to him. 'We're going to be orphans.'

Tom looked at her. In their own ways, they both cared about her. Neil was all hyperbole and the camp aside while Tom's warmth was more obvious and pleasing to shelter in. He said nothing, but gave a very tiny smile and nod of the head, approving. Emma felt embarrassed and the centre of unwarranted attention, wishing she'd never mentioned anything to Neil, but knowing she had been bursting to tell him since she had spent her first afternoon with Matt. After four years of dodging bullets on Wall Street, she had almost forgotten how it felt to lust after someone, to want to see them again.

'I think Tom's giving his blessing,' Neil said. 'I'll kiss his ring later. Tell your boyfriend he has to ask us for your hand in marriage.'

Emma and Tom gave an exasperated sigh at precisely the same moment, leaving Neil holding the underwear as they went to look at Tom's jacket.

When the boys were off looking at china, Emma went and bought the Donna Karan jacket for Neil and hid it one of her own bags. She would find a good moment to give it to him. The day ran away from them quickly. Emma purchased some shoes, two pairs of trousers and a suit that she would be able to wear for Lomax.

They ended the day in a cinema, Emma between Neil and Tom, holding what seemed to her a small bucket of popcorn compared to New York-sized ones. It was a comedy and all three of them laughed hard, Neil the loudest, Tom the longest and Emma the happiest. In the darkness of the cinema, she fiddled with the shopping bags and moved the Donna Karan jacket into one of the boys' bags.

'When will we see you again?' Neil asked outside the cinema, darkness around them. 'Never?'

'I'll give you a call next week,' she said.

'Now that you've met Mr Right, when do we get to?' he asked mischievously.

'All in good time.'

'Neil, stop hassling her,' Tom interrupted. 'You're pressuring her. She only just met him.'

'But she knows. Don't you?' Neil looked to her for support.

'I'm not getting in the middle of this,' she said. 'I'll call you guys next week.'

'But you *are* the middle, Mother,' Neil protested.

Emma laughed and backed away. 'I'll speak to you soon.'

'Wait!' Neil said urgently, reaching into a bag. 'I've got a present for you. Well, sort of for you. And I want *details*.'

'Promise,' she said kissing him and then Tom, knowing that the bag contained the briefs from earlier. Neil loved to have the upper hand.

When she was ten paces from them, she turned.

'Oh Neil,' she called.

He turned around.

'Say hi to Donna for me.'

Emma laughed aloud at his bemused look and went to hail a taxi.

Chapter Eleven

CATHERINE LOMAX WAS already behind her desk when Emma arrived. It seemed like she was always there. It was just before nine and one or two people were at their desks but for the most part, the Lomax Property Agency had yet to burst into life. The meeting later that morning with Nic Lawson had given her the chance to upscale her dress slightly and she was wearing a soft, nicely textured one-piece by Calvin Klein. It was surprising the difference it made to her and the reactions of other people. Allowing herself the extravagance of her favourite Chanel coat, Emma had strutted down the Kings Road pleased to have the odd head turn. Catherine, by contrast, looked tired.

'Good morning,' Emma said to her, closing the door as she entered.

Catherine checked her watch, seeming confused about the time.

'It's a Wednesday,' Emma said gently and playfully. 'Tell me you haven't been here all night, Catherine?'

'It feels like I have. How are things? One of the gang yet?'

'Not quite. They're wary of me, but I'm working on them.'

'Ed certainly seems better behaved with you. I don't

know what you said to him when you were off measuring up, but it worked,' Catherine said.

'We have an understanding,' Emma smiled. 'Catherine, looking at the records of transactions over the last few months, I'm struck by the sketchy level of detail. Does Sonia do any sort of analysis of trends over a long period?'

'No, we're much more intuitive than that. We know at what points in the year the business will peak and when it will trough. Sonia keeps track of cashflow.'

'How far back do your records go, ones that are kept here rather than archived?' Emma asked.

'I'm not entirely sure. I'd have to check with Sonia, but I'm sure we have at least eighteen months.'

'Is there a way you could find out if I could see records going back three years without arousing any suspicion about it?'

Catherine thought for a moment. 'I'll see what I can do. Doesn't that sound ridiculous? I own this business.'

'In my old job, we were fascinated with ownership versus control, what one really meant against the other. You can control through information, Catherine.'

'Are you looking for anything specific in the records?'

'Not at the moment,' Emma said. 'In my old job, I had a reputation for finding patterns and trends in information. We thrived on information. I realised quickly that it wasn't a shortage of raw data that was the issue but how clever you were in interpreting and manipulating it.'

'Sometimes I'm glad you're on my side. You're looking very smart today. Is this for our friend Mr Lawson?'

'I thought some effort would be in order. Are we going to have a briefing meeting with Malcolm and Dominic?'

'Yes. I thought in about half an hour?'

'Fine,' Emma said, leaving.

Nic Lawson was a client the agency was keen to attract. He was new money and self-made. Whether the old money liked it or not, people like Nic Lawson were a part of the new order. Emma had found out a little about him, partly via Neil. 'He manages one of those boy bands that Tom likes, all torsos and pectorals. Tom's a tit man, you know,' Neil had told her. Nic Lawson's interests stemmed beyond the music business into computer technologies. This seemed to be where his new interests lay. To gather some more information, she called Chris, spent some time thanking him for the welcome-home time they had together in her flat and then asked him to pull any clippings he could from his firm's online system. As always, Chris had been obliging.

More at issue was what had happened between Lomax and Nic Lawson. From what Emma had been able to glean, Malcolm had let Dominic Lester look after him and it had not worked out, leaving Malcolm to take over. Unfortunately, that had been a similar failure. Nic Lawson, rather charitably Emma thought, was giving Lomax a third chance. Before she and Catherine met with him, Emma wanted to get to the root of the problem.

When she re-entered the main office most people had arrived, apart from Jane Bennett. Emma wanted to look over some of the foreign transactions to get a feel for the way they were structured. It would have been easy to wait and ask Jane, but Nicola was there and Emma was not one to shirk a difficult interaction.

'Hi Nicola,' Emma said, smiling as she approached her desk.

Emma saw Nicola's face darken as she neared her, her eyes running appraisingly over the Calvin Klein dress. If there was an international body language for 'you bitch', Nicola was using it at that moment.

'Hello,' Nicola said flatly.

'I'd like to have a look at a few files from the foreign section if I could. Jane tells me you're a stickler for documenting them. It's just to give me an idea of how this part of the agency works.'

'We don't need any help on foreign,' she said shortly.

'Nicola, I'm only asking for a few files, not offering to help.'

'I know what you're up to,' Nicola said, her voice low.

There was a beat of silence while Emma considered and she did not respond, merely raising her eyebrows as if to tell Nicola to continue.

'You think they're going to make you a senior agent, don't you? That you can just come in here and bat your eyelids and everyone will fall over themselves. They need me here and there's nothing you can do about it. If you want files, ask Jane.'

Emma leaned closer into Nicola and made direct eye contact with her.

'Nicola,' she began in a soft and warm tone, 'if I had wanted your job, I would have taken it by now. As far as I know, you do a good job, so don't spoil it over an issue like this. You've got a husband and a boyfriend to keep, so why take risks? If I want files, I'll ask either you or I'll go and ask Catherine – you can choose. Why don't you give me the fucking files?'

Emma stood upright again, a serene smile on her face as though they were girlfriends exchanging dating secrets. Nicola was gawping at her, fiddling unconsciously with a paper clip on her desk.

'I've got a client meeting in an hour, so sometime after that would be good. Thank you, Nicola,' Emma said, heading for the kitchen and not bothering to see if there was a response.

Ian Cameron was in there changing the bottle on the water cooler.

'It has to be put on so you can see the label,' he said, taking it very seriously. 'Malcolm puts it on anyhow and I hate that.'

He heaved the bottle up and dropped it onto the cooler with familiarity.

'Can I pour you a coffee?' he asked her, lifting the pot from the hot-plate.

'Please.'

A second coffee maker was brewing away quietly and on it a Post-it note read 'Client Coffee – Hands Off!'

Ian saw her looking at it.

'I have to put that on there or everyone drinks it. And we use a better blend for clients, but don't tell anyone.'

'So are you the master brewer?' she asked him.

'Someone has to be. No one here can make coffee.'

'I'm not too bad,' she said. She was about to start telling him about a place near Times Square in New York that did amazing lattes when she caught herself. 'You should let me make it sometime.'

'Emma, about the other night . . .' Ian blurted.

'Ian, it's okay. I was flattered, honestly. I'm sort of involved at the moment. I could still use a friend here, though,' she said, smiling at him.

'I just feel stupid, that's all,' he said, his eyes downcast.

'You shouldn't. Tell me you won't, okay?'

'Okay then,' he said.

At her desk and making sure she could not be observed, Emma wrote down the details of the people in the agency she wanted Tom to gather information on. She included everyone in the agency and the bank details of the agency itself. Tom was reliable when it came to things of a practical nature. Emma simply put at the bottom, 'Please write to your mother soon.'

While she had prepared the list of names, she eyed

the Post-it note on her screen that said Matt had called. When she was done with the information for Tom, she returned his call and arranged to meet him later that evening. On the phone, he sounded as though he was holding back and not wanting to push too fast. On her return to England from Wall Street, Emma had made a promise to herself not to fall for anyone. Now, with Matt, she sensed she was near to toppling over. Involvement with him would not be easy until she had finished her research at Lomax. Even then, she would have to explain herself to him, given that she had misled him. Still, her secret was not such a bad one to keep from somebody. 'Oh, by the way, I forgot to tell you, darling, I'm a multi-millionaire. Must have slipped my mind, sorry.'

'Shall we do this meeting?'

She looked up. It was Malcolm.

The meeting rooms used for Lomax clients were as plush as any Emma had ever been in. Nic Lawson would get star treatment in Room One. The rooms reminded Emma of those used by lawyers in the City, where you made sure you ate every biscuit and drank all the coffee you could to get full value for money. The difference with the Lomax rooms was they had a touch of elegance about them. Twelve feet square, they were neither too big nor too intimate and were all furnished in bright maple that made a valiant attempt to look like a Frank Lloyd Wright design. The meeting table could accommodate six and pads with the Lomax logo and good quality pens were laid out at each place, marked by a leather blotter pad. Tasteful watercolours of the West and South-West of London adorned the walls and a side table was laid out with a china service. Lomax gave clients what they expected.

Dominic Lester was already waiting in the room with Catherine, chatting amiably. Emma had not had much to do with Dominic so far but she had found him to be helpful whenever she had spoken to him. Thirty years old, he was Lomax's resident bachelor. Emma had heard speculation that he was gay. He was not. From the first time he had smiled at her, she was certain. Emma knew enough gay men and enough men who were attracted to her to be able to tell the difference. Dominic rose to his feet when she entered with Malcolm. Good mornings exchanged, they got to business.

'Malcolm, can you update us?' Catherine said.

'Nic Lawson could be a very important client for us.' Malcolm fiddled with the buff-coloured folder on the table. 'He's in the music and entertainment business, quite wide interests from what I could gather.'

'What does he want from Lomax?' Emma asked.

'I don't think he really knew at first,' Dominic broke in. 'Obviously he wants a house, but he didn't know where or what. He sort of expected us to come up with all of that for him. I'm afraid he and I are rather different and everything I suggested seemed wrong. Seemed to infuriate him in fact.'

'I think, being honest,' Malcolm added, 'we were a little too hot to get him on our books and we lost sight of him. He's very well connected. His network could open up a new area of business for us. But that's part of the difficulty in itself.'

'We don't have any connections to him at all?' Emma asked.

'One or two,' Catherine said. 'We have to be discreet about how we use word of mouth. He's heard good things about us and that's why he's giving us another chance. All of our best business comes out of relationship management, but building that takes time.'

'I don't feel that Dominic or I are the right people to do that, to be frank,' said Malcolm.

'What about Ed?' Catherine asked.

Malcolm rubbed his right temple. 'Catherine, you know Ed. I think he might overwhelm Nic a touch. Nic's very self-made,' Malcolm said, turning to Emma. 'He's a tad conscious of his roots and we don't want to parade Ed in front of him like a banner to remind him. God knows, we all love Ed, but horses for courses.'

'Ed is prettier than us though, Malcolm,' Dominic said, throwaway fashion.

'What do you mean?' Emma asked.

'Just a feeling I have, that's all,' said Dominic.

'Just coming down to facts,' Catherine said, moving on, 'what do we have?'

Malcom opened the file. 'He has a large house he had built specially in Essex. He doesn't need to off-load that but he wouldn't mind. I can't see who would want it, but the land might be worth something. It's got the lot – guitar-shaped pool, you name it. In terms of the new place, somewhere in London. I'm guessing, but five to six million plus he's ready to spend on changes. We just haven't found the right pigeonhole to put him in.'

'He's due in at eleven-thirty,' Catherine said. 'I suggest you boys be scarce at that point.'

'Don't be offended if it's a short meeting,' Malcolm said. 'He can be abrupt.'

The arrival of Nic Lawson sent an apparent tremor through the Lomax Property Agency. There was a low-level commotion, the sense that something important was happening. He arrived with an entourage of four people, all of whom he promptly dispatched with a few words barked in a broad London accent that was hard to pin down, part-East and part-South.

Looking well kept for a thirty-eight-year-old, he was dressed in a tweed suit that was cut in a sixties style, making him look like an early Beatle – if you didn't look at his hair. Long and black, it was tied into a pony-tail that fell between his shoulder blades. His face was strong and square, upper and lower lips seemingly identical in size, giving him the look of someone ready to snarl. Average height and quite broad, the squareness of his face extended to the rest of him. Overall, Emma could only think of the word square. In his way, however, he was harshly attractive.

'Hello, Catherine,' he said sticking a hand out to her.

'Nic, hello. This is Emma Fox. She's recently joined Lomax and will be with us this morning.'

'Lovely,' he said, his hand moving from Catherine and towards her.

'Emma Fox. Pleased to meet you,' she said to him, making full eye contact, noticing how dark his were.

'And you. I was going to bring all the hangers-on, but they just confuse things,' Nic Lawson said, falling into a chair. 'Catherine, I just want a bloody house. How hard can that be?'

'The boys showed you a few. Nothing you liked?'

'No. Most of them were horrible. I can't make a career out of looking at houses, Catherine.'

'What are you looking to do by moving?' Emma asked.

'Basically? I want to get out of Essex without ending up in bloody Surrey.'

Emma wondered if his Michael Caine accent was contrived or not. It seemed to shift through a sentence and end up somewhere else.

The door opened and Ian came in with a tray of coffee and biscuits. As he leaned over the side table to place the tray down, Emma watched Nic's gaze. It travelled casually and carefully across the room and scanned from Ian's feet up to his rear. As Ian turned, Nic's face changed from the brute to the charmer, the lips moving up into a smile, the eyes shining. Ian was unaware or unconcerned as he left the room without ever glancing at Nic Lawson. Nic seemed a little deflated.

123

'Is the house in Essex your only one?' Emma asked him.

'No. I've got one in Spain and one in Los Angeles.'

'Is the Spanish one a villa?'

'Sort of. I don't get out there very much.'

As he spoke, his eyes were wandering over the front of her dress in much the same way they had just done Ian's trousers. A sexuality seemed to beat just below the surface with him, waiting to be unbound. She leaned forward to give him a better view and was certain she saw his pupils dilate.

'Where's your house in LA?' she asked him.

'In West Hollywood, off Sunset.'

'Near La Cienega?'

'Not far. Well, nearer Griffith Park. You go to LA much?' he asked her, seeming impressed.

'Once in a while. What's the house there like?'

'Great. It's my favourite. I don't spend enough time there. I've got some video game interests out there and I'm still convinced I'll sign a surfer band. A grunge version of the Beach Boys.' He gave her a smile.

'Would something like that, if it were in London, be what you wanted?' she questioned.

'It might be. There's quite a few unusual features to it. I spent a bundle getting it done up.'

'Does anything you've looked at,' Catherine asked, picking up where Emma was leading, 'come close to it?'

'Not even near.'

'If we were able to find something that gave you the same sort of scope as the LA house, but a chance to improve on it, would that be interesting?' Catherine asked.

He thought for a moment, colonising the idea and making it seem like his own. His face lit up and he spoke quickly.

'If we could find something like my house in

124

Hollywood, do it up a bit, it would be like being there and being here, wherever I was.'

He was pleased with himself. He drummed on his lips with his fingers.

'Would it be possible for me to see the house in LA?' Emma asked, aware of Catherine's sideways glance at her.

'You'd fly out, just to see it?' he asked, a flattered smile spreading across the roughly hewn features.

'I'd love to,' she replied.

'I'm going out next week for a few days. I could see you there, show you round.'

'That would be excellent. It will give me a feel for what you're after.'

'What a great idea,' he said, sounding like a little boy on Christmas morning.

And that was it. With a tremor of equal significance, Nic Lawson swept through the Lomax Property Agency and was gone.

Chapter Twelve

MATT HAD BEEN in Emma's flat for under five minutes and already she was uncomfortable. He was impressed by the Chelsea address, its proximity to the Kings Road and the decor. Emma was sure her explanation of it had been too faltering, apologetic almost. Fortunately, he was pleased enough to see her and this smothered any awkward questions that may have been raising themselves in his mind. This did not alleviate her own sense of discomfort at his being in the flat. It was a strange irony, he wondering how she could afford to live there yet not knowing that she could have bought the place if she desired. Emma was determined not to let negative feelings get the better of the evening. She had sat him down on the sofa and fetched beers. Still willingly unfamiliar with her temporary kitchen, she had not cooked. They would eat out later that night. Food was on neither of their minds and what was going through their heads hung in the air between them, finding its way between the music that played quietly. Sometimes, she thought, the second time with someone can be more delicate than the first.

'You've convinced your parents about the loft then?' she asked him.

'Told you I would.'

'How soon will you want it?'

He thought about it, taking a drink from the beer bottle. As casual as each time she had seen him, he wore a cream-coloured sweat-top with brown borders on the cuffs and collar and a more chocolate-coloured T-shirt underneath it. His jeans ran the contour of his legs perfectly, the cloth lying on the skin as though comfortable there. Emma longed to take off his clumpy black walking boots, pop the buttons on his jeans and unwrap him.

'I could move next week. Both Mother and Father are out of town, which will make it a good time. Can Lomax organise the lease for then?'

'I can set it up for you, no problem. I'm away myself next week but I'll leave it with someone,' she said.

'Really? Where are you going?' he asked.

'To look at a rock star mansion in Los Angeles,' Emma said.

'Why Los Angeles?'

'Long story,' she said. 'Basically, we're stroking the ego of a client we want to bring us some other business. He manages some boy bands, has a few other interests. Nic Lawson. I'd never heard of him.'

'Oh, I see,' he said. 'Nic Lawson. Those boy bands.'

Emma wondered what he was thinking. She put her hand on his knee and he sat still and listened to the music. He put his hand on hers and then pulled it nearer to his crotch. Emma felt the heat from him. She broke her hand free from his and touched him through the heavy fabric of his trousers.

'You have a great cock,' she whispered to him dirtily, excited as much by the tone of her voice as her words.

Leaning on him, she kissed his cheek as demurely as she had when opening the door to him. Then their mouths found each other and it was like meeting him

127

all over again, the sudden change of tension in the situation, the switch from calm to storm. She kissed him in a violent way, chewing on his lips and poking her tongue roughly into his mouth, feeling the ridge of his teeth and the caustic surface of his tongue. Emma could taste the beer they had been drinking and she pulled the back of his head hard, the bones in their faces touching, lipstick smearing Matt's face and around her own mouth. It became hard to breathe and it got hotter between them. Emma was oblivious to every part of Matt except his mouth as she turned her head to one side and clamped her open mouth over his, feeling the strain in her cheeks.

They pulled away, getting their breath back.

'I think we should go to bed,' Matt said, as though the exertion of the kissing had been too much for him and he was retiring early as a result.

Emma left the music playing and led him upstairs to the bedroom. They were very calm and organised, she turning back the covers and he removing his sweat-shirt. He sat on the edge of the bed and leaned forward to take off his boots.

'Let me do that, please,' Emma said.

She sat at his feet and undid the double bows on the boots. They were heavy walking boots and the black leather was nicely worn. Emma released the laces, pulling them through the eyes until they hung loosely over the front of each boot. She took the heel and toe of a boot with her hands and slid it off. She repeated the motion with his other foot and then removed his socks, the tops of his feet smooth and hairless, veins near the surface.

Reaching up, Emma undid his belt and the buttons on the fly of his jeans. She stood up and removed his T-shirt, eager to see more of his flesh. It was exactly how she remembered it, the outline of his chest, his nipples and his abdomen. She wanted to kiss him again but was unwilling to slow down his progress to nudity. She brought him to his feet and stood close to him, putting her palms into the side of his boxer shorts. It would have been wonderful simply to have stood there, hands warm against his hips, but she wanted him naked. Keeping her body close to him to make the action intimate, she slithered his jeans and underwear off, freeing him. Taking his rear in her hands, she pulled him close to her, letting his skin rub against her dress, savouring his nakedness against her clothing. She kissed his shoulder, biting into it and feeling the warmth of his skin in the heat of her mouth.

Emma turned and asked him to unzip her dress. The sound of the zipper and the vibration it made sent a shiver along her spine. The back of the dress gaped open, revealing the line of her sheer knickers. His hands opened the dress wide across her shoulder blades and pushed it forward so it fell in a heap at her ankles. She was left wearing only knickers. His body was close to hers once more, the sensation now skin on skin. Matt's cock touched her rear. Emma reached her arms over her head and back, finding his hair and playing with it. As he took her knickers down, they traced a delicious scratch over her rear and along her legs.

'Let's get into bed,' Matt said.

Lying on her side and facing him, she ran her hand along his jaw. His face was clean shaven and her hand glided over it easily. They were under the heavy covers of a densely patterned cotton duvet that trapped their body heat and warmed them. The room was lit only by a lamp in the far corner, light from it casting across the room and illuminating them with its fading yellow. There was a dark space between them where their bodies raised the covers from the bed but did not touch each other. Emma looked down into it and saw the dark shadowy profile of Matt's body. She moved closer to him, closing the gap between them, her body docking with his.

Matt ran his fingers over her leg and her behind, moving swiftly and never lingering for very long in one region of her. When he moved his hand between her legs, she raised one knee to allow him greater access to her. Touching her labia and running his finger along the graze of her lips made Emma grow moist as he deftly operated on her. Inside, her pussy was alive with the sensation brought on by his touch and by her own expectations, the juices she produced trickling through her pussy-lips as Matt opened them fractionally with a finger.

With a single sweep of his arm, powerful and decisive, Matt threw back the covers, revealing himself to her in the low light of the room. Emma looked at him, his eyes burning into her skin like the brightest thing in the room. The draught of the covers and the suddenness of their removal had startled her. Matt was sitting up, his behind resting on his ankles, and he towered over her on the bed. His long cock was fully extended and she reached for it, moving herself down the bed so her head came off the pillow and onto the mattress. Matt leaned over her and pushed his cock towards her face, his balls tight and his thigh muscles solid. Keeping her mouth closed, Emma ran the tip of his cock along her lips, smelling the tangy clear come that had seeped from him.

Adjusting his position, Matt kneeled at the side of her shoulders, one of her arms stretched through his open legs. Emma turned her head and opened her mouth so that Matt could fuck it with his cock. She lifted the arm that ran under his legs and placed it on his behind, pushing him so his cock came towards her. Matt fell forward and supported himself on his hands. He was now leaning almost sideways across her, knees one side of her shoulders, hands the other. From above, they would have looked like a cross shape.

Now able to see only his cock clearly, Emma took it through her opened lips, relaxing her mouth and throat. She closed her mouth gently when the first third of it was in, drawing on the head and rolling her tongue round, wetting him and blending his fluids with those in her mouth, lubricating his shaft. He picked her head up and slid in further. Emma felt it touch the back of her throat and mouth, and she slackened there, making it an inviting and flexible orifice for him. Bracing herself, she took the remainder of him in, the last two inches or so, bringing her face into his pubic hair. She could hear him groaning and feel the swelling movement of his cock in her mouth.

The mattress rocked and squeaked from Matt's movements as he thrust himself in and out of her mouth, trailing his shaft along her lips and over her tongue. When he sank it in and held it there, Emma squirmed her tongue about in what space she had left in her mouth, licking him and flicking at the underside of his shaft. His stomach flexed as he drove himself in and out of her, the trail of hair under his navel thickening into the mass of fine brown pubic hair. His movements were controlled, and he was pleasuring himself on her mouth. Emma stroked his behind with a hand, his buttocks stiffening and releasing with each backward movement.

Had her desire for him to penetrate her pussy been less, she might have let him continue in her mouth until he came, letting him lose control and come violently in an orifice that was so delicate and feeling. It would have been nice to watch the strained muscles of his arms and legs become whipped up by the surge of his orgasm, the way his thrusts would lose their regularity as he could no longer contain himself. And while he was thrashing away, desperate for it to last and more desperate for it to end, Emma would lie and

131

drink his come as it filled her mouth, swallowing the hot and heavy fluid that came from the very depths of him.

But she wanted him inside her pussy. And soon she would let him, but first she wanted to toy with him some more.

'Come here, you,' she said, when she had removed him from her mouth and was sitting up on the bed.

He kneeled close to her and kissed her, under her spell and ready to please. Emma wondered how ready as she touched one of his buttocks and then held both of them in her hands, pulling them wide. His breath exhaled in the midst of the kiss, seeming partly surprised by what she was doing, but not enough to stop kissing her. She pulled him apart again, this time with her hands closer to the centre, near to the puckered crease that was a way into him she suspected had gone unexplored. Emma, ever bold, decided it was time to mount at least a small exploratory expedition.

Still kissing him, she worked the opening of his rear with a dry finger, feeling the wrinkled skin. She did not intend to enter him, just to alert him to the possibility. They continued to couple at the mouth, feeding on each other, while she used her thumb and middle finger to spread the outer ring of muscle and then probed her index finger at the clenched inner sphincter. She let go with the thumb and middle digit, allowing him to close on the remaining finger she kept there, buried by him. In a fast movement, she prodded backwards and forwards with the finger, stretching the muscle but never breaching it. The stabbing motion of her finger set his whole behind in motion and massaged the gland deep in him that caused his cock to strain.

For several minutes she held him under the spell. This beautiful twenty-two-year-old boy, someone

132

whom only three weeks earlier she had never even seen before. Now, naked, he knelt on her bed as she kissed him and lightly worked on the opening between his exquisitely taut buttocks.

'Did you like that?' she asked.

He nodded shyly.

Once again they lay on their sides, facing each other, bodies as close as they could be without his body actually being inside hers. Emma raised one leg and pushed her other knee under him. Matt raised himself up and allowed her to put her leg under before carefully resting his weight on it. Emma lifted her other leg over his hip so that she lay on her side clasping him between her legs. It was as though they had been making love with him on top of her, her legs drawn up, and they had rolled onto their side. The outer edge of Matt's torso, just above his hip, rested on her leg and his cock pushed against her groin.

They held each other but did not move. Several times, she almost spoke, but did not. Frozen like a sculpture, they lay and stared at each other, noses almost touching. A rush of feeling went through her and she pushed her face into his shoulder, resting the side of her face on his, Matt's hair lying fanned on the pillow. She could sense the beat of his heart and the rising of his chest, feel his breath escaping over her back. She let her arm fall across his back.

Matt was gently putting his hand down and manoeuvring his cock so that its tip touched the lips of her pussy, moving his body to make the necessary space. The position of Emma's legs had opened a crevice between her buttocks and pulled at her labia. She was ready to be penetrated by him. The undersides of her thighs were pressed by his hip bones and their stomachs were touching. As close as she was to him, with as much of her skin touching him as there was, she still wanted him inside her. The closeness

133

extended beyond the physical proximity and Emma felt part of his whole ambience. This close, she felt a physical and an emotional closeness to him that belied the newness of their relationship. Something had fallen into place with him and felt right.

Emma's eyelids became heavy as though she was being hypnotised as Matt entered her, parting her labia and pushing through into her vagina. When she had eased his foreskin back, it revealed a zeal for her that shone out of the warm intimacy they shared in the faint light of her cosy bedroom. She doused him with herself, her pussy cooling the flames of his passion and satisfying her own appetite for him. In her, it burned away like an ember ready to rekindle a fire. Emma felt it, solid and pulsing, filling her vagina. His legs were lying straight out on the bed and as he raised the top leg, so he was deeper in her. Slowly, he slid his leg up the bed and his cock further into her until a point had been reached where she felt perfectly penetrated. At other times, she might want him deeper or not as deep, slow or fast; but at that moment, she held him steady, whispering to him not to move, allowing her to hold onto the sensation for a few moments before he started thrusting into her.

When she had held onto enough of the feeling, she relaxed her body and let him start. Her top leg, flung over his side, jiggled with his movements, her foot swinging loosely. Emma raised her leg to open her pussy further and the sensation of him thrusting at her while she lay so open to him was delicious. His weight was carefully distributed on his hip and his arm so that he rested on her leg with just the right force. His groin pounded into her and his cock filled her, the friction sparking tension deep within her.

Emma's clitoris was engorged, swelling from her and sent into dizziness by his movements. She gripped him tightly, with her hands, her legs and her pussy, waiting for him to come inside her, knowing her own orgasm was becoming more tangible by the second. His actions lost some of their relaxed pace and gained an urgency, not a rushing as such, but a definite indication of desire to arrive at a point somewhere soon. She recalled from the week before his first orgasm with her in the loft in Soho, the way it had assaulted him and electrified him as though he were wired into some arcane power source. When he had been coming, she was struck by the sense that he had vacated his body and was letting it be taken over by the waves of sheer energy, possessed by his orgasm.

Picking up on the powerful storm that was building in him, Emma was excited by the thought of him coming and by the feel of him inside her, the way movements that brought her so much pleasure would also do the same for him. It was as though she too were tuning into the force that had driven Matt this far and would shortly push him out of himself. She closed her eyes and concentrated on his sounds and movements, the push of him in her and the weight of him on her leg. Emma retreated into the grey and white world beneath her eyelids, blocking the visual stimulus and using her other senses to produce a feeling that was unbounded.

In her pussy, deep within, there was movement. The walls of her vagina were opening and closing around his shaft, compressing it and feeling it nudging her along to climax via her clitoris. As she came, the presence of his cock was so pronounced in her and her pussy so sensitive that she cried out, holding tightly onto him and using the movement of his body to mould her orgasm around it. Every part of him that touched her now felt hotter and more pronounced. Tingles ran the length of her body and her head filled with the buzz as she clenched him with her pussy and came in almost painfully prolonged spasms.

As his orgasm followed in the wake of Emma's own,

Matt's shoulders heaved on the bed and in the air, his groin slapping against her as he desperately tried to force semen from himself and into her. She was lost in the sensation of fluid warmth in her pussy, feeling like it was flooding in a long unbroken deluge rather than spouting from him in several short successive blasts. Emma drank him into her as surely as if he had been in her mouth, making him a part of her, feeling his come moving in her with a life-force of its own. She let it subside and continued to hold onto him, pulling his shoulders so he was close to her and feeling him soften inside her.

Matt lay on his back, his feet stuck under what remained of the covers at the bottom of the bed. His cock gave the occasional quiver, still fraught from its recent experience.

'Oh, that was great,' he said. 'You're great. Where did you come from?' he asked, more to himself. 'Go on, tell me a secret about yourself that no one else knows.'

Emma shifted uncomfortably, thinking of one secret about her that she really should share with him.

He looked at her.

'I feel like I could tell you anything, right now,' he continued, speaking quickly and apparently not expecting her to tell him anything. 'There's no bullshit with you, no playing games, or lies. I like it. I like you.'

Emma stared into space, chewing her bottom lip and unable to say anything in response.

Chapter Thirteen

EMMA LOOKED DEEP into Matt's eyes and saw a flicker in them, a movement far off as though they were infinite, like space. She placed a fingertip in the cleft above his top lip, stroking and then running it around his mouth. He nipped playfully at her and continued to move himself inside her. The bone of his jaw was so gorgeously long and perfect that Emma could not resist feeling its line with her fingers. As she toyed with his face, he moved his head around in time with her movements. Up so close, she could view the slightly asymmetrical shape of his nose, the snub that made it so cute from a distance. All of these small details, the thin line of his eyebrows that could appear so deceptively heavy when he furrowed his brow, the high cheekbones that traced a similar path to his jawline, all of these added up to Matt. Again, she saw the glimmer in his eyes and she knew he was close.

Squeezing him with her legs as he moved on top of her, she had lost count of the times they had made love in the last days. This would be the last chance for a while. The next morning she was going to Los Angeles to see Nic Lawson and his house. Matt was giving her something to remember him by. They had been making love for almost two hours, starting as soon as she had arrived home. It was now nearly eight in the evening. For the last two hours he had stimulated her, sometimes gently and other times roughly. In her mind, the previous hours were a long stream of gradually more connected and closer together orgasms as he seemed to mould and manipulate her, enjoying her pleasure in and of itself. He had caressed her, licked her, nibbled at her, even very gently spanked her behind.

For a long time, his mouth had worked at her pussy and she had enjoyed letting herself be exposed and open to him as he explored and familiarised himself with her. The inquiring nature of his tongue, the way he had strained it into her, had left Emma feeling different. He had made her conscious of different patterns and movements her body was capable of.

It was the kind of sex she had with someone when she knew they had gone beyond that initial stage of simply fucking. The quiet and brooding intensity with which he made love to her seemed to scare him, as though he knew he was letting himself go but was powerless to resist. Matt brought just the right degree of confidence, shyness, experience and awe to the situation and it sent feelings through her that were hard to vocalise. Together, they were a potent mix. He startled her with his finesse in bed, the way he touched her and handled himself, belying his years. She had not asked him about his sexual past, but she wondered what it must have been like, how he had become the sort of lover he was. The fantasies that she manufactured in place of knowing the truth were as intense as anything she imagined he might be able to tell her about himself.

That was it, she thought, as he slowly and carefully reamed her with himself. He seemed to have a secret. Not one that would be shocking, but one that she would like to know. More to the point, it was one she

138

felt she could discover if she spent enough time making love to him. It was not a secret that would be conveyed in words, the simple telling of a tale. Emma suspected he did not know himself what secrets he had buried in him like treasure. If she chose to, she could end up knowing more about him in this way than even he did himself. Was she ready to go down that track with him? She had a secret of her own, of course. One that she had yet to tell him. What if his reaction to her had been based on the perception that she was plain Emma Fox. How would it change things?

Matt kissed her and let out a tiny sound. His cock throbbed inside her, his orgasm seconds away. It obliterated all questions and words for Emma. There was a point where these needed to be suspended and she had to trust to the moment. The face she had been studying and pondering in close-up now changed. His features twitched, the eyes scrunching and the lips disappearing into his mouth. His hair fell onto her face and she smoothed it with her hands, resting one on the back of his neck, feeling the tension there and the bucking of his hips against her, the desperate way he fought to reach his climax.

Emma held him tightly as he came. His body was a wire of sexual energy, every muscle moving in concert to exert his desire on her and for himself. She clung onto his body, the one that had spent so much time tending to her and looking after her. Now it was his time and she let him ride and writhe over her, his head buried into her collarbone, muffled cries and half-formed words. She laid a hand on the warm flesh of his hip, resting it on the side between the front of his groin and a cheek of his behind. The flesh was smooth and was moving from his pumping into her. Matt shivered and exhaled, pulling his head up to look at her, a smile and a warmth on his face.

For a moment, they looked at each other. The words hovered near both of them, neither wanting to say it or complicate the situation. For a second, his lips pursed as though he were about to speak, but he seemed to pull himself back. It was as they continued to look at each other that it occurred to Emma, in an obvious and forceful way, almost troubling, that they needed no words.

An hour later, they walked along the Kings Road hand in hand.

'I still can't get over your place. Is it a perk for everyone at Lomax?' Matt asked her, his hip casually bumping hers.

'I needed somewhere to live and they helped me out. It's only temporary,' she said to him. 'I'm sure they'll put me in some hovel when one becomes available. I'm looking for somewhere on my own as well.'

'Not as nice as here, though. I'd be trying to hold out for as long as I could.'

'Your place is lovely, Matt, don't you think?'

'Are you asking in your professional or personal capacity?' he asked.

'A bit of both?' she ventured.

'It is lovely. You're right. You were definitely wasted at a bank.' He squeezed her hand.

'I know,' she said quietly.

It felt uncomfortable when she lied to him. With everyone else, it was easy. It rolled out of her, embellished a little more each time she told it. Not with Matt.

'Do you want to go for ice-cream? I'll pay. It can be my treat before you fly away,' he asked her, seeming to accept what she had told him about the apartment.

'Why not? Just let me go to that autobank.'

'I've got money,' he insisted. 'I can afford to buy you

140

an ice-cream, you know.'

'It'll only take a second,' she said, producing her card.

They sat across from each other over the shining glass surface of a small circular table. They had ordered and were waiting for ice-cream. Drinks had arrived and Emma took a sip of her Purdey's while Matt toyed with a straw at the ice in his Coke. They had been pleasantly silent for the last few minutes.

'You must be excited about going to Los Angeles,' he said from nowhere.

'Of course I am.'

'Have you been before?'

She faltered for a second too long. 'Um, yes.'

'You don't seem sure,' he said lightly.

'Sorry. I'm not with it. I went there on a holiday once.' More lies.

'Have you travelled very much?'

He looked at her as he asked, his eyes concentrating on her. It was hard to hold his gaze and think up an answer.

'Holidays here and there, the usual stuff. You must have been lots of places,' she said, trying to deflect attention back to him.

'Yes. My parents have been very good. How long did you work at the bank?'

'Matt,' she said, a trace of terseness in her voice, 'this is like an interrogation.'

'I don't know very much about you, that's all. I'm sorry.' He looked back down at the Coke.

She reached out and touched his hand, which was cold from where he had been holding onto the glass. She gave it a squeeze and he looked up at her. Again, she felt herself shrink from his gaze. What would it take for her to be able to look him straight in the eyes and feel no tension?

'Matt . . .'

The ice-cream arrived. Emma played with it, her appetite gone. Matt dug in and took hearty mouthfuls and she watched the way he ate, the movements of his jaws, how he twitched his nose. He looked up and caught her staring at him.

'What?' he asked, the spoon midway to his mouth.

Emma said nothing and he carried on eating, showing no sign of self-consciousness. Tomorrow she would be in Los Angeles. Already, in such a short period, it felt too far to be away from him and even the few days of the trip seemed too long. Emma let out a slow breath and reached down into her bag. She retrieved a small slip of paper and slid it across the table to Matt. He picked it up and looked at it as Emma watched, trying to gauge his reaction. It was the slip of paper the autobank had given her when she requested a balance. He looked up at her, more intrigued than surprised.

'You have twenty-eight thousand pounds in your bank account?' he asked.

'That's my current account. I use it for day-to-day things, the general running of my life. It's transferred over from my investment account on a monthly basis – mostly interest earnings but some of the principle if I need it. I pull over enough so the balance never drops under twenty-five thousand, plus there's an overdraft of half a million available. I call it an investment account, but it's actually a whole portfolio. The risk is very well spread.'

'Your redundancy money from the bank's invested?' Now he seemed confused.

'Just under five million sterling is held in the portfolio, the majority of it in very pedestrian safe investments – gilts and the like. About a million goes for higher-yield, high-risk stuff. There's a further account in the Caymans that runs through a whole manner of legitimate shelters. That's much more liquid, so I can get to it very quickly. Just over three and a half million in there. There's six hundred thousand I use to play equities when the mood takes me, but I don't count that in.'

He stared at her, eyes wide. She would explain, but she wanted to finish it off.

'There's a few illiquid things plus some property and art, difficult to value. If you were someone official, I wouldn't tell you this, but I suppose my net worth is sitting at about thirteen and a half million pounds. You should let me buy the ice-cream, don't you think?' She smiled.

'Did you work at the bank or rob it?'

'I did work at a bank and I didn't rob it. I worked for a bank on Wall Street called Morse Callahan. Have you heard of them?'

He shook his head. 'I thought you worked in London?'

'I was an investment banker. I worked at Morse Callahan in their Mergers and Acquisition section. Do you know what M&A is?'

'Corporate raiding and all that stuff?'

'I suppose so,' she said, slightly surprised that he knew what she was talking about. 'I earned enough to stop working and I did something that really shocked them. I actually did stop working.'

'They pay you that sort of money?'

She nodded. 'People don't realise, Matt. The first year I was there, my bonus was almost two million dollars.'

He leaned closer to her. 'So what are you doing at Lomax? Do they know all of this? Am I the only one who doesn't?'

'Of course not. You won't tell your father this, promise?' she said, feeling herself being drawn in. It might have been easier not to tell him. 'Catherine is a friend and I'm thinking of investing in the agency. I

143

wanted to do some research on it before I parted with any money and this seemed like a good way to do it.'

'Thirteen and a half million pounds and you're sitting here eating ice-cream, working for an estate agent's?'

'Where else would I be? I can't just take off to the Moon. It's only money. Come on, Matt, you don't go short of money.'

'We're well off, I know that. Father doesn't talk about it, but I know I don't have to worry. I'm not sure if we're as rich as you. Emma, Jesus Christ.'

'What?' she asked.

'Why didn't you tell me?'

'I am telling you,' she said.

'Why did you tell me?' he asked, an exasperated tone in his voice.

'What does it change?' she asked.

'It could change a whole lot for you,' he said. 'How do I know what you want to do?'

'Is it because I have more money than you?' she asked. 'Tell me it isn't that.'

'The money doesn't matter. I just . . .' He paused, a pained expression on his face. 'I knew there was something about you. You seem out of place at Lomax. With all that money, you could do anything, it just makes me feel . . .' His words trailed off again.

'Matt,' she said. She couldn't think of anything else to say.

Matt inhaled. 'I feel like I like you more than I should already. I know you don't want to hear that and you're probably going to think I'm weird. I'm sorry.'

'Stop apologising, Matt. I like you too. If you want to know the truth, and I'm being honest here, I feel like I'm in too deep already, but it's a good feeling. I just wanted to tell you because I felt uncomfortable lying to you. That's all. I'm telling you all this for a positive reason.'

'Thirteen million? And you tell me tonight. Emma.'

'It doesn't change anything. Just focus on that,' she said to him firmly.

'It makes things feel different. That's all,' he said. 'It's like your whole life is taken care of and sealed up. Is there a space in there for someone?'

His question hung in the air.

'When I come back, I'll take some time off and we'll spend it together. I could have waited to tell you, but it's been on my mind. I wanted you to know before I went to LA.'

'And you have been there before? Your name really is Emma Fox?'

Emma leaned across the small distance and gave him a gentle kiss on the cheek. She held her position and then kissed him less gently on the mouth.

'Why don't you take me back home and show me that it makes no difference?' she whispered to him.

Chapter Fourteen

EMMA SMILED AT the good-looking valet in front of
the hotel as she pulled away in her rented convertible,
turning onto Sunset Boulevard and off into the
direction of Nic Lawson's house. From the map and
her previous experience of the city, she knew Nic's
house nestled between Sunset and Griffith Park and it
was just a question of finding the correct left turn
shortly after La Brea. It was ten in the morning and it
almost felt like it, time difference notwithstanding.
Emma had slept well in the hotel Nic Lawson had
recommended, after she had politely declined his offer
to stay at the house. She had made it from LAX to the
hotel in Bel Air in a single fluid movement, her passage
smoothed by first-class travel. Emma had paid for the
trip herself, not wanting to burden Lomax with the
cost and not wanting to appear uncharitable about
Catherine's offer to fly her business class. From
England to the West Coast of the United States – that
had to be first class, Emma thought.

At that time of the morning, Los Angeles was
pleasant. The weather was cooking up towards a good
heat, burning off the smog, and the traffic of the
morning had drawn a breath as the roads waited for
the lunchtime rush. The wind played with her hair and

she put on her sunglasses. A wish that Matt were with her gnawed at her. Now she had been honest with him, she just wanted him more than ever. And he her, if their last encounter had been any measure. She saw the road that was her marker for the left, found her turn and after several minutes and two more turns she was at the gates to Nic's house. It was ten-fifteen.

Behind the large iron gates she could not see the house. She pushed the buzzer from the car and announced herself; the gates buzzed and swung open. She passed a man with a dog, both of whom looked at her impassively as she drove slowly by. At the end of a small gravel incline sat the house. It was as square as its owner and looked like a brick that had been dropped out of the sky and had landed there by accident. The building seemed to be all glass like a solar panel or a pair of highway Patrol mirror shades.

Emma parked the car and was met by a woman who introduced herself in a slow California brogue as Nina, an assistant of Nic's.

'Mr Lawson will see you right away,' she informed Emma, leading her round the side of the glass cube.

At her side, Emma's leather briefcase tapped against her leg. In it were several papers relating to Nic and a whole manner of material concerning Lomax that Emma had used the long flight to study. A pattern was emerging and she would speak to Catherine face to face when she got back. She was wearing a cool cotton two-piece by Bijan which had seemed the most appropriately Beverly Hills thing to throw in her suitcase.

A man and a woman were splashing around in a large swimming pool with water as blue as the sky. They were both the same shade of sun-kissed blonde and laughed and giggled as they splashed and grabbed at each other. On a lounger set back from the pool, a man in a black polo-neck was leafing through a

147

magazine, a mobile phone at rest on a glass-topped side table.

Nic Lawson, wearing sunglasses, sat at the head of the pool, as though it were a dining table. He stood, smiling, and approached her. Dressed expensively in varying shades of grey and black, he looked like a drug dealer. The whole set-up looked like something from a movie, which Emma suspected was the effect he was trying to create.

'Well, here's the pool. I wouldn't want one in London anyway.'

He looked at the splashing in the pool and then at her.

'They're twins,' he said, raising his eyebrows above the frames of the Wayfarers. 'Oh my. Thank you for coming, Emma.'

Definitely turning on the charm, Emma thought.

'It's a pleasure. Good to see you again, Nic.'

'I called the hotel and they said you got in okay last night. I wasn't gonna disturb you. Everything all right with the room and stuff?'

'Fine. This is an amazing place. I can't wait to see it all.'

'Nina, is the house clear?' he barked.

'Yes, Mr Lawson.'

'Good.'

Nic held his arm up, indicating she should rest her hand on his forearm. She did.

'First stop, the bar, I think,' he said, leading her towards the glass house.

The bar was in a mock solarium environment, the sun's rays rendered mauve by the glass. The bar itself was neat and well stocked. Nic went behind it and his torso virtually disappeared into a huge fridge. He returned with two bottles.

'Have one of these. Smart cocktail. Do you the world of good.'

148

'Tell me this isn't spiked,' she said.

'Course it ain't. This is LA.'

They sat on two stools. The top of the counter was a clear plastic material that encased the gold and silver discs of various artists.

'Are these all your artists?'

'One way or another. You know LA well, don't you? I can tell. When I first came, it knocked me right back, but you seem at home here.'

'I spent about four months here once. And I've spent time in other parts of the States,' she said.

'I can tell. Let me explain the house before we troop off. Basically, it's three floors and a basement. Half the basement is like a sort of nuclear fallout anti-riot shelter. The bloke who had the house before me was a nutter, one of those survivalist types with his sperm frozen in ice-cube trays in case of holocaust. Mind you, there were riots not long after I bought this and the bunker was already there so I thought I'd just quietly leave it. Just in case. The rest of the basement is for music, videos and fun. There's a cinema and a listening room down there. I'll show you all that last. The rest is pretty obvious. You married?' he finished, clumsily.

'No. Not even divorced,' she informed him.

'Sensible. The top floor is only half the size of the others. It's got four bedrooms, all with bathrooms and a couple of living areas with televisions and music. You can close off the doors so that it makes two self-contained living areas, one of which you would have been more than welcome to stay in. See, you wouldn't even have had to share with me.'

Emma had removed her sunglasses before they had entered the house. Nic finally took his off and she preferred being able to see his eyes.

'And the second floor, Nic?' she asked, ignoring his imploring look, the need to be patted on the head and liked. She took another pull on the fruity liquid.

'My sleeping area, basically. Lots of huge bedrooms, loads of bathrooms, lots of stucco. One room with a bed that's the size of a room, full of mirrors. I call that the fuck room, pardon the language. Six bedrooms up there, all different designs, depends how I feel and where I want to sleep. And who with.'

She drained the bottle. 'Shall we have a look around down here?'

He led her from room to room, carefully opening doors for her and politely describing the sums of money he'd spent on every change. Emma had to admit to herself that the house was impressive, not as gaudy as she would have expected based on the façade Nic seemed keen to present to the world. On the ground floor there was an enormous living room designed for large parties that had a spectacular view out to the gardens and the city just visible over the distant high walls. In its corner, the obligatory white grand piano made a cameo appearance. All of the rooms and spaces worked well together, some of the floors wooden and others stone tiles with rugs on them. All of the decorations were carefully colour-coordinated, one room seeming to flow into another. The ground floor had a study, a library, several separate reception rooms and a pool room. Other sundry rooms seemed to be sprinkled about the area.

It took less time to cover the top and second floors. The door system for the guest area on the top floor of the house was ingenious and Emma sensed Nic was proud of it and enjoyed playing the host. The bedrooms on what he had called the sleeping floor were indeed different. One was old English Tudor, another like a log cabin, one like a monastery and one done out like a fifteen-year-old boy's room. Then she came to what he had so aptly called the fuck room. It was some thirty feet square and half of it was taken up by a bed. It was gargantuan.

'No need to tell me which this room is,' she said to him, smiling.

Surprisingly, he was very well behaved in the room, pointing out structural features and talking about where he had had the bed made and, of course, how much it had cost. What had gone on in this room, she asked herself?

There was a lift that descended into the basement and it opened out into a small, well lit stone hall with three doors leading off it.

'That's the cinema and it leads to the bunker,' Nic said, pointing at the door in front of them. 'That's the music room, two hundred grand of audio equipment in there.'

'And this room?'

'This is what I like to call the cyber room.'

'Why?'

'Let me show you.'

He opened the door and she stepped through.

The room was spartan, the floor a warm rubber and the walls some sort of acoustic material. The light was pleasant, at a table-lamp kind of level, and it was relaxing. A workbench against one wall housed a computer and a console, various wires trailing from it and into a box in the centre of the room. Two single wires, quite thick, ran from the other end of the box and over into the corner. There, discarded almost, and linked to the wire, were what looked like two wet suits.

'What's this room for?' she quizzed, her curiosity sparked.

'It's linked to a computer in the fallout shelter. This is some of the most advanced technology there is at the moment. It's being developed by my video and computer games division. It won't even be prototyped properly for another two years, released in about four and probably six to eight before it's generally available.'

'It being?' she asked.

'Cyber-sex, darling. Care to try?'

'Sex with a computer?'

'No. Much more and much better than that. These suits read you and you read them. Believe me, it's like a synergy between you and it. I know this sounds like science fiction, but trust me. Think about it. It can be almost anyone you want. Sex with anyone you want, huh? The technology learns and understands. You just sit and tap in a few things at the console and it will do the rest.'

'Are you serious?'

'At least let me show you how the console works.'

Nic flicked a switch, tapped at the keyboard and displayed menus listing a whole range of sexual possibilities. It was fascinating to Emma. The screen flashed examples and she was amazed at how real it all looked.

'What about sounds and feelings?' she asked.

'It's a clever mix. The headgear will pump noise at you, even release the odd vapour that you choose. The suits feel as real as you or I and there's a few mechanical tricks in them to shift things along.'

'I might sound crude, but why go to all this trouble when you can have the real thing?'

'I might sound like a cliché,' he came back, 'but this is better than the real thing. Trust me. I've fucked Marilyn Monroe and James Dean using this. I want them both together next. A threesome. That's what I've got the nerds in the lab working on. They're really pleased about that,' he said sarcastically.

Something flicked past on the screen that caught her attention and she told him to stop. She put her hand on his and removed it from the mouse, using it to select a new sub-menu. He turned to look at her as she made several selections.

'Now, there's my kind of girl,' he said to her.

Nic was right. The suits did feel real. The headset was light and comfortable to wear, feeding her sound, vision and vapour from the computer. She moved her head around, the vision tracking with her. The environment was fairly basic, like the monastery bedroom she had seen on the second floor of the house. He had told her it would take a few minutes to get used to the suit and he had been right about that too, but now she felt it start to tune in with her.

Emma looked down at herself and gave the cock that was dangling between her legs a squeeze. It seemed to pulse, somewhere in her, like a rush of blood, and in her hand it firmed up. As the erection grew, she moved her hand up and down the shaft, marvelling at the feel of it, so life-like that it was hard to believe it was part of a suit attached to her like a second skin, a small probe in her vagina replicating the feeling. She moved the foreskin back and forth, the head of the cock swelling. It became harder and she could sense the stiffness, the slight pain, a feeling that it might erupt. In place of her breasts, when she looked down, she had a finely muscled chest with a light smattering of hair. Her arms were muscular and her hands looked bigger.

The smell of Chanel perfume and a faint tinge of clean sweat pervaded the atmosphere. Emma heard the husky feminine breathing and looked ahead of her. There, in front of her, was a luscious woman with long brunette hair. She sat on the floor, her legs parted, and toyed with her pussy which glistened with moisture. The woman smiled at her and popped a finger into herself. Emma felt a pang of desire in her, and as she did, the cock throbbed. She looked down at it, stiff and ready. Utterly lost in a virtual world, it was no longer *the* cock or even *a* cock. It was *her* cock.

The brunette turned and kneeled on all fours, pushing her rear into the air and spreading her pussy.

'Oh, fuck me,' she said in a slow drawl.

Emma knelt on the floor behind the woman and reached a hand out to touch her pussy. It was wet and pliable to the touch and Emma toyed with it before sinking a finger solidly into the warm smooth passage. The woman cried out as Emma pushed in deep, another finger finding the clitoris and moving it gently from side to side. Her finger continued to work on the woman and the odour of the Chanel became more intimate the closer she got to her. Emma leaned over and kissed one of the cheeks of the woman's behind, the feel of it warm and soft to her lips. She withdrew her finger.

Positioning herself carefully behind the woman, Emma took her cock in her hand and probed it at the woman's vagina. The pussy felt hot on the tip of her cock and Emma no longer cared how or why this was. She pushed the tip in and watched it disappear into the woman. Eventually, the whole of it was buried in the woman and she cried out. Emma smiled. She reached her hands under the woman and fondled the dangling breasts, tweaking the erect nipples.

Starting with a slow and deliberate tempo, Emma reamed her cock in and out of the vagina. It felt hot around her and her cock tingled and swelled painfully as she continued to fuck the woman doggy-style. Emma was not certain why she had let the computer generate so obvious an image, a lusty vivacious brunette, but it was working for her. She drove her cock in deeper, feeling her pubic hair against the woman's behind. The force of her thrusts was driving the woman forward and she was grunting each time Emma drove her cock home.

The woman's vagina contracted rhythmically around her cock and the feeling made Emma want to come. She wanted to drive on at the woman from behind, keep shoving roughly into her until the woman had a long and loud orgasm and she too came. The woman groaned as Emma increased the speed of her invasion, jerking her hips about and varying the depth and angle at which her cock entered the woman. The cock was swollen painfully and felt ready to burst inside the vagina, flooding it with come.

Letting out a loud and desperate cry, the woman yelled, 'I'm coming! Oh God, that's it, fuck me.'

It was the strangest of sensations. Emma had no way of telling where it started or exactly what it felt like. A tension, in a whole wave, cloaked her body and then she felt the cock quiver a few times. It made a long and aching twitch and she felt it start to pump. She could hardly believe it. The faster she stabbed into the woman, the better the sensation got. The cries of the woman, who was coming violently and squeezing Emma's cock with her pussy, were drowned by her own shouts.

Emma could not resist. She withdrew and pumped at the shaft of her cock. She cried out and came in a profound spasm that sent smaller waves through her whole body. She stared down and watched herself ejaculate several long streams of semen and she pointed her cock at the woman's behind, watching it splatter onto her cheeks. She continued to pull and squeeze at her cock until the last of the semen dribbled from it.

So this is what all the fuss is about, she thought?

For several long moments, Emma knelt, catching her breath. She reached to the switch on the side of the headset and flicked it.

The programme came to a halt and the wonderful virtual world was replaced. The headset might as well have been a pair of sunglasses. She pulled it off, abruptly back in the real world, the suit and its dangling piece of rubber no longer so real. In front of her, Nic was on his hands and knees encased in a rubber suit, gasping for air. He looked round at her and laughed.

'Not bad for your first time with a cock,' he said. 'And I knew you'd have a big one.'

Chapter Fifteen

EMMA REACHED INTO an unfamiliar darkness, trying to find the ringing phone somewhere at the bedside in the hotel room. Being disoriented by the jet-lag made it hard to tell what time it was. The air-conditioning in the room was burring efficiently and there was a pleasant crispness to the air, matched by the linen of the sheets and contrasted to the scorch of the atmosphere in the city itself. Her mind tuned in. She found the phone.

'Hello,' she said, not bothering to try and find a bedside light.

'Hi, sexy.'

She paused. 'Matt?'

'Your first guess. I'm flattered,' he said.

'What time is it?' she asked.

'Depends where you are,' Matt replied.

'Where are you? This is a very good transatlantic line,' she said, sitting up in bed, the room becoming clearer as her night vision adjusted.

'I'm in New Hampshire.'

'I thought you were going to move house? Didn't you call Malcolm? What are you doing on the East Coast, Matt?' she asked him, surprised at her twinge of excitement at learning he was on the same continent as her.

'Missing you, mostly. My parents have a place here. Their honeymoon hideaway. I wanted to talk to you.'

'I tried calling but you weren't there, obviously.'

'I'm missing you, Emma.'

She smiled in the semi-darkness and moved herself in the cool hotel sheet, his words bringing back consciousness of her nudity to her.

'I'm missing you too. I'll be back in a couple of days. How long are you there for?'

'Only a few days. Can you hold on a second?'

She waited a few moments and then he was back on the line.

'That's better,' he said.

'What are you doing?'

'I was just undoing the buttons on my jeans,' he said.

Emma imagined a pair of lightly faded jeans hugging Matt's narrow hips and behind, cut close into his crotch and the bulge of his cock, the silver buttons of the fly covering him.

'Why did you do that?' she asked him.

'So I can reach into my underwear while I talk to you. Listen.'

At the end of the line, she heard the sound of fabric moving and she knew he was holding the phone into his lap, letting her hear what he was doing. Then she heard his breathing again.

'Where are you in the house?'

'I'm, um, sitting in an old armchair, one of my favourites when I was a boy. You're in bed, I take it?'

'Yes.'

'On your own, I'm assuming.'

'Of course. Just you, me and your underwear.'

'Are you wearing any underwear?'

'I'm naked, just a white sheet covering me. Is your cock hard yet?'

'It has been since I thought of calling you. My cock is very hard.'

'You have a gorgeous prick,' she told him.

'Do you like it?'

'Yes.'

'Do you like it inside you?'

'Yes.'

'And in your mouth?'

'Especially in my mouth.'

'Why?'

'I like the taste of you and of your come. There's another place I'd like your cock that we haven't tried yet,' she told him.

'You'd like it there, would you?'

'Please. How would you give it to me?'

'I'd make you strip. Then you would have to lubricate yourself and my cock. I'd make you bend over and then I'd finger you for a bit, but not too much. I wouldn't want it to go in too easy.'

'Would you come in there?'

'I'd fill you right up,' he told her.

'Will it hurt?'

'A bit, maybe. Are you touching yourself?'

'Yes. I'm stroking my clit. My pussy's wet. Are you touching yourself?'

'Yes,' he replied.

'Pull your foreskin all the way back,' she said. 'Have you?'

'Yes,' he said.

'Is there fluid on the tip?'

'Lots.'

'Take some on a fingertip and lick it off. What does it taste like?' she asked him.

'Bitter,' was his response.

'Matt, what's it like when you come?' Emma asked him, feeling warm in the cool room.

'Oh, I don't know really. It's like someone's tied you in a knot. One of those slip knots and they've pulled it really tight. The knot closes and then all of a sudden it

159

disappears. It just wipes me out. I love coming with you.'

'Do you do it to yourself much?'

'Too much. The last couple of days especially.'

'Why's that?' she purred into the phone.

'All I've thought about is fucking with you. Doing all sorts of things I never would have thought of before. These ideas just come tó me.'

His breathing was irregular.

'Tell me some of them,' she instructed him.

'Coming,' he said. 'I want to come with you, on you, all over you, everywhere I can. I want you to tie me up and I want to tie you up. To use toys. Other people. To eat you out. For you to suck me. Do you get the picture?'

'I'm getting a picture, certainly.'

Emma slid her middle finger into herself in a familiar and precise motion, letting it travel in quickly and feeling the invasion of it. Matt's words, knowing he was at the other end of the phone, jeans splayed open and hand in his underwear, had sent her pussy into action. She shuddered, a tingle running up her back and her muscles closing around the finger as she worked it along her passage. Had Matt been there, she would have put her hands into his hair and guided his head down between her legs, allowing him to lap away at her. She thought about forcing his face into her, making him one with her and allowing him access to herself. The distance he was away from her at that moment, despite being less than it could have been, made her desire so potent she was barely able to hold onto it. Emma longed to clamber over his lithe young body, the virtually hairless torso, the faintest muscle definition. And his face. That alone would have been enough to ensure her endless orgasms.

'Oh,' she cried out.

'How many fingers are you using?'

160

'Just one,' she told him.

'Put another one in,' he directed her.

As she did, she gasped at the enlargement of her vagina.

'Are you thumbing your clit?'

'Yes,' she whispered.

'My cock feel's like it'll explode soon. It hasn't been so hard for ages. I might save it for you. Would you like that? You can suck me off when you get back.'

'Oh Matt.' She was hoarse.

'Open your legs wide and put three fingers in. I want to hear you groan and come.'

Less delicately than the second, the third finger entered her, her voice raising almost an octave. It was like having him inside her, but not quite. At least she had him at the end of the phone. Her hand ached, a feeling of cramp developing, and she pressed her rear into the mattress, legs apart and slightly back to form a linen tent over her pussy. The bed gave a slight creak and it moved back and forth in time with her exertions. That noise was mostly covered by the noises she herself made. Together, all the disparate tones which were building slowly from a cacophony of passion would culminate in the blissful harmony of her orgasm.

'Hold onto it,' Matt was saying.

'Matt, talk dirty to me.'

'What do you want most?' he asked her.

'For you to be here.'

'Would that be a nice surprise?' he asked.

'Oh yes,' she replied, sinking into the spreading passion. 'Please talk dirty to me, Matt.'

There was no response.

'Matt?'

Still no response.

'Are you there?'

The door to her room opened slowly and an

unmistakable silhouette crossed it, hair hanging down the forehead. Emma was dazed and confused, thinking she was in a dream. He approached the bed and instantly reached under the sheet, replacing her fingers with two of his own. Longer and bonier, they found a greater depth inside her than she had been able to manage. The interruption had taken her off the boil and his fingers toiled to reheat her. Her vagina was supple and when he slipped a third finger into her, she was easily able to accommodate it. The phone discarded against her collarbone, Emma let her hands lie limp on the pillow and allowed him to labour at her. She seethed when his little finger joined the other three and her body felt overrun and opened by the skilful young hand.

Throwing the sheet fully off her, he lifted the receiver of the phone from her. Her eyes were closed and for a second she opened them and then scrunched them tightly shut and writhed against the sheet, her throat gurgling as he introduced the earpiece of the phone into her vagina. The plastic was warm and smooth, the wide roundness of it a strange shape in her, opening and stretching her without any real penetration. His fingers had readied her well and the earpiece eased itself through her opening and she closed around its narrow shaft.

'You bastard,' she hissed at him.

With her vagina stuffed, he turned his attention to her clitoris, now full and rapt. Carefully he tweaked at it and massaged his fingers around it, coaxing her along. The earlier delayed orgasm was ready to return with a vengeance, fortified by the wait. She was ready for it to take her over and to possess her as surely as she felt possessed by Matt. For a few delightful moments, Emma would surrender willingly to it. Matt's fingers were deft on her, so loving and so careful. She wished she could have seen his face properly in the room, but made do with the outline of it and her own imagination. It was not an image that required embellishment in any fashion. With Matt, the reality far outstripped any fantasy she might have concocted.

The vision of the face etched into her mind, Emma ran her hands through her own hair and felt the orgasm tremble. As though balancing on a high wire, she was ready to topple. It was the feeling of almost falling and just catching herself in time. One single, almost immeasurable microsecond of release would be recorded and replayed for long and agonisingly pleasurable moments as she wrestled with her orgasm, ready to let it throw her over.

Emma contracted tightly around the plastic. She felt herself shrink onto it and then it was forgotten as she palpitated around it, the long waves of her orgasm loosening off every muscle in her body, bringing her down to a deep and peaceful level while Matt continued to worry at her clitoris with his dexterous fingers.

An hour later, she was resting her head on Matt's chest, feeling the warm movement of his recently spent fluid inside of her.

'Of all the hotel rooms in all the towns in all the world,' she said to him. 'I think an explanation would be useful at this point.'

His breathing was slow and even, chest rising and falling in time with it.

'I'm a friend of Nic's. He told me about this trip and where you'd be staying. I got him to arrange it with the staff here so I could have the room next to yours. I thought it would be a nice surprise.'

She squeezed his frame. 'It is. How did you get a key to the room?'

'Nic's well connected here.'

'That's good to know. Do your parents really have a honeymoon hideaway in New England?'

163

'Yes. In the White Mountains of New Hampshire. I thought we might do a stopover there en route to London.'

'Oh really,' she said to him.

'If you think it's a good idea. Just over the weekend. Unless you have other plans?'

'No. I just need to finalise things with Nic tomorrow and then I'm finished here.'

'I'll see if I can help you there.'

'How?' she asked.

'I know Nic and what buttons to push,' he said. 'We'll see.'

In the whiteness of the linen and the freshness of the room, she held onto his firm body and as the city pulsed and throbbed around her, she drifted into a tranquil sleep.

Chapter Sixteen

THE GENTLE BREEZE of mid-morning crept around their ankles and lifted the light edges of Emma's hotel robe as she and Matt sat on the balcony, the remnants of a recently shared brunch casually littering the table. The sun was perfectly positioned to pleasantly bathe them without the need to squint. The frantic rhythm of people and freeways that was Los Angeles drummed in what seemed a far distance, barely audible but ever present. Muffins, orange and cranberry juice, some pancakes, bagels and scrambled eggs had all been eaten in an unhurried way, their senses still oscillating from the exertions of the previous night's sex. Soon, they would need to go and visit Nic Lawson, enabling Emma to finish what had been interrupted by their computer-controlled liaison. For the next few minutes, however, Emma wanted to take her time with Matt and with the strange serenity of her surroundings. It was almost like a holiday, she thought.

Emma had woken before Matt that morning. When she did, she was neither disoriented by a strange room nor surprised at having someone next to her. It felt like where she was supposed to be and with whom she expected to be. Emma had spent half an hour lying close to him as he slept, appreciating the resting warmth of what she knew so well when in motion. She had huddled close to his back, cheek resting on a shoulder blade, and thought of nothing at all but what she was doing there and then, completely tuned out from everything else. When he too awoke, he appeared to slip casually from the world of sleep, looking at her as though about to respond to a just-asked question, like he'd never been away.

Slipping from the bed, she had run a bath and poured fragrant gel into the water, softening it. Then, she had simply bathed him. Using more of the gel directly onto his skin, Emma let it lubricate her caress over his chest and stomach, along his legs and between his legs, holding and tenderly washing him. The whole time, he was responsive and obedient, moving his body around in the tub to allow her to clean him. The continual sexual tension between them was oddly smoothed away by the delicate passage of her hands over his lithe and virile body. She dried him off, scuffing the towel pleasantly against the soft manly skin, before she massaged creams into him, rendering the skin supple and fresh. Sitting him on the end of the bed, Emma carefully dried his hair and traced some gel through it, teasing at it with a brush as he sat silent and still as a portrait. Finally, she left his naked body in a fine mist of Calvin Klein's Escape, watching as it settled on him in minute droplets.

Now, he sat on the balcony in familiar denim jeans and a shirt in a green shade of the same material, the blues and greens accentuating the gold of his skin. The shirt had flapped open enough at the top to reveal a hairless contour of his chest which was far more arousing than when he had been naked earlier. The sweet fragrance she had sprayed him with lingered in the air and was picked up on the wind and wafted to her, and she realised this would become a smell with which she forever associated him and Los Angeles.

Before speaking, she let the memory of the smell flourish and store itself away.

'Are the tickets going to be at the airport?' she asked.

'The concierge is arranging for them. He wanted to have them sent here. I think he's just trying to be helpful. I told him it would be easier for us to pick them up at the airport.'

'I only need to make some notes at Nic's and take a few snaps. It won't be more than two hours. Are you sure you want to come?'

'Of course,' he said. 'I've known Nic since I was ten years old. He loves me.'

'Why didn't you tell me this when you first knew I would be seeing him? It might have been useful.'

'I didn't really know you that well then – I still don't – but I didn't want it to seem as though I was showing off or pulling strings.'

'Catherine Lomax is keen to get him as a client. It could open up a new area for the agency,' she told him.

'What, jaded old rock stars and their managers? Nic moves in some funny circles.'

'How does a genteel child like you end up knowing him?'

'It's weird, really. He arranged for a band to play at my tenth birthday party. Nic was unknown back then. My parents wanted to make a fuss, show me off to everyone, that sort of thing.'

'And you stayed in touch?'

'Nic's arranged things for my sixteenth, eighteenth and twenty-first birthdays. The last two at my behest, not my parents'. They get grander as Nic gets more successful,' he said.

'He sounds more like your godfather.'

'I only see him every now and then. When you get to know Nic, you'll find that when you're with him, you're the most important person in the world. Then he forgets you and moves on.'

'A user, you mean?'

'In the nicest way,' he said.

'I really want to see this parental love-nest in New Hampshire,' she said, pouring more coffee into her mug. The need to mainline several shots of caffeine was one of her Wall Street habits she had yet to shake.

'You'll like it, I know you will.'

Matt grinned at her. The easy smile that was growing more familiar to her. Between that grin and their conversation over ice-cream in the Kings Road, he had said very little about her purpose at Lomax, or the amount of money she was worth. He did not seem to be brooding on it, she thought, so she hoped it was not going to become any sort of issue between them. With an easiness similar to his smile, he had taken it in his stride.

On the breakfast table in front of her was the buff file containing the information Catherine had provided. Glancing at its cover sent Emma's mind off in a different direction, anchoring it in some sort of reality. Several times since arriving in Los Angeles and on her way there, Emma had opened the file and looked over the multitude of poorly constructed figures. She rethought the numbers using her own logic, trying to spot anything that would give a clue as to the small and gradual decline in agency revenue outside of obvious market factors and seasonal variations. It was barely noticeable and that was what troubled her about it. Still a pattern eluded her. Perhaps she was being too analytical. Emma decided to leave it alone for a while, hoping that in coming back to it, something would suggest itself or take her by surprise.

'Matty!' Nic Lawson said, a happy tone accenting his voice more than normal as he greeted them in the impressive entrance hall. 'How's it going?'

Before Matt or Emma could respond, Nic's eyes had shifted between them knowingly, reading their body language.

'Come here,' Nic said, pulling Matt to him in a 'that's my boy' sort of hug and planting a kiss on his cheek as he released him. 'He was in short trousers first time I met him,' he said to Emma.

Nic danced around, playfully shadow-boxing at Matt. They were like two adolescents messing around. Emma twisted on the heel of one of her pumps and touched the side of her Katherine Hamnett shift dress, the lightness of it so right for the close heat of LA. She felt a little spare and unneeded standing there as Nic and Matt bantered on. A strange feeling came over her and for a moment she thought she was actually jealous. Then, the emotion seemed to make itself clear to her as she watched them. She was aroused by the two of them. It was as though two complete opposites had been mixed and the result was something unexpected and strong. Emma was clear enough about how titillated she was but did not know if that should make her feel guilty.

'I'm going to make some notes and take a few pictures,' she said briskly. 'You boys can play and I'll see you in a while.'

Padding quickly away, she made for the guest area that had so impressed her on first sight. It still did, but she was now quicker and more business-like in her movements. Aside from the brief meeting with Matt's parents on her first day at Lomax, Emma realised she knew very little about him. Seeing him with Nic was the first suggestion of any kind of life he might have had outside the world of fantasy the pair of them had so willingly inhabited in the previous days.

Emma wandered from bedroom to bedroom on the upper floor, uncertain of what Nic Lawson had been trying to do by creating so many differently styled rooms. There might have been any number of clever psychological reasons she could have used to explain his nomadic sleeping habits in this large house, but she did not judge him. In the room with the oversized bed, she sat down. The environment was garish, and not a little exciting. In an area some thirty feet square, the bed must have been twenty feet square, planted in the centre like a boxing ring. Stretched across the expanse was a black silk sheet that fitted perfectly. Emma could not see a seam anywhere, as though it were one great silk square. An archaic wooden dresser with finely carved details on the doors stood unobtrusively in one corner and Emma wondered what might be in it. With only large cushions scattered here and there and the squareness of the bed giving no indication of where, if at all, to sleep, the room seemed to be designed for only one thing.

The quiet of the room was eerie. The walls and ceiling were tiled in a polystyrene-like material, so that every move and breath was audible in the flat, un-resonant acoustics that threw every sound back on itself with equal force. Emma ran a hand over the silk as she sat on the corner of the bed. The feel of it under her palm reminded her of Matt's skin in the hotel earlier as she had tended to it. She moved so she was sitting on a corner of the bed, the right angle of the mattress protruding between her legs. In the silence of the room, the careful movement of her hand under her dress seemed loud. Idly and as though she were not really aware of herself, she slipped her hand into her knickers and fondled herself.

Even as she heard the door open and the sound of their laughing conspiratorial voices, she had already removed her hands and was standing, a guilty look on her face.

'Fancy finding you here,' Nic said, no trace of irony in his voice.

'I was just . . .' her voice trailed off as she felt no need to explain herself.

'It's the room, right?' Nic asked.

'How do you mean?' she said, now demure.

'If there's one thing I absolutely need in a London house, it's a room like this. I couldn't tell those old blokes from the agency that, could I?' Nic said.

'What sort of room is this?' Matt piped up innocently.

Emma and Nic Lawson looked at him. Nic raised his eyes.

'Where'd you find him?' Nic asked her.

'This room is very affecting, Nic. There's something about it,' Emma said.

'Yeah, there's sort of, I don't know.' Nic struggled for a word.

'An ambience?' Emma suggested.

'Yeah. I used to use it for recording. Just simple stuff, demos and all that. Whenever I was in here on my own, listening to stuff, I'd end up playing with myself. That's when I decided to use it for what it seemed best for.' Nic imparted the information with cheerful candour.

There was silence.

'If you really must know, I was sitting on the bed with my hand in my underwear. There definitely must be something about this room.'

She was glad to have it out in the open. Matt, at Nic's side, had not spoken. He looked at her and she returned the gaze, letting her eyes drop to the crotch of his jeans.

'I can sort of feel it too, really,' Matt said finally, as though he wanted to be part of it.

'Shall I leave you two lovebirds alone?' Nic asked gleefully.

Emma looked at Nic and at Matt, the camaraderie between them like happy schoolboys. How to ask, she wondered. Was it on their minds too? Why had they come to the room when they did?

'I don't know about you two,' she said, kicking off her shoes and sitting back down on the bed, 'but I'm staying right here for a while.'

Ignoring them, she sat first and then lay back on the corner of the bed and put her feet up on it, the short dress easily revealing her underwear. Emma genuinely did not mind what they did. She *had* been happy enough on her own. Again, with the same composure, she explored herself, closing her eyes and rubbing her shoulders against the silk. They could do whatever they wanted, but she was happy where she was. When she felt hands under her dress, removing her underwear, her eyes remained closed. Emma did not want to know who it was and did not even try to guess. Even as the dress was pulled off, she did not look, enjoying the thrill of not knowing. It was like a game of hide and seek. The only sounds in the room were those made by her clothing as it was removed.

Naked and eyes shut, she rolled herself around on the expanse of the silk, so cool on her skin and so easy to slide over. The simple and almost pornographic feeling of being on a bed so huge was exciting and as she rolled around, Emma touched at herself when the position of her body allowed it. She stretched her arms and legs, feeling the muscles elongated and liberated as her body woke to itself.

The naked body that joined her was unmistakably Matt's and she opened her eyes to look at him. He was laughing as he wrestled friskily with her, gripping and squeezing her waist, lightly mauling her breasts and tousling her hair. The smiles became broader and broader as they rolled around, giggling like naughty children. Matt's cock flopped freely but heavily about as he moved and his body was warm to the touch, rubbery almost. The gel on his hair was not sufficient to keep it in check and, instead, it fell in all sorts of directions, giving him a wild look. Emma kissed him, her tongue exploring the soft cavern of his mouth.

Off to one side, near the bed, Nic Lawson was standing naked, a large erection protruding from his groin. He was boggle-eyed as he looked at the pair of them tumbling about on the bed. He reached down and gripped himself, the shaft and head full of blood. Working his hand back and forth, there was a look of hunger on his face. Emma ignored him and continued to frolic with Matt, grabbing handfuls of his behind and squeezing. She could hear Nic's breathing, accelerating gradually in time with the motion of his hand.

They ended near one corner of the bed, Emma on her back. Matt sat on top of her, his legs straddling her hips and his cock resting across her damp pubic hair, riding her almost. She held him close to her and explored his buttocks where she could reach and he looked into her eyes. Each time she was joined to this boy, there was something new in the midst of the well-known. The fragrant aftershave was still powerful and it assailed her, making her grip him as tightly as she could without hurting him. Emma wanted him in so many different ways, for him to do so many different things to her sexually, that it made her want to rush through them all in case they ran out of time. Matt had given her a renewed sense of urgency and she was devouring him at every opportunity.

Emma heard a creaking sound and her attention was distracted from Matt. It must have been the ornate wooden dresser. She was unable to see from where they were. Slowly and with a mix of caution and hesitancy, Nic sat down on the edge of the bed. In a faltering motion, his hand reached out and touched Matt's long hair, smoothing through the back and on over to his forehead. As though he may even have

173

expected it, Matt's expression was unchanged, his lips the same dainty pout and his eyes the mild opals. Gently, as if stretching his neck, Matt circled his head, moving his hair around Nic's hand. All the while, Emma watched in close-up the look on Matt's face, the feel of his body warm on her, his weight carefully spread. He leaned in closer and kissed her, a long breath exhaling from his nose as he did.

Nic's hand rested on the back of Matt's neck for a brief moment and then Emma watched it trace down over his back, kneading the base of Matt's spine. As she watched, Nic's hand moved lower and disappeared behind Matt. As it did so, Matt arched his back. Her neck ached from craning around Matt's shoulders and she let it come back down onto the bed to rest, restoring her view of Matt, hair wisping around his face. Emma sensed a sudden shift in Matt's composure and heard the sound of skin touching skin. She seemed to be balancing finely on a line that was a division between pleasure and pain; the throb of his cock communicating the former while his scrunched-up nose indicated something of the latter.

While Nic's hand was at work, Matt's muscles slackened against Emma and he seemed to go fluid on her. A tiny, winnowy cry escaped him and she felt the heat of his breath on her neck. The whimper grew to a long and satisfied moan, coming from the base of his throat. His cock, hard and hot, now rested itself directly on the fold of skin where her labia met. Matt raised his body, the air cold on Emma's own as he did, and she felt the tip of his cock aim itself at her centre.

Matt kissed her all about her face, biting at her nose, running his tongue along her cheek. His eyes were now lightly closed, and he talked to her in a quiet voice. His cock pressed a fraction forward, barely parting her, but it was tangible nonetheless. Emma reached down and held him, trailing his phallus over her labia and blending their fluids together. She wanted him to enter her, but sensed that this was not the right moment, although she was sure that he would, soon. Emma was content to use his member to tickle and cajole herself, to ready her pussy for him.

Nic Lawson's face was rapt with concentration and his arm was moving more forcefully. Matt was the crossover point, the thing they were sharing in common. She did not feel particularly connected to Nic and she was sure he did not to her. Through Matt, however, they were part of the same process and would, for a short time and in a strange way, be joined. This was the second time she had been involved with Nic, she thought, without actually *feeling* involved with him. Perhaps she would never experience him first-hand. As she was thinking this, Nic Lawson stopped and stood up, looking down at her and Matt, the same hunger on his face, stronger even. He looked at Emma and spoke in a certain and confident tone, not ordering but more asking.

'Stand on the floor, there, facing the end of the bed,' Nic motioned, 'and bend to touch your toes.'

Her back stretched as she leaned forward and grasped her ankles, the elasticity of her body assuming the position easily. Her buttocks were taut across her, her pussy pressing through her legs. For all the space of the bed which dominated the whole room, he wanted her to stand in the small area by its side. Hands roamed over behind as she clutched her ankles and enjoyed the sudden rush of blood towards her head. A tongue flicked at her sensitive areas, leaping from place to place. A finger traced her spine, making her conscious of the small bumps of bone nestling just below the surface of her skin, the narrowness of her waist spreading out to her ribs and up to her shoulders. Her short hair hung as free as it could.

'Stand behind her, Matt,' she heard Nic say, and

then she felt familiar hands on the sides of her behind.

As Matt entered her, she felt Nic's hand holding and guiding his cock into her. She opened her eyes and saw Matt's feet, near to her own. Emma spluttered a breath as he continued to enter her and she raised herself up away from her ankles, to rest a hand on the end of the bed. With a final careful push, Matt was inside her. He held her by the hips.

'Oh my,' Nic was saying again and again. 'Oh my.'

There were a few moments of silence and then Matt gave a sharp groan, his grip on her hips tightening. His body was pushing against Emma's, driving her forward. Nic was moaning and talking to himself, Matt sighing as his cock pulsed and jumped inside her. Matt's body bumped against hers and rubbed his cock inside of her, a hot friction between them. From him, there emanated what sounded like a long and unbroken sob as the force of Nic's body pushed his own into Emma. A method developed between them and soon Matt was thrusting himself in and out of her.

The head of Matt's cock was wide and substantial as it opened her pussy from the rear and soon Emma had joined Matt in his low howl of pleasure, the pair of them singing in dazed unison. She knew her orgasm would not hide from her. There would be no need to look for it, to coax it delicately from herself. Rather, she was holding herself back, trying to keep it to herself for a while longer, enjoying the feel of Matt inside her and of the desperate sounds he made, his cock throbbing forcefully. Her clitoris did not need her and she left it to its own devices, willing to let it lead her where it wanted. Matt's hands still steadied themselves on her hips, while her own hands gripped the bed, bearing the brunt of all the downward force. It gave Matt's shafting a greater weight and she felt it each time he sank into her, the power behind the lunge.

In the midst of his drone, Matt hissed and then gave

176

a short high-pitched noise that sounded as though it came from his nose. He held her and swore, Emma feeling his cock pumping his come along the shaft. As it did and he shouted, so too did Nic Lawson, giving loud encouragement to him. Soon both of them were roaring and Matt's body twisted and convulsed behind her, his cock barely managing to stay in her.

And then she lost the noise.

Emma's orgasm had the effect of deafening her. Down in her pussy she was aware of Matt and the warm pulses of his lust, but even that faded as all that was important, once again, was herself. In a movement that belied Matt's into her, Emma tensed and untensed in turns as the orgasm that she had tried to contain was now free and out of her power. Her arms sagged and she fell slowly and carefully forwards onto the bed, Matt embedded in her and following her, smothering her into the mattress. Despite the discomfort it obviously gave him, he continued to move himself in her, giving momentum to the orgasm. She buried her face into the silk and seethed against it, rubbing her cheek on its coolness while the elation made her as light as silk itself.

Later, when Nic had discreetly left the room, in the middle of the vast bed, Emma and Matt huddled together as though they were on a tiny single, sleeping.

Chapter Seventeen

FOR OVER TEN minutes, Emma and Matt had been driving into what seemed like a wilderness. Having just left Interstate 93 in New Hampshire, they were heading towards Matt's parents' honeymoon hideaway in the White Mountains. They had flown into Manchester airport in the south of the state, near the border with Massachusetts, picking up a rental car. A top of the range Lexus, it carried them along the highway with the precision and certainty of an ocean liner, the engine silent and the ride hovercraft-smooth. Matt had been giving an intermittent commentary about Bretton Woods, Old Men of the Mountain, Flumes and Ski Museums, showing all the enthusiastic knowledge of someone who had known the place as a child and now surveyed it as an adult.

When she had worked on Wall Street, Emma spent one Fall in Vermont, watching the leaves wane gracefully through gold and ever deepening reds and browns, the landscape different every day, as though red snow had fallen in the night. Harvard, of course, had been suburban leafiness par excellence and she had hardly noticed it by the end of her time. Compared to the concrete forest of Los Angeles, where they had been not so long ago, there was something discernibly more relaxed about the East Coast of the States. New York and Boston, the cities she knew best, were little different from the freneticism of any major city, but once she escaped that and headed into the New England countryside, the contrast screamed out.

'We're nearly there,' Matt said.

The last of the sun lingered behind a mountain and the shadow of dusk was gradually casting itself across them. Matt slowed the car as they approached a mailbox and then turned into a driveway that Emma would never have noticed.

'Well, what do you think?' he asked as they approached the house. 'You'll just see it before we lose the light.'

It looked like a small ski lodge or a chalet in a winter Olympic village. Just to look at the wooden construction and its arrangement of windows suggested skiing, the outdoors and a bracing chill wind.

'It's enchanting,' she said to him as they stood next to the car. 'And so secluded.'

'Everything out here is. But it's handy for the skiing on Cannon Mountain and they make snow early for it from Echo Lake. I'll show you all of that tomorrow. It's a shame we're on such a flying visit.'

Emma nodded in agreement. Three days did seem short. 'I have to get back to Lomax, Matt. I don't want Catherine to think I've lost interest.'

'I know. Let me rush you round on a quick tour, then we can get settled.'

It could almost have been a small hotel. The front hall was like a reception and there was a large dining room with a kitchen adjoined to it by swing doors with porthole windows. A larger room had a dance floor and there was a smaller den with a big television, a sofa that looked comfortably lived in and lots of throw blankets. The elegant wide staircase led up to a landing and long corridor that had three bedrooms leading off each side, all with their own bathrooms. One of the bedrooms had models and cars in it, the bedroom of a young boy. Emma did not ask, but she could tell by Matt's face that it was the room he used. They both jumped and then laughed when a tiny frog hopped along the upstairs passage, obviously perturbed by their presence. Emma felt she could comfortably slip into the place and let it cosset her.

'The gardens are great. I'll show you them tomorrow.'

'Why is it so warm in here?' she asked.

'There's a local man who looks after a few of the places. I called ahead and he came and opened up. This is a fraction earlier in the year than normal for us to be here. Which bedroom do you want to use?'

'They're all lovely. Why don't you choose? I'd hate to pick one with a terrible negative childhood association,' she said to him, rubbing the sleeve of his jacket.

'There are no bad memories of this place for me.'

'Have you brought girlfriends here before?' she asked.

He thought for a moment. 'Do you know, I don't think I have. You should be honoured.'

'Does that mean I'm your girlfriend?' she asked him playfully.

Matt gave a bashful look. 'I'll get the bags.'

Not much more than an hour later, they were sitting in the den drinking coffee they had brewed with beans retrieved from a huge walk-in freezer. There were enough containers in the freezer to combine with the various tins so that they would be able to concoct a makeshift dinner later on. They sat next to each other on the sofa, the sound on the television low.

'Do your folks ever rent this place out?' Emma asked.

'They let friends stay here, but they've never

charged anyone that I know of. We'd spend a month or two here some years. Often, my father would go back to England and I'd stay here with my mum.'

He took another mouthful of the hot coffee and swallowed thoughtfully. Despite the varied and plentiful sex of the last few days, she still hungered for him. She reached and tousled his hair, unable to keep her hands off him.

'I think they'll retire here,' Matt continued, unflustered by the attention. 'They might buy a small hotel or use this as one. I could see them doing that. A few years ago, I thought they were going to. They even spoke to Lomax about selling off our house in London.'

'Really?'

'Nothing came of it. It's a shame. I think they didn't want to do it while I was at university. If they had, I might have come out here to do postgraduate work.'

'My MBA is from Harvard,' she told him casually.

'You have an MBA?' he asked.

'Didn't I tell you?'

'I suppose you would have, really. What's your degree in?' he asked.

'Economics.'

'You're something, you know that?' he said, looking at her.

'Why?' she asked.

'You just are.'

Matt picked up the remote and found a rerun of *I Love Lucy* which, to their dismay, they had both seen.

'I must have seen this every time I've been here,' Matt said. 'It's always on somewhere in the world at some time.'

'How old were you when you first came here?'

'Nine. It was so exciting. The room upstairs with the aeroplanes and stuff is mine. I keep it that way still. Is that weird?'

'I don't think so,' she said, setting her cup down and moving closer to him.

'It's just so great when it snows and you're in the warm inside, building a fire and sitting round it. When you're nine years old, that doesn't seem as trite,' he said.

'Well,' Emma said, sidling up to him and biting at his earlobe. 'What shall we do now?'

'The hot tub and sauna have been on for a while. We could adjourn there,' he suggested.

'I didn't know there was a hot tub,' she said.

'You say that as though fond memories are harboured.'

She smiled at him. 'I'll put on some more coffee for the tub. Then you can show me this sauna.'

The dining room had large double doors that opened into the gardens, which were a cavern of darkness. Only the courtyard could be seen, with the help of the glowing yellow garden lights mounted on the trellis fence that ran along one side of the hot tub. A large square of some ten feet, the tub was lit from below and emitted light refracted by the water. The tub bubbled and hissed like a geyser, vapour rising into the chill air. The sauna was a log cabin that had a shower in the entrance and then a second door leading into the sauna.

'I used to pretend this was an airlock when I was a kid,' Matt said. 'Like going into the secret sauna from the outside world.'

Casually, they undressed and showered, getting close to each other under the warm spray of the water jet.

The heat of the sauna wafted up and hit Emma in the face as she walked in. She sat on one of the slatted benches, the wood hot on her rear. Naked, Matt followed her in and closed the door, sitting next to her. Still wet from the shower, the water on their bodies became hot and then pure and clean sweat began to glisten on their skin. Emma was getting used to seeing Matt sweaty, but that was normally after sex. She used her hands on his body, sitting her self sideways on the bench to allow herself better access to him. Her hands slipped easily about him and his skin was hot to the touch and taut to the feel. Almost the colour of sand, it was a single, unblemished sheath and she brushed her cheek against the outline of his chest, his nipple prominent. She kissed it and rolled her tongue about it.

It was too hot to make love in the sauna. They both knew that, but did not want to leave it, preferring to let the temperature in the small room and the heat between them build. Matt's hair was wet and clung to his head and the sides of his face. Emma smoothed it back and ran her hands over his shoulders, kissing him as she did. Between his open legs, his balls dangled weightily on the wooden slats, his cock elongated by the intense heat and the simmering lust. Emma picked up his balls in her hand, suspending them away from his body and feeling their shape as she closed her hand on them and gave a squeeze. Matt looked at her as he did, his cock growing erect.

Emma sat back and let him touch her, not wanting to arouse him too fully in the extreme heat of the sauna. As always, he was gentle on her, using his long fingers and strong hands to explore and arouse her. It was when she found him at his most masculine, as he held himself in check and concentrated on her, focusing on certain areas and making her sigh or sometimes gasp, preparing her. Emma generated heat of her own, unconnected to that given off by the sauna. Her body boiled as he manipulated her, his hands touching her breasts, kneading them, wandering over her stomach and toying with her labia. Here, he merely traced his fingers over the top, making motions with them which he might have echoed inside her. But he did not enter her with his fingers, continuing to bait her with them, the threat and the promise of what would follow.

Matt stood and held his hands out to her. She gripped them and he pulled her to her feet. They embraced each other, clinging on and feeling the fevered hotness that had been so slowly building out of their mutual caresses. He gripped her behind and ran his hand down the join of her buttocks, caressing the underside of her pussy. They broke away from each other and she led Matt out of the sauna and under the shower again, letting the cool water dampen the passionate fire, leaving embers of longing burning in her and ready to flare again.

Sitting neck-high in the hot and soothing water of the tub, Emma watched Matt as he brought coffee and wine on a tray. There were loungers by the tub and several small side tables. Matt set the tray down, removed the small towel that covered his midriff and carefully stepped into the pool. She scrutinised him as his body disappeared into the water, the outline of it exciting below the surface, distorted and sexual in a way that made her feel voyeuristic. She could see the strong legs, the cock floating away from his body, his stomach and his chest. Soon, he too was neck-high in the water and he approached her.

'It's cold out there,' he said, shivering theatrically.

Dipping his head under the water, he resurfaced and slicked his hair back like a mane.

'Hello,' she said to him as he moved to stand up facing her, the water lapping at their chins.

They kissed. Around them, the night was like a heavy blanket. Stars sparkled in the clear sky and their breath was visible in front of them, carried off by the rising vapour of the pool. Matt used his thumbs on her pelvis, massaging the skin around the bones of her hips. In the hotness of the water, Emma's pussy was aroused, alive to sensation like the rest of her body but yearning so much more to be touched and teased. Matt picked her up and she folded her legs around his waist, leaning back against the poolside. His cock brushed her pussy and the skin between it and her rear. Her breasts were squashed up against him as he continued to kiss her, their mouths making noises in the night as he did. Under his shoulder-blades, the muscles of his back rippled as he pulled her closer to him.

Matt's hand reached down and furrowed at her pubic hair, the water swishing around her. He stood upright and his collarbone appeared above the waterline, heavy droplets clinging to him like rainfall. Cautiously he side-stepped to the ladder at the deepest end of the small pool. The metal handrails came up into a large arc out of the tub and onto the side, similar to a conventional swimming pool. As he backed her towards the steps, Emma put an arm around each rail and set her rear against one of the steps, releasing her legs from around Matt's waist. When she was certain of her arm hold, she let her legs hang and her rear slip off the step. She hung off the ladder, supported only by her arms and Matt quickly approached her and continued to touch at her.

When he finally touched it, her clitoris seemed to jump from the sensation. He firmly worked at it, determinedly massaging and pressing at it with his fingers. The muscles in Emma's arms were deliciously strained as she hung on to the handrails, wanting to come as she flailed about in the tub. She spoke words of encouragement to Matt, telling him harder and then telling him faster. With his other hand he reached around her side and used two fingers to open the cheeks of her behind and expose her anus to the water. It puckered and quivered, the hot water feeling inexplicably cool around the orifice. Several times he opened and closed her rear in this fashion, each time stretching her a fraction wider.

Turning all of his attention back to her pussy, he jogged her clitoris furiously with his fingers, his shoulder moving about on the surface of the water, his arm a watery blur beneath and his fingers invisible to her but so prominent in her feelings. Her arms ached and she pulled herself tighter, her legs agonisingly close to the bottom of the pool. The steps pushed into her shoudler, her back, her behind and her legs as she clung on and felt her orgasm tremor within. She sighed and flicked her legs about, just enough to encourage the release. The tension in her arms became a tension all through her and the effort required to keep a hold became less important than the hold she tried to keep over herself as waves spread from her pussy and echoed throughout her.

Showing no mercy, Matt was relentless, playing her body at a steady pace. No concession was shown by him to the painful ardour that gripped her and held her tighter than she could hold herself. His fingers coaxed her and then they refused her, pulling back before pressing on again. Emma held on to a scream and pulled herself tightly back against the wall, sweat running down her face and dispersing into the water.

Finally, her muscles gave way and she hung from the wall by virtue only of the position of her arms, not from any effort she could make. She was beyond effort as her body heaved and jerked, her orgasm ravaging her pussy which throbbed in the surrounding water. The muscles of her back and her arms were useless to her, all her energy concentrated into a single point, flowing out of her as easily as water. The thrashing of her body sent waves into the water, tangible representations of the feelings that flowed over her. Emma held on for several more seconds, the orgasm flushing through her, her pussy quavering.

The waves in the water and in her body dissipated. Her strength returned and she pulled herself, found a step with the back of her foot and gratefully rested her weight on it.

'I've a good mind to do the same to you,' she said to him, referring to the handrails.

'You'd have to tie me to them.'

'That could be arranged,' she said.

They were silent for a moment. The only sound was the pump, whirring away and recycling the water. Matt poured some wine into two small heavy tumblers. They sat on one of the ledges at the side of the shallow part of the tub, still fully covered by water. They drank. It was Chianti and the taste of it was warming.

'Thanks for bringing me here,' Emma said as she looked at Matt.

'Look at that sky,' he said, his voice clear in the night air.

Emma looked up, her body still loose from her orgasm. The wine had flowed into her quickly, warming and relaxing her in the water. Emma gazed into the vastness above, feeling big and small at the same time. Matt took the tumbler from her hand and placed it on the tray. As she stared up at the heavens, he moved near to her and then hugged her. She turned her attention to him, almost surprised by the gesture, the way he had intimated himself into her space. As she looked at him, she saw the passion in his eyes and the set of his jaw, the way he nuzzled at her. At that moment, she wanted only to make him come, to force him to shoot forth in long, painful seconds of pleasure.

Standing, the air cold on her back, Emma arranged Matt on the ledge so he was close to the edge of it, his legs outstretched in front of him. She knelt, the water covering her again. Through the water, she moved her hand and found his erect member. As she squeezed

187

the shaft, firm in her grasp, he closed his eyes and the lids wrinkled as he pushed them tighter together. Loosening her fingers, she let his shaft move freely in her grip and stroked up and down it, the sides lighting against her fingers as it moved freely around in the space she had permitted it. His balls which in the sauna earlier had fallen so freely were now more tightly drawn to his groin. Emma pulled at them and freed them up, compressing them in her hand.

Through the lens of the water, his pubic hair looked like a neat triangle and his cock a large protrusion from it. Emma eased his foreskin back over the glans. Placing her thumb over the eye on the tip, she felt, even in the heat of the tub water, a heavier and stickier fluid. She gathered what she could on the thumb and pressed her index finger over it to save it. When she pulled her hand up, some of it remained between her fingers, a glistening string as she parted her fingers a fraction and licked the gap in between them. Matt had opened his eyes and was watching her. She savoured the fluid, pressing it to the roof of her mouth with her tongue.

Back under the water, she placed her hand on him, fingers on the underside of his shaft just below the glans and her thumb on top, near the ridge of his phallus. She used his foreskin, pulling it over the head and then back again, her fingers tight on him, maximising the sensation she gave to the tip of his cock. He was rigid in her clasp and she knew he was not far from releasing himself. Emma pushed his cock at a downwards angle, feeling it strain as she did. She continued her motions, back and forth over the head of his cock, a fast pace and a solid grip on him. She was going to ask him if it was how he liked it, but Matt was fidgeting about and shivering, an orgasm ready to burst forth.

Emma watched him with fascination as he started to

come. It built slowly and only small clues were there. His posture changed imperceptibly, his legs sagging wider and his hips pressed forward more. His shoulders fell lightly backwards and his neck loosened. It was as though he were sagging away only to be tugged up from his groin, the only part of him seeming to have direction at that moment. She looked hard into his face, watching the features stiffen and the expectation cover him. It was almost a look of panic, of going over the edge and not being able to control it. Then his cock pulsated, a faint tremor, not the forceful spasm that would send his come along the shaft and out of the tip. Rather, it was an indication that he was readying himself.

The body which had sagged now stood rigidly to attention, as though on parade. Emma could sense he was seconds from ejaculating. She looked at him and then down at the water, her hand moving on him in the depths. When he ejaculated, she thought, it would be lost in the enormous pool of water, his semen floating and diluted in it. Emma took a deep breath and disappeared under the water.

Opening her mouth and quickly putting his cock into it, Emma closed herself on him and forced the water from her mouth using only a minimum of air. She held her remaining breath tightly and ruthlessly worked his phallus on the inside of her mouth, no pretence of teasing or coaxing. In the watery silence, he let his come go into her mouth. Emma kept her mouth closed and felt the hot jets on the roof of her mouth. She kept herself on him, letting him release all he had into her. As soon as the force had gone from his spurts, Emma stood upright and shook her hair, swallowing his come in a single greedy gulp, relishing the chance to take him in this way.

For half an hour or more, they held each other in silence, the water lapping around them and purifying them. Emma clung to Matt and he kissed the nape of her neck and whispered in her ear. She ran her hands over his face, feeling his features, certain she would recognise them even if blindfolded. He nipped at her fingers when she put them to his mouth. As each moment passed, Emma felt herself more and more familiar with him, this boy she had never seen until a few weeks earlier. She had left her old life behind but she had never expected the prospect of a new and more exciting one to reveal itself so suddenly.

They both jumped, rudely stirred from their reverie by an unexpected noise. Their concerned faces turned to laughter when they saw the source of the noise. Making another scratchy sound with its throat, a frog, identical to the one they had seen upstairs, hopped away from the side of the pool.

Chapter Eighteen

EMMA HAULED HER luggage through the door and dropped it heavily in the hall, going to the alarm box and tapping in the code to stop it. She had left the tranquillity of Franconia behind her and brought back some warm memories of Matt. Her time with him in Los Angeles had been hot and the few days in New England had cooled them down, in an increasing intimacy fostered by the isolation of their environment. They had spent the time talking, making love, cooking and watching television. It had been that simple and that relaxing. He was a good travelling companion and she was growing accustomed to seeing him first thing in the morning, listening to the sound of his breathing as he slept or turning and speaking to him, knowing she would find him there seated on her right.

In their long talks, far into the dense New England night and even into the dawn on one occasion, they had skirted only one subject. What would happen next. Emma was ready to tell Catherine that she was prepared to become a sleeping partner in the Lomax Property Agency. But that was all she would ever be, a sleeping partner. Her few weeks at Lomax had been enjoyable, but it was not where her future lay. When she had left Roger Metz, head of M&A, standing on the tarmac of the Morse Callahan heliport, her future had been Lomax. A very short future, but one that was tangible. Emma knew at the time that beyond the property agency, there would come a point when the future opened up again. What she had not expected, in such a short space of time, was the possibility of someone else in that future. Yet, she and Matt had not discussed it, letting their pasts be the subject of discussion and their enjoyment of the present an excuse to make endless love. No mention of the future.

On the plane back to England, it had been there, in the gaps in their conversations, even in the gaps between the words of their sentences. It was pervading all the things they did.

At that moment, Matt was behind her and he closed the door, picking up two envelopes from the floor, one large and one small.

'Letters for you,' he said.

She was not expecting mail. No one knew she was living in the flat apart from Tom and Neil and Catherine. She took the envelopes and played the usual guessing game with the postmarks. One, from North London, was the information from Tom, the credit and background checks he had offered to run on Lomax and its staff. It was heavy. The other did not even need the postmark. It was from Lomax, she saw – the heavyweight envelope and the standard Lomax typeface.

'You have a phone message too,' Matt said from over her shoulder.

Emma turned up the volume and replayed it.

'Hi Emma, it's Tom. Just to let you know the information you wanted is in the post to you. You should have it by the time you get back. Call me.'

She went to the living-room and sat on the sofa, pulling open the large envelope. A whole sheaf of computer printouts tumbled eagerly into her lap. There was a cover note from Tom. In his unmistakable handwriting, so neat she could hear him saying it, he explained the way he had conducted the searches, the level of detail he had gone into and the accuracy of the data. Shrewdly, he had not signed the note with his own name, simply putting at the bottom, 'To my loving mother from your devoted son.' She grinned. The note also said that he had looked at the data himself and made a few dispassionate comments that might be helpful to her.

All the sheets for each individual were stapled into a separate bunch. Emma glanced at them, amazed and then shocked at the level of detail that was available if a person knew how to access it. She had not pressed Tom on his methods of gathering the information, but she knew herself that there were specialist companies which would seek out such information, not revealing how they did, of course. It was a whole trail of ignorance, no one wishing to know how the other link in the chain came across the information. Emma was tempted to ask Tom to run one on herself.

Emma was tired, needed to rest, and would have to go over the data in fine detail later. Still, she was curious enough to look at what Tom had written on the front of each of the collections of paper. On Malcolm's, it noted a large loan to build an extension to his house. Very homely, Emma thought. Sonia Morgan had spent over five thousand pounds on one holiday. That was rather indulgent for the cautious Sonia, Emma thought, but supposed she was allowed a little fun. Ed's finances looked like a mess. Overdrafts, loans and credit cards stretched him beyond any sensible limit. Dominic Lester and Nicola Morris were unexciting. Emma smiled at the amount of money Jane Bennett spent on store cards. It didn't show. Ian Cameron, on a cursory glance, was the diligent and careful saver.

The information on Lomax was more scanty. The agency was not a living and breathing person and did not, as such, do things. All she had for Lomax were bank statements going back three years. It was hard to put any real meaning into a collection of credits and debits in a column. Besides, she was too tired to make any sense of it.

Emma stopped.

She re-read the throwaway line Tom had written on Tony Wilson.

'Divorce seems to have done this one some good.'

Rifling through the sheets on Tony Wilson, she saw that joint bank accounts had become accounts in his name only. The house had been sold, proceeds divided. Tony's profit from the sale had been invested in a long-term savings account. On a form he had filled out applying for a connection to a mobile phone network, he listed himself as a tenant living in rented accommodation in Whitton. Tracking back over his bank statements, Emma could see no outgoings that looked like rent. Very few standing orders at all but a lot of cash withdrawals. To the back of the information, Tom had appended a summary check on Tony's ex-wife. Emma was at least relieved to find that she was alive, recalling Ed's drunkenly bragging about his theory that Tony had murdered her. Why would Tony Wilson want to pretend he was still married if he was not, she asked herself? Was he embarrassed about it? He had the kind of shy demeanour that might make him keep it to himself. But, Emma thought not. There had to be more to it. On Wall Street, a maxim of Emma's had been that it all comes down to money or fucking. If you can link the two, even better. Emma realised she was not the only person at the Lomax Property Agency who was not what she seemed.

Matt came into the room and sat on an armchair. Emma stared at him. He looked tired and inviting.

'What was in your letters?' he asked her nosily.

She remembered the other letter, the one from Lomax, and opened it.

On a folded sheet of headed paper was a short two-line message in a swirling script font. Not the standard typeface Lomax used in all its correspondence. Even before she read what it said, the shape of the letters on the page were familiar. She tried to recall when she had seen them. It would come to her. The note read:

> *I know who you are (Morse Callahan)*
> *and what you are doing here.*
> *Are you going to tell everyone or shall I?*

It was unsigned.

She remembered where she had seen the typeface.

'Bastard,' said Emma.

'What?' asked Matt.

'Someone thinks they're on to me at Lomax,' she said.

'How do you know that?'

She showed him the note.

'What are you going to do?' he asked.

'Use it to my advantage. I'm not going to let him threaten me,' Emma said.

'How do you know it's a he?'

'I just do. Trust me.'

Another wave of tiredness hit her, soothed away by the vision of Matt sitting back in the armchair. He was a relief from Lomax, unconnected to it in any real way. His legs were sprawled open and revealing the blue material that had started to wear white on the crotch of his jeans. It was late as far as their body clocks were concerned and there was nothing she could or wanted to do about Lomax at that moment.

'Take me upstairs and do something dirty to me,' she said to him.

Ten minutes later, having wordlessly led her up to the bedroom and removed all of her and his clothing, Matt was standing behind her as she knelt on the end of the bed, knees wide and shoulders low, her bottom on display for him. The house had been chilly when they arrived and the heating was only just taking effect, the air still cool around her naked and tired body. Afternoon light leaked into the room from behind the drawn curtains and the room was still and quiet. Her muscles were stiff from long-haul travel and she was on the verge of sleep but not quite tired enough to drop into a slumber.

'How dirty?' Matt asked her, devilment in his voice.

'That's a good question,' she replied.

His hands pulled at her behind and she felt him kiss the cheeks. His hands were flat on each cheek, as though they had just landed after a spank, and his mouth was biting at the fleshy rounds, his tongue flicking at the skin. In all of his caresses and kisses, he remained on her rear, not venturing towards her pussy at any time. He was sending her a silent signal that it was not her pussy that interested him this time. His tongue flicked over the crevice of her behind, leaving moisture there, and she knew what he wanted to do to her.

'You'll need something to lubricate me with,' she said. 'Try the bathroom. And hurry.'

In a matter of moments, he was gone and then back again, a plastic bottle in his hand.

'Is this all right?' he asked her.

She turned and looked at the bottle. 'Yes.'

'Not the cream,' he said. 'I meant this.'

'If it's what you want to do to me,' she said to him coyly, as though a little afraid and unwilling.

Matt took the top off the bottle and she heard the gurgling sound as he applied some cream to his fingers. It was cold on her behind, the room no longer so cold by comparison. The first lot of cream he worked directly into her anus, not lingering to smooth any around her or to play with the skin around the opening. Instead, he inserted his lubricated finger directly into her behind. She relaxed herself and allowed him to probe, her anus unprepared for such a deep exploration so quickly. His finger darted in different directions, forcing into her and touching her deep inside, the fingertip coarse on the smooth skin. As he moved his finger, his hand made a liquid sound, slick and oiled as he massaged her. He slid his finger back and forth, using its full length on her rear end and the tiny opening, hidden between her buttocks, which he had found and was plundering with no mercy.

Emma kept her head and shoulders close to the bed and her backside high in the air, squirming away from him at one moment and then backing onto him in another. Without removing his finger or stopping his movements, he poured more cream on with his other hand. There was a lot of it and Emma felt it flow like cool lava over her buttocks and trickle through her legs onto the underside of her pussy. Using the extra lubrication and the increased pliability of her orifice, Matt introduced a second finger. It opened her doubly wide but the increase in the delicately aching expansion was multiplied many more times. It was as though he had opened her up for him to see and she felt that he was working away at the very depths of her, using his fingers to find places she had thought were hidden from anyone.

The intensity of it made her light-headed, Matt's fingers hard and relentless. Another flood of the cream and one of his fingers disappeared. The remaining one was soon joined by the finger of his other hand. Now, with one finger from each hand in her, he delved deeply into her behind. He inserted his fingers until they were up to the knuckle and then he stopped.

Emma let out a long gasp as he opened his fingers, stretching the muscles of her anus as he did. It was a slow and excruciating pleasure as he parted her, opening a small gap with his fingers as though creating a second tiny orifice between his digits. Emma felt the air, cool inside her as it rushed in. She cried out and tried desperately to relax herself, letting him open her wide and yet fill her with nothing. It was the delight of penetration without being penetrated at all. With his fingers, he was able to make her anal muscles mimic the movements they would make when he entered her, but with nothing tangible inside her. It was doubly cruel and much more exciting.

Matt allowed her to close as he withdrew his fingers. He put still more cream on her and into her, until she felt full of it, her behind a slick lubricated zone eager for his cock.

There was the sound of cream being applied yet again, but this time it was not to her. He was covering his cock with a veneer of white cream. Emma could not resist turning to look at his long member covered in the lotion. He was casual and confident in his movement on his cock, not manipulating himself or attempting to make it any harder.

'Put your knees together,' he said to her.

Emma did so and it was as though her anus had beat a retreat between the firm muscular globes of her rear, hiding from him. But there was no escaping it and the tip of his cock was hot in the crease of her buttocks where they joined to cover and protect her. He came to rest on the entrance, his tip leaning bluntly against her. As he positioned himself to get the best angle of penetration, he bent his legs to adjust his height. After a few moments of experimental movement in the cheeks of her behind, he was ready.

In her position, knees tightly together, Emma's

behind was stretched into a firm round shape, a tiny quivering weak spot at its centre. It was this spot that he focused on and then entered her through. With her head on the bed, her position made her feel completely self-contained and he completely alien to her. The first few inches of him could have been connected to anyone as it was the only part of his body connecting with her. Into the tiny ring of her anus he pushed his long and hard cock until he was in as far as he could go. When he was fully inside her, his legs came to rest on the outsides of hers, his inner thighs strong against her hips.

They were both tired and horny as hell. His fingering had loosened her and aroused him sufficiently. This was not going to take long, she thought. Emma put her forehead onto the bed so from her bent position she could stare at her pussy. Using her head and one hand as balance, she reached her right hand down and found her engorged clitoris. With all his concentration on her rear, her pussy had become a wet but unnoticed place. She would work on that herself and leave him to deal with her behind, which he seemed more than capable of.

Matt's strokes into her were deep from the start, but they were also very fast, orgasmic almost. Perhaps she had underestimated the excitement he had obtained from using his hands on her the way he had. His cock was a hard intrusion into a sensitive region and she was filled with him in a dark and powerful way as he slid his cock along her back passage. The muscles of her anus had long since given up resistance to him and now relished his presence, enjoying the shift in focus to a new area in which they could both take pleasure. Matt's thrusts kept up their brisk pace, coming perhaps every half a second, barely time for her to adjust to the absence or the presence of him in her. The speed made her feelings a blur, rushing past too fast to feel, Emma no longer able to distinguish from the painful expansion of a thrust in or the exquisite relinquishment of her muscles as he pulled out of her. So close together, the movements became as one, serving a single purpose as the tingling and warm sensation gathered inside her.

Emma came, gasping as she did, massaging the bud of her clitoris and feeling it seem to explode with the force of the orgasm, the sensation enhanced by the feeling of having Matt buried in her behind and shafting her with his stiff cock. He was impervious to her orgasm, unwilling to let it send him over the edge and he continued to ride her as she came. She fluttered off with the orgasm like a piece of paper lifted by the wind, as light and as delicate as air itself. Now she wanted him to complete the feeling by letting himself go inside her.

He did not disappoint her.

It was an impressive and frightening orgasm. Wild shouts and harsh jabs were followed by mumbled, incomprehensible words and the jerking and twitching of him inside her. His inner thighs trembled and his hands, resting passively on her hips moments earlier, now clutched her frantically. Finally, the warm flow followed. He had brought it from deep within him and used her to force it through himself and out of him and he was now firing it into her as he jerked passionately and called her name. In that painful second, Emma realised that he was doing it as much for her as for himself.

The sleep that followed for Emma was full of dreams and half-thoughts. She jerked awake after an hour and nestled into Matt's sleeping body, holding one of his hands while he slept. For almost twenty minutes she simply looked at him, inches from his face.

Emma sat up in bed, releasing Matt's hand. She moved herself around so she was still looking at him.

Later she would go through the information Tom had sent. She would need to arrive at Lomax early the next morning to check what she wanted and then she would have an interesting little conversation with the author of her threatening note. Then she would talk to Catherine. These things were the future, she told herself unconvincingly. No, she said, aloud. They were tomorrow, she thought, but they were not the future.

What *was* the future?

She looked back at Matt.

Chapter Nineteen

AT A FEW minutes before eight o'clock on a Tuesday morning, Emma Fox slipped into the Lomax Property Agency. Like the first time she had seen it, late at night six months earlier with only Catherine Lomax for company, the feel of the place was the same. The empty and silent office was gloomy in the light of morning, the atmosphere quite fresh enough, the air-conditioning probably not due to start for another half an hour. She carefully re-locked the door, making it seem as though no one was there.

For a moment, she stood behind the reception desk and surveyed the scene. She was glad that her time at Lomax was almost over. There had been some high moments such as whipping Ed Shields into line, the bizarreness of Nic Lawson and the whole Los Angeles episode, the chance to help Catherine and, of course, there had been Matt. There still was Matt, in fact. Today, she had several things to accomplish before she was ready to be on her way. By the end of the week, she would be out of Lomax as surely as she had been out of Morse Callahan. Out of another game. It was not the time to get sentimental, she knew.

Making her way through the office she glanced at the desks, noticing that the tidy people, herself included, had fastidiously cleared theirs before leaving. Emma had done this a week ago, before Los Angeles. Ed's desk was a shambling wreck of paper, Dominic Lester's a clear expanse of walnut. With her briefcase in hand, she went past the coffee area, scrubbed and made antiseptic by the cleaners.

Only three personal computers in the office were of interest to her and they all had their own hard disk drives, unlike several of the other diskless nodes that hung off the network. Emma wondered if she would find anything of use as she went to each desk in turn and fired up the PCs. As she started the third, she returned to the first which had by then gone through its initialisation procedure. No one at Lomax was as computer literate as Emma. The network, Catherine told her, had been set up at great expense by an outside consultant who'd driven the biggest Mercedes in living memory. The files on all the personal drives had been organised in a shabby fashion. Were Emma to attempt a fraud, her office PC would be one of the last places on which she would store information, but stupider things had happened.

Her search revealed nothing.

Emma entered Catherine's office where she could be hidden from view. She adjusted the slats of the blinds covering the internal windows, enabling her to see through them. She sat at the PC and switched it on, waiting impatiently for it to run through its boot-up. Emma logged in under her own network name and password. From her very first day, she had been surprised and disappointed by the lack of security around the small network of personal computers used by Lomax. It was typical, she knew, of small companies. Using her own identification and password to access the system did not concern her. She was going to snoop around on the net and it did not worry her if anyone found out about it. She doubted anyone would check a system administrator audit file and, besides, in a few days, she would own almost half of the Lomax Property Agency and would do as she pleased.

No private data areas had been created on the network data disks, meaning that it was possible to set her directory to any other person in Lomax, effectively becoming them as far as the system was concerned. This was not quite what was meant by open systems, she thought, but then no one in Lomax should have anything to hide. Based on her close study of all the information Tom had supplied her, she knew exactly what she was looking for and in whose directories to look for it. Her confidence in achieving a positive outcome from this course of action was not strong. Again, it would have surprised her if anyone had been stupid enough to leave their tracks so visible.

Scanning through lots of word processing documents in the relevant directories for Lomax employees, there was nothing. She located the holiday and sick logs and found the data she needed from them. Emma switched to the spreadsheets and looked through these. Three of them were password-protected and had file names that signified nothing to Emma. There was no way to beat that level of encryption with her knowledge. The computer network had been a longer shot than the personal hard drives. Likewise, it revealed nothing to her.

The front door of Lomax opened. It was eight twenty-five. Emma had spoken to Catherine on the phone the night before, telling her she was going to snoop around the network and asking her to make a call for her. She wanted Catherine to arrange for someone to arrive early that morning. They had not disappointed her.

Getting up quietly, Emma observed him through the slats in the blind. He sat at his desk and switched on his computer. Emma waited until he was fully logged in, so his e-mail messages would be displayed. When he was, she returned to Catherine's desk and typed a message that would broadcast to his screen:

You might know who I am, but you don't know where I am. . .

Emma stood and went to the front of Catherine's desk, pressing the send key while leaning over it, ready to dart to the blind to see his reaction.

When the message flashed, the beep audible to Emma, he literally jumped an inch or two out of his seat. She smiled. He looked around, scared and confused. He stood up and was fidgeting uncomfortably, shuffling his feet and running his fingertips over the surface of his desk. Emma picked two pieces of paper from her file and went slowly out into the main office.

'Good morning,' she said, sarcastically.

'Hi,' he said, weakly.

Emma unfolded the anonymous note she had received on her return the day before and handed it to Ian Cameron.

'What's this?' Ian asked.

Emma did not even bother to answer, instead giving him an impatient stare.

As he looked at the swirling script of the note he had sent her, she handed him another note, the one he had left on her desk on her very first day at Lomax, the one informing her that her password had been set to *good morning*.

'I wouldn't advise a career in extortion,' she said. 'You may as well have signed it. No one else in Lomax uses this stupid typeface.'

This time, he did not answer.

'How did you find out?' she asked.

This time, he did.

'I saw a letter that you wrote to Catherine. I shouldn't

have seen it. I came across it in some papers she wanted copying,' Ian said. 'I started to read it and I got carried away.'

'What would make you want to go through Catherine's desk?' Emma asked, unimpressed.

He shook his head feebly and said, 'I just like to know what's going on, that's all.'

'And what did you think you'd gain by sending me this? We had this conversation on the night of my welcoming drinks, remember? After we had dinner and you made a bloody scene,' she snapped, her voice rising with anger.

He nodded. Ian was blushing and Emma did nothing with the tone of her voice or her body posture that would help him out. On the night of the agency drinks, after everyone had left, she had gone to dinner with Ian, knowing it was a bad idea and feeling she should not have, particularly in view of her burgeoning involvement with Matt. She had been right and most of the evening was spent fending off his clumsy but affable advances and ended up in an unfortunate and difficult scene with him at Sloane Square tube station. The next day at the agency, however, he had been fine. Emma had thought that would be the last of it.

'What are you going to do?' he asked her forlornly.

'What are *you* going to do?' she asked him emphatically. 'Or put it another way, what do you think I should do?'

'Are you really going to buy the agency? Do you have enough money?'

'Question one, not all of it, just a share. Question two, more than enough. I could ask Catherine to fire you,' she said.

'It was only a note. I don't care who you are or what you're going to do. I just wanted you to know that I knew. I might be able to help,' he said.

'I've already thought of that,' she replied.

'Can I? Help?'

Emma decided she had let him suffer enough; his face was too red for her liking. He was not involved, she knew that.

'How much do you know about Tony Wilson's wife?' she asked.

'As much as everyone else: nothing. No one ever sees her. Sonia's the only one who's talked to her. They're friends, I think,' said Ian.

'Do you have access to any of Sonia's files that you shouldn't?' Emma asked.

'No,' was his short reply.

'Ian,' she said in a disbelieving tone.

'She keeps some stuff locked away in that fire-proof file cabinet, the small one by the side of her desk.'

'Does she always keep it locked?' asked Emma.

'Always. There's another key, though. I found it along with a whole bunch of spares that were kept.'

'So you found a bunch of keys and systematically went and tried them all until you opened it?' Emma asked, incredulous.

Ian had a look of pride on his face.

'And Sonia, obviously, knows nothing about this?' she asked.

'Nothing,' he said.

'What was in there?'

'A bit of a disappointment. The personnel files, but I know what everyone earns because some months I process payroll. A lot of other papers, invoices, things like that. Nothing that made much sense.'

Not to him, thought Emma, but she needed to see in the cabinet and check for herself.

'I'd like the key,' she said.

He hesitated and she saw he was about to object.

'Ian, all I want to hear you say right now is, "Here's the key." Do you understand that?'

207

He nodded, swallowing tightly as he did.

'If you say a word, a single word, to anyone about this, you're out. That simple.'

'I won't. I told you, I just want to help.'

Emma looked at him, saw his enthusiasm, his willingness. Just what I need, she thought with a mental sigh – a loyal sidekick.

Just prior to nine o'clock, still in Catherine's office and now in possession of the key to Sonia's file cabinet, Emma called Tom.

'Hi, Tom, it's Emma,' she said.

'Hello, Mother,' he said.

'Can you check something else for me?' she asked.

'I might be able to. Tell me what it is.'

Catherine Lomax entered her office and smiled at Emma. She closed the door behind her and set her case down on the floor, seating herself in one of the guest chairs. Emma hoped Catherine would not take offence to find her at her desk, as though assuming charge through a coup.

'I need to know who owns a house that someone's renting and I need more detailed bank information for two people.'

'That shouldn't be a problem,' he said.

'And, can you search for any company directorships held by anyone here at Lomax?'

Catherine frowned at her.

'Who do you want the bank statements on?' Tom asked.

'Tony Wilson and Sonia Morgan,' Emma said. She read out the rented address listed for Tony Wilson in Whitton and asked Tom to find out who owned it. She also specified the level of bank detail she required. 'How soon can you get back to me?'

'You want this today, yes?'

'If possible,' she said.

'I'll call around lunchtime.'

Catherine was looking at her when she put the phone down.

'I have the creeping feeling I am missing something here,' Catherine said.

'We need to talk,' Emma said.

'Talk to me,' she replied.

'I'm waiting for information to confirm this, but I think there is a fraud going on here at Lomax,' Emma said.

Catherine seemed neither surprised nor angry. Emma waited for her to speak, but she did not.

'I don't think it's huge, but it's still a fraud, stealing from the agency,' Emma continued.

'Who?' Catherine asked.

'The only person at Lomax it could possibly be is Sonia. She's the only one close enough to the business. Sonia holds the records and the files for everything. No accountant, the company doesn't file public accounts because it's structured as a private partnership. That puzzled me, because when Victor was alive, the agency was a subsidiary of the Lomax Group. When things were sold off and the group dissolved, the agency went back to a private status. Of course, that means there's no way of getting information.'

'But I get the financial information from Sonia on a monthly basis. You've had access to everything I have,' Catherine said.

'The invoicing and billing, I haven't seen. That's all done by Sonia and so is the banking. She's in a prime position.'

'I can't believe it of Sonia. You have no proof?'

Catherine was asking the question in a way that held out hope that Emma was wrong. Emma knew that she was not.

'I need to get some more information. If you look at a company like Lomax, there's no cash turnover, so it's not as simple as taking cash. There needs to be a vehicle for this type of fraud. I suspect there's a company somewhere that belongs to Sonia and which bills the Lomax Property Agency on a consultative basis. This is an assumption, based on a close analysis of Lomax cashflow. A regular irregularity, you could say. Even the biggest and most complex scandals that hit Wall Street in the eighties rested on similarly tenuous threads. In the final analysis someone always has to be paid and there has to be a mechanism for doing that. Cash is not that mechanism any more. And all the other mechanisms leave a footprint.'

'That's a lot of opportunity for Sonia to do something like that. Anyone in her position has the potential to do that, I accept that. But why would Sonia do it?' asked Catherine.

'We used to have a saying at my old firm: it's all money and fucking. If you can link the two, even better. I think she's having an affair with Tony Wilson,' Emma finished.

Catherine laughed loudly. 'Not Sonia and definitely not Tony. He's such a family man.'

'His wife left him two years ago, Catherine. Tony doesn't even live at the house he tells you he does. He's living rent free at a house in Whitton. How could that be? How could Tony keep that a secret from Lomax? Only Sonia could help him do that,' Emma said.

'But Tony's still married. He talked to me about his wife a couple of days ago. Sonia spoke to her last week . . .'

Catherine's words trailed off.

'Did you know that Sonia had been to the Seychelles on holiday last year?' Emma asked.

'No,' Catherine said, now intrigued.

'She was there three weeks, last two of June and first week of July.'

'No, that was to visit her brother in New Zealand,' Catherine said.

'Tony Wilson was off sick the last week of June and the first week of July last year. I haven't checked, but I wouldn't be surprised if he was with her.'

'Wouldn't he have come back with a tan?' Catherine asked.

'Maybe he did,' Emma said.

'Are you going to be able to prove any of this?'

'There will be a paper trail. There has to be. It's a question of finding it. I think I know how, but I need your help.'

'What would you like me to do?'

'Call a staff meeting this morning at ten. It must be about time to announce there is to be a substantial investment in the agency. Let them know someone is interested but, obviously, don't let them know it's me just yet. We'll save that particular surprise. If you can keep them busy for forty minutes, that will be all the time I need. Leave Ian on the front desk to answer phones.'

'Fine,' Catherine said.

At ten o'clock, the whole agency was in the meeting room and Emma opened the file cabinet by the side of Sonia Morgan's desk. Ian had put up the closed sign on the door of the agency to prevent unwanted passing trade and the answering machine had been switched on to fend off calls. Emma flicked through the files, discarding those that dealt with personnel, the lease on the building and other agency details. She came to the information she suspected would be there and made photocopies of everything, replacing it in the same order and re-locking the cabinet. The whole process took less than twenty-five minutes and when the staff came out of Catherine's meeting, their faces alive with the news and slightly concerned at the prospect of outside involvement, it was as though nothing had happened. The open sign was back on the door, the answering machine off.

Emma spent the rest of the morning waiting for Tom to call back. At lunchtime, he did.

'I've got some interesting information for you, Mother.'

Chapter Twenty

THE LIFT CARRIED Emma swiftly to the top of the large building in Soho. Even though no contracts had been signed for the loft apartment, Emma had given Matt a key and kept one for herself. An afternoon spent on the phone and with Catherine had tired her out and she wanted to see Matt. Leaving the lift, she went to the door and opened it.

The room was in half darkness, lit only by the glare of London, but filled by music as surely and completely as it could have been by light. The music system was wired into the very foundations of the loft, speakers hidden everywhere. A syncopated bass drum thumped with a hefty insistence on the offbeat and over a syrupy blend of synthesis and voice, there was a higher-pitched bitter-sweet whistle with a melancholy tune.

The heels of her shoes clicked on the wooden floor as she approached the window out of which Matt was staring, his profile a silhouette with tinges of red and green from the lights outside. His nose and mouth were unmistakable, the jawline cutting sharply into the semi-dark. His fringe was tousled carelessly over his forehead and he ran a hand through it before resting back on the window-sill, leaning forward and

213

surveying the scene below, the action flickering on his face as though projected onto a movie screen.

Emma stood behind him and embraced him. His body was warm and firm and even though he did not move or speak, she could feel him responding to her touch. Emma pulled him tightly, his back pressing into her front, his behind into her groin. Matt turned his head to one side and kissed her. She rested her chin on his shoulder.

'How was today?' he asked her.

'Good. Did you get your stuff moved in?'

'No,' he said, cutting the volume of the speakers by half with a touch of the remote pad.

'Why not?' she asked him gently, nuzzling his shoulder and feeling the heat.

'How much longer will you need to be at the agency?'

'Not long. Why?' asked Emma.

'I thought we could go somewhere, you and me,' Matt replied.

Emma thought for a moment. She glanced around the shadowy loft and saw nothing that looked like Matt's. The place was as spartan as when they had first viewed it.

'You'll still need somewhere to live. When we get back from wherever we're going,' she said.

'Will I?' he asked, turning and sitting on the ledge.

Emma leaned against him, letting her head sag tiredly onto his shoulder.

'Where do you want to go?' she asked.

'Nic Lawson has a boat. A big one. It's in the Caymans at the moment. Nic's not using it and he said we could.'

'How long for?' she asked.

'Nic said it was free for almost four months. We could fly out, spend some time and work out what we want to do next or where we go next,' Matt said.

214

Emma knew that when he said *where* they went next, he was not referring to a place.

'Is it what you'd like to do?' she asked.

'Yes. How much longer will you be at the agency?'

'I could be out of there by the end of the week.'

Matt looked at her, his eyes shining through the dim light. He drew a breath in through his nose and then picked her hands up with his. He squeezed them and stroked his thumbs over the palms, looking down at them as he did. He looked back up at her and narrowed his mouth into a tiny smile.

'Can I say something to you?' he asked.

Emma knew what he was going to say.

'I know,' she said. 'Why don't you hold onto it and say it to me later on? Is that okay?'

'Of course it is,' he said. 'As long as you know, that's all. I don't even have to say it ever.'

Emma drew him close to her and unbuttoned his shirt, fiddling with the buttons. She took the shirt off him and stroked his flesh, the supple warmth encasing hard muscle. Emma unbuckled his belt and opened his trousers, running her fingers over the waistband of his underwear and the skin on his belly. As they kissed, Emma made trails along his back with the ends of her fingernails, feeling his body tense away from her at the sharpness of the touch, the breath of the kiss more laboured.

She removed his trousers and as he stood before her in only his underwear, she took a step back and looked at him. The loft was where it had started, where she had stood apart from him and thought about him. Where she had made the first step towards him, uncertain of what lay ahead. That was *when* it had begun and this was *where* it had begun, she thought. It was ending here too, in some other way. Not where she and Matt would end, but rather where this short phase of her life would come to a close. With all of it behind her, free of the tissue that surrounded her life, she would be left simply with Matt.

With the same excitement as the first time plus the certain knowledge of what would lie beyond, Emma took a step towards Matt.

She kept him in his underwear for a while longer, not needing to rush and enjoying the expectation of his naked body, ready for her. His undressing of her was sped along by the youthful fervour of his years and she was soon naked, the wood floor warming quickly under her bare feet. When she removed his boxer shorts, working them slowly over his behind and down his legs, his cock hung but was starting to point away from him, the force of his desire raising him. Emma held it and fondled it, the skin soft and flexible in her fingers. Through this, she felt the core of his cock harden as it filled, desire pumping through him. She lifted his balls, the hairs on his sac tickling her fingers. Emma wanted to possess his cock, to coax and manipulate it, to smother it and make it her own. As it hardened in her grasp, she recalled the pleasure it had given her, how she had held it in her mouth, her behind and her pussy. She remembered all of these times and most of all she remembered Matt, the sensitive and shy way that he made love to her, the fire she had been able to coax from him and the yearnings she had unlocked in him.

Matt rested back on the window-sill as Emma dropped to her knees, wanting to taste him and to make him as hard as she could before she let him inside her. She worked his foreskin back and licked the head of his cock, wanting to stimulate him immediately and choosing not to tease him. She closed her mouth over the head and felt its shape, the underside rubbing against her tongue and the ridge over the top of his phallus resting in the roof of her mouth. She slithered her tongue over him, wetting the head and

216

licking the underside. She gripped the base of his cock, holding it aloft, and rhythmically moved her mouth over him, noises escaping from him as she did.

The taste and the feel of him in her mouth made a hunger deep within her, and she could feel her labia damp and swollen, her clitoris as excited as Matt's cock. Soon she would touch herself down there or be touched by him, but she was content to let the feeling build inside her and to nurture it by feeding on him. In her mouth, his member strained and distended, unable to process all at once all the sensation she was giving him. She could tell he was helpless in her mouth, unable to control himself. Were she to continue for much longer, she knew he would willingly and gratefully relinquish himself to her.

Emma led him to a large rug and they sat on it. Matt's cock stuck up bone-like from his lap as they sat prayer-fashion on the soft threads. Emma reached over and kneaded the tip of his cock with eager fingers, the head wet from her mouth and from his own fluid. There were times when she had enjoyed bringing Matt to his orgasm by hand, watching the way he came and able to savour the sight of his powerful ejaculation. It excited her to do to him something she had imagined and fantasised about him doing to himself, with his own practised and familiar hand. The feel of him coming while he was inside her was a different and more complex pleasure, the mixture of their bodies and motion, the way they worked themselves to a climax, the closeness of Matt to her as he let himself go, willing to abandon himself so wantonly and in her full view. She liked it when he was on display to her, the way his features would dissolve and he would thrash almost in denial of the joy he was experiencing.

Kneeling up, with her knees apart, Emma offered her pussy to his touch. Matt needed no encouragement, words not required between them as he reached for her. She closed her eyes at the moment of contact, realising how wet she had become. It was a delicate blend of the familiar and the strange as he stroked her and explored her labia. When he touched her, it was as though the possibility of him entering her had only just suggested itself. Her desire for him filled every sense that she had, overpowering her, and it was only through his touch on her that she became focused on the idea of him penetrating her with himself. A doorway to her was opened by his tender caress.

Resting her hands on his shoulders for support, Emma allowed him to probe her, his fingers going gradually deeper, making a path for his cock. She shuffled her knees wider and in turn he put his fingers, two of them, inside her. His thumb tormented her clitoris, soothing and worsening the ache at the same time. Strain ebbed away from her and was replaced by the tightly coiled mechanism of passion. Matt's fingers, his very presence, replaced the one sensation with the other.

The groans she made filtered through the music in the darkened room. The rug was near enough to the window to light their bodies in a soft glow. Though too high to be seen by anyone, Emma wondered if there were not, through one of the city's many windows, eyes that watched the graceful movements of their naked shadows as their bodies prepared to couple. Were a passive observer able to see only the motion of their darkened forms against the grey background of the room, it would have been obvious from their movements what was about to happen and the depth and intensity of the act for the two figures involved. Emma wanted Matt inside her. She wanted his cock in her pussy, buried in as far as it would go. In the large and high-ceilinged room, she wanted to cry out louder than anything else in or around it, reaching the rafters as she came. With her mouth and with her hand, she had made Matt ready and he had done the same for her with his careful ministrations to her wet sex, his hands always careful and almost respectful of her. Now, she was ready for him.

Emma pushed Matt onto his back and leaned over him to kiss him. With no pillow supporting his head, he was spread out flat on the square of carpet, his neck stretching to reveal the Adam's apple. Under his collarbone, the muscles of his chest rose in gentle bumps that gave way to the stomach. Where his behind was on the floor, the sides of his buttocks were dented as the tops of his legs began. Emma rested a palm briefly in the cavity. His legs were long and at their end his feet lay on their sides, the skin on his insteps an accordion of soft crinkles.

Taking another look at his face, Emma kissed him one more time before turning with her back to him and squatting over his cock, still erect and tight against his stomach as though glued there. Emma pulled it upright as though it were a lever. It stood up straight in her hand, and she was conscious of the pressure required to keep it in that position. His foreskin had rolled forward a fraction as if trying to protect him, so Emma eased it gently back, watching from above. Then she was left just looking down on the large head, the view from above making the shaft invisible to her. There it was, just below her, so close to her pussy, Matt's swollen phallus ready to enter her as she squatted over it.

She moved herself forward to position him under her and she felt herself open almost indiscernibly, ready to accept him. Matt's hand joined hers on his cock and she left it to him, resting her fists on the floor and letting the tip of his cock tickle at the lips of her pussy. He was barely inside her, tantalising her labia. Emma lowered herself and allowed his cock to begin to enter her. As it pushed her open, she paused at the exact moment of his entry and held him tight inside her lips for several seconds, savouring the motion and letting him see himself partly inside her. His cock throbbed, starting from deep within him and ending up as a pulse that pushed against the muscles of her vagina.

Half of his cock was in her now. Emma was in no rush, wanting to appreciate the differing sensations, taking him into her gradually and letting herself become accustomed to his presence. Her breath escaped her as she continued to sink slowly onto Matt's shaft, feeling it touch every part of her, slick against the front of her vagina. She felt his fingers, where he was holding his cock steady, and sensed he was nearly inside her. Matt's fingers moved away and she knew that she had only an inch or two more of him to take. It was a satisfying feeling as she sat on the last of him, his hands holding her waist above the hips. Again, she waited, the same slow approach she had taken when introducing him into her. Now he was hers. She sat on him and moved her muscles around him, possessing him. Matt lay, still and silent, letting her do what she wished.

Emma used her fists and her feet as pivots on which to rock herself back and forth on him, as gentle as if she were rocking a baby. The squatting posture left her knees high and her face close to them. Her pussy merely moved his cock back and forth lightly, no pressure or friction to bring him to the boil. Emma imagined this sensation to be much more teasing, her pussy barely stimulating him, rocking over him with a cruel slowness. Her whole body only moved back and forth perhaps three or four inches, Matt's cock barely slipping from her as she did. She did this to him as though he were a bomb, volatile and about to explode.

Carefully, Emma put her legs out in front of her so

that rather than crouching over him, she was now sitting on him, using his groin as a seat. Her feet were on the floor and to the outside of his legs, either side of each shin. She steadied herself by gripping his legs above the knees. She was able to move herself backwards and forwards on him with ease, his cock rubbing at the front wall of her vagina, brushing at her sensitive spot.

Eyes now adjusted to the dark and ears used to the music, Emma felt a part of the room, a piece in the dark tableau, however transient. She became one with the dark in the room, slipping into it, finding her way between the beats of the music. She melded with Matt, amplifying each aspect of him in her consciousness until he became all present to her. Emma held him clenched within her and lost sense of time and place, wanting only that moment with him, to share the experience with him and to go on sharing it.

In contrast to the sensitive and tender passage she had made over him only moments earlier, she now rode him with violent lunges, the bulk of the force from the muscles in her stomach and back. She reached down and cupped his balls, making him groan and reminding herself that he was still there physically. She gripped his legs tightly and used her rear and his groin as the focal point from which to create the movements on his cock. Matt's hands rested unmoving on her behind. Apart from the noise he had made when Emma touched his balls, he had been silent throughout, content for her to set the pace and take him where she wanted.

Emma touched her clitoris, so susceptible in her current pose, ready to be fondled. She ran her hand in the opposing direction to her body, a sensuous friction brought on by her fingers rubbing the intimate folds of skin, Matt inside her the whole time. The movements gave rise to intense sensation between Emma's legs and in turn these physical sensations developed gradually into powerful mental images, switching her body on and awakening it to the possibility of all her faculties working in concert towards a single goal.

Matt gave a sigh of contentment and squeezed her bottom, his hands fitting around it and moving with her. Emma shook her head, freeing the short strands of hair from her face. As her head was stretched back, the neck and shoulder muscles elongating and then loosening, she gave a cry of her own, guttural and unexpected as though from somewhere deep within her, beyond her control. She ground herself on him, wanting him in her, needing him in order to find release for herself and desperate for him to release into her.

The music finished abruptly. They were left only with the noises they made. In the sudden silence, their cries were amplified beyond all expectation as though they had blared from nowhere. The room consumed them as the harmony of bodies was made audible by their eager shouts and howls. Where the music had soothed and held back, the soundtrack of their own voices pushed Emma further, nearing her to the edge. She was determined to make her orgasm as close to Matt's as she could.

She told him as she was about to come. He begged for her to hold on for a few moments longer. She changed the pattern of her fingers, delaying herself by seconds. Matt's body juddered beneath her and he tensed his behind, lifting it higher and Emma with it. She thought about his cock, inside her and in the early throes of an orgasm. Her eyes closed, she saw herself sitting on Matt, her back to him and upper body arched forward towards his feet, her hands gripping him and her whole body jockeying on him. Emma wanted to come as his cock exploded into her, thrashing back and forth on his member as it unloaded his hot young come into her pussy.

Matt gave a gasp that Emma knew meant only one thing. She rubbed hard at her clitoris, sensing her orgasm before she actually felt it. Matt's orgasm seemed to punish him and he begged for its forgiveness as it had its cruel way with him. Emma was partly responsible for it, she knew, and showed him little sympathy as she used his cock and the movements of her body to ensure her own climax.

Emma's movements became erratic and desperate, her cries so high pitched she could barely issue them. She came, feeling her pussy cling onto Matt, the pleasure of it beyond words or even sounds. Whether she continued to shout, she could not tell. The obliteration was total and she floated through it, an endless falling through a seemingly bottomless space. It seemed as though, halfway through the free fall, she met with him.

Their orgasms fused into one, a joint pleasure. Juices mingled as Emma came around his cock which slipped about inside her. She contracted and undulated whilst she felt his cock pulse and throb. Smelted together in the fire of lovemaking, their agile bodies were a single entity, joined at the physical and the emotional level. Having given so much to each other, they stayed together long after their orgasms had subsided, pulled tightly together on the rug, oblivious to all around them.

Emma turned to look at her young lover, spent and happy. She nuzzled up to him, rubbing his stomach and tickling the sticky mat of his pubic hair. She felt him, his warm and heavy fluid inside her and she quivered, kissing him on the shoulder. Their sex had made Emma forget all the past and future and in her climax had even wiped out her sense of the present. Now, as she lay with Matt, these things came back to her, but they were reordered and sensible. Things of the past she had done, things she needed to do right away and things they would do in the future. In some way, he was now a part of it, be it past, present or future. She was ready to give all of it to him and she knew he would do the same for her.

'Matt,' she said.

'Hmm?' he murmured, hugging her.

'I love you,' she said, the words reverberating into silence.

Chapter Twenty-One

TODAY WAS THE day. Emma entered the Lomax Agency on Friday morning at eight-forty. She had spent the previous day at home with Matt, keeping out of the agency's way and making several important phone calls. Tomorrow, she would be on a plane heading for the Caymans and to rendezvous with Nic Lawson's boat. But today, she thought, is the day. For the last time, she had crossed the threshold at Lomax as plain Emma Fox. To bridge the gap of the plain and the real, Emma had donned an appropriately business-like suit by Donna Karan, bought specially for this occasion, the jacket not unlike the one she had purchased for Neil. The effect was a devastating transformation and Matt had already taken her out of the suit once that morning. Emma felt blood in her veins, almost like old times. Almost like being back in the game.

A staff meeting had been scheduled by Catherine for ten-thirty with the promise of more information regarding the investment in Lomax. Appointments had been hastily cancelled and, according to Catherine, there had been much anxious whispering. The prospect of a takeover or buyout of part of the agency must, she thought, have sent a ripple of worry through

Sonia Morgan and Tony Wilson. Unless they believed they had covered their tracks effectively. The pattern of the morning's events would tell.

Using Catherine's office, she dialled Chris's number. A pang of guilt went through her as she knew she would have spent more time with Chris had she not met Matt. Still, Chris did look after various of her funds and the fact that they occasionally had sex had never clouded this. To the contrary, it had made her trust him more.

'Hello,' said Chris's familiar voice.

'Chris, it's Emma.'

'Hello. How you doing?'

'Fine. I'm about to send you a fax, so stand by the machine when we've finished,' she said.

'Sure. What's in it?' he asked.

'About the investment we discussed in the Lomax Property Agency – which of my accounts to make the transfer from and who to make it to. It's important not to make any transfers until I call you. We've got a few things to sort out here. I'm also sending a basic offer letter, so can you check over it and maybe get a lawyer to look at it?'

'Easy,' he said.

This was one of the things she liked about Chris. Nothing was difficult.

'I'm going away for a few months,' she said.

'Anyone nice?' he asked slyly.

'Yes, thank you,' she said, passing over the comment and getting back to the purpose. 'One other thing. The deposit account, the one that accrues the rent from my house in Islington?'

'Yes.'

'I want to close it down. There's almost nine thousand in there. Close it and process a cheque to Tom Brien, his details are on the third page of the fax.'

'What are you going to do with the house?' he asked.

'Give it to them.'

'Emma, charity? That's never been your style.'

'I know. Getting old, I guess.'

'It's a good job you got out when you did. You'd be easy prey,' Chris said.

'I'll call you Monday to give the go-ahead on the transfer. Thanks for all your help, Chris. You keep on making money for me, okay?'

'Not a problem. I'll go stand by the fax.'

Emma was pouring herself a coffee when Ed Shields sidled up to her.

'What do you think about all this?' he asked her.

'All what?' she said, innocently.

'Catherine bringing someone in. I don't suppose it worries you, being only temporary.'

Emma looked at him but did not speak. He took the silence as agreement.

'I'm surprised there's been no due dilligence,' Ed said.

'What's that?' Emma asked, trying to appear blank.

'When somebody buys a company, they want to look it over and make sure they're not getting a pup. Bit like a survey on a house. Normally, lawyers and accountants come in, talk to all the key players, look at the books, that sort of stuff. I'd tell them a thing or two.'

'You seem to know a lot about it,' Emma said, doing her best impression of being impressed.

'A bit,' he said, with the familiar swagger.

Malcolm joined them, getting a cup from the cupboard.

'What's news?' asked Malcolm.

'Ed's just been explaining to me how you buy companies,' Emma said.

Malcolm was unconcerned. 'I hear the Rayner boy is not going to take the loft in Soho. He called yesterday and said his plans had changed,' he remarked.

'I guess I lost that one,' Emma said.

The atmosphere in the agency was tense. Emma had been on innumerable due diligence teams, where she had been the enemy, the evil banker ready to asset strip an old family company, leaving mass unemployment in her wake. The smallest company she had ever been involved in at Morse Callahan had been twenty times the size of Lomax. However big or small, Emma had learned, the atmosphere was the same. Fear and uncertainty. In fact there were only two people who should have feared anything, and it was these two who were trying their hardest to act cheerfully. Sonia had beamed beatifically at her, commenting on her attire. Tony Wilson's façade was a wafer-thin veneer of calm barely concealing a powder keg of anxiety. He would weaken long before Sonia. But with the staff meeting only fifteen minutes away, neither of them had very long.

The phone on her desk rang.

'Emma Fox,' she said briskly.

'Emma, it's Nic Lawson,' his voice crackled.

'Hello,' she said, not wanting to use his name in the office.

'It's two in the morning here and I'm trashed. Anyway, Matty tells me you're definitely going to use the boat.'

'That's right. Thank you,' she said.

'No worries. About time somebody used it. The last two times I did, I was puking over the side most of the time. Hope you've got sea legs. Who's gonna find me a house in London now you're gone?'

'We'll put someone else on it,' she said.

'Bet they won't give your level of personal attention,' he laughed.

'Probably not,' she answered, thinking of Malcolm.

'When I get back, I'd like to talk to you about how you could help the agency out. Would that be okay?'

'No worries. Send me a postcard or drop a message in a bottle,' he said. 'My love to Matty.'

No one had any worries or problems, it seemed, on that Friday.

Five minutes before ten-thirty, the meeting room was full, the agency empty. Catherine's office door had been closed since she arrived that morning. Emma imagined she had been studying the information Emma had given her. She had wanted to let Catherine view it for herself, unimpeded by her presence. Emma went to her door, knocked softly and entered.

'Nearly time,' Emma said, closing the door behind her.

Catherine looked up and Emma was certain she saw a redness to her eyes, as though she had been crying. That was possible. Sonia Morgan had been with the agency a long time. It must have been a shock to Catherine.

'Are you okay?' Emma asked.

'I will be,' she said. 'I feel so angry. How could she? This goes all the way back, right to when Victor died. It was his death that gave her the chance. She used that time and my state as an opportunity to do this.'

'Have you decided what you want to do?' Emma asked.

Emma had told Catherine that it should be her call. Catherine should resolve the issue prior to her taking a stake in the agency. That was her only stipulation to Catherine that had resulted from the secret due diligence. Sonia and Tony should not be a part of the agency. Beyond that, it was up to Catherine.

'I just want her and him out. I don't even care about the money. I would have given it to her if she'd asked me for it. After the meeting, we talk to the two of them,' Catherine said.

'You know that your involvement in the business is going to have to increase again? Sonia holds all the cards at the moment. Once she's gone, it's down to you. I'll support you, but I don't want to run this place,' Emma said.

'It will be like starting again. I think it's a good thing. After Victor died, I became a figurehead here. Don't get me wrong, I was glad for that to happen, but I feel partly responsible. Now I want to take the reins again.'

'Once we've sorted them out and we're certain there are no loopholes, I'll be having the money transferred. But now, I think we should go and put some people out of their misery and a couple of others through it, don't you?' Emma said with a smile.

Emma and Catherine entered the meeting room together, met by a frieze of expectant faces.

'This is Emma Fox,' Catherine said with the faintest hint of drama, 'and very soon she will be my partner in the Lomax Property Agency. Well. Lomax-Fox, we think,' she finished with a smile, obviously having just thought up this particular twist.

Sonia and Tony were seated well apart from each other. Emma looked from one to the other and then around the room, not wanting to linger too long on Sonia or Tony. Colour was draining from both their faces as though they were dissolving. For the first time ever, Ed did not look on the verge of speech. Malcolm was nodding insistently, checking it with himself no doubt. Emma gave Nicola Morris a long and ice-cold glance before speaking.

'I think I owe you all an explanation,' she said.

Malcolm continued nodding and Dominic Lester smiled at her, as did Ian Cameron. It rallied her to at least have some support. Jane Bennett's eyes betrayed the computer-like calculations that were going through her mind. These, she could sense, were going through every mind in the room. Questions like: What did I say her? Was I ever rude to her? Will she fire me now? Every face in the room searched for answers. Emma looked around at them again, remembering her run-in over files with Nicola, the way she had literally taken Ed in hand, the threats she had made to Ian in order to keep him quiet. In fact, of all the people, it was Tony and Sonia who had kept out of her way.

'I've known Catherine for some time,' she began. 'As I'm sure you will all have gathered, the estate agency world is not my primary business experience. I have a background in finance which I have recently retired from. I will be taking forty-nine per cent of Lomax, leaving the remaining fifty-one to Catherine. My purpose is purely to be an investor, a sleeping partner. If there are areas in which I can help, I will, but it is my intention to leave the running of the business to someone who properly understands it. Catherine.'

As Emma said Catherine's name, she looked at Sonia, whose smile had evaporated.

'The reason for not telling you the real purpose for my working here was my own idea. In my previous life, I bought a lot of companies on behalf of other people, using their money, and most of the time we knew very little about what they were getting for their money. This time, as it was my money, and because I had the chance, I decided it would be interesting to observe a company close-up and really understand what goes on there.'

Tony Wilson was sweating and eyeing Sonia edgily. Emma thought he might actually make a bolt for the door.

'I'm sorry if anyone feels somewhat misled. My real concern was to observe the business, not the people. This was a business transaction, not a psychology experiment. I've enjoyed the time here and think that the people in this agency are a great asset to it. Outside of that, I have no interest in personnel issues. As I say, I will be a sleeping partner only.'

For a second, she saw Tony Wilson relax, as though it was all going to be okay.

'I imagine you may have questions,' Catherine broke in.

There was an awkward silence.

'Perhaps,' Catherine said, 'we could reconvene this afternoon or this evening after work. As Emma has indicated, she will be taking a stake, forty-nine per cent to be exact, in the agency. Prior to her doing this, we have agreed that preferential share options for the purpose of this investment only will be distributed to everyone as a mark of recognition. I am still putting the final details together, but it is my intention that everyone will benefit from this new involvement.'

There were nods and murmurs and they all stood almost in time with each other.

'Sonia, might I have a word?' asked Catherine when she was close to her.

Tony Wilson eyed them and then cast his gaze to the floor as he and the others left the room.

Sonia sat smiling at them.

'Congratulations,' Sonia said to Emma.

'Sonia.' Emma paused. 'What can you tell me about Morgan-Court Consulting?'

Sonia swallowed tightly but said nothing.

'I've been looking at the detailed figures for Lomax and there are payments made to Morgan-Court Consulting, described as consulting fees. In the last six years, as far as I can see, the Lomax Property Agency has made payments totalling one hundred and twenty-seven thousand pounds. You are the signatory on Morgan-Court's bank account and also on Lomax. There is, let me see, eighty-seven thousand pounds in the account at the moment. Is this some sort of nest egg? A very private pension scheme?'

'I don't know what you're talking about,' Sonia said, looking at Catherine, waiting for her to intervene.

'The house Tony Wilson lives in was bought on a company basis by Lomax,' Emma continued, 'and then transferred over to Morgan-Court. At that point, the value of the house was one hundred and eight thousand pounds, although the sale price for the transfer to Morgan-Court was forty-seven thousand. I spoke to Tony's wife yesterday and she has not seen him in nearly a year. They're divorced. As far as I can tell, Tony has never paid any rent on the place and the house he lived in with his wife was sold. There's no point in looking at Catherine, Sonia, she knows all this.'

'What do you know?' Sonia asked her viciously. 'You swan in here in a suit and think you can buy the place. Do you know how long I've worked here? I've given my life to Lomax.'

'And taken a hundred and twenty thousand pounds and a house that didn't belong to you in the bargain,' Emma retorted. 'You actually started this when Victor died and the holding company dissolved, the subsidiaries de-grouped and wound up. No accounts filed, you in control, Catherine distraught. Jesus, you are a cold bitch.'

'I don't want this to collapse into a stand-up row,' Catherine said in a quiet and controlled voice.

'Do you know how much it is?' Sonia asked. 'It's less than thirty thousand pounds a year over the six years.'

'You have never been badly paid, Sonia. Victor included you in the pension fund. What more did you want?' Catherine asked.

'I always ran this place, Catherine. You know that and when Victor was alive, he knew that too. He couldn't admit it, but he knew I made a better job of it than you could. Everything you know about this business is because of me.'

'And everything she doesn't know,' Emma said.

'And when did I ever say it wasn't, Sonia?' Catherine asked, shaking her head.

'When did Tony become involved?' Emma asked, softening her tone a shade.

'He was having problems with Julia, his wife. He'd kept it hidden for so long. He was embarrassed about it, as though he'd failed when she left him. The first I knew was when he asked for advice about the property. God knows why he asked, he knows enough about the legal side. I think he wanted someone to confide in. We went from there,' Sonia said.

'And the Seychelles?' asked Emma.

Sonia gave her a surprised look and then laughed.

'We toyed with the idea of trying to open a bank account there. We didn't even know how to or what the advantage would be, but it seemed so glamorous, like a John Grisham novel. In the end, all we had was sunburn.'

'You know that I can't keep you on, don't you?' Catherine said.

'Can't or won't?' Sonia replied, cutting Emma a glance.

'Both. I could go to the police with this. But I won't do that either. I would like you to leave and to not expect me to give you a reference,' Catherine said.

'And the money?' asked Sonia.

'I think Lomax-Fox will be sending Morgan-Court a large bill for consulting services. When we get a good accountant on board, we'll see what's the most tax-efficient way of getting it back into the company, but for now, I think you should transfer it to a holding account,' said Emma. 'I'll give you the details.'

'What about Tony?' asked Sonia.

'I'll be asking him to leave also. Same terms as yourself,' Catherine said.

'And that's it, is it? This is what it comes to?' Sonia asked, looking both of them over. 'Do you think the agency will run without me?'

'It'll certainly be a lot more profitable,' Emma said.

'You really think you're hot stuff, don't you? I could tell that, the way you strutted around the office like you owned the place.' Sonia spat the words.

'Well, you were forty-nine per cent right, weren't you?' Emma replied crisply.

Sonia stood. No words left, attempting to retain her decency through a strident posture.

'We'll see how long it lasts. Lomax-Fox,' Sonia said with a snort and left the room.

'That went well,' Emma said ironically after a few moments.

'It could have gone a lot worse,' Catherine said.

'Lomax-Fox?' Emma asked.

'Yes, I thought it would piss her off,' Catherine said.

Their laughter broke the tension.

'I suppose it's all down to you now. Do you want me to attend this meeting tonight?'

'Do you want to?' Catherine asked.

'People might find it easier to speak if I'm not there. I don't want to be an oppressive presence. You might want to say that Sonia and Tony resigned, something about the investment.'

'Are you certain about this share idea?' Catherine asked. 'It's your money, but all it amounts to is you giving them some of it.'

'It's our money. A little for them is less for you. Let's see if we can do a plan based on the amount we think we will get back from Sonia. I think it will be good for morale. People will feel they have a stake or they can make a quick cash-in on them. Either way, they'll feel good.'

'What are you going to do next?' Catherine asked.

'Take a holiday,' Emma replied.

Chapter Twenty-Two

THE WATER IN which the boat lolled was so clear, they could have been floating in the air. Each time Emma had dived off the side, she had been unable to judge exactly when she was going to hit the water.

Sitting naked on a lounger, the sun drying her body, Emma Fox lay back and thought about nothing. They had been cruising on Nic Lawson's boat for nearly six weeks, letting their bodies brown and living in a pleasant haze of cool drinks and suntan lotion, and still had no plans made about what they would do when they got home, unsure of where home even was.

Matt appeared, a pair of long shorts clinging to his small waist and billowing out at the bottom. He carried a piece of paper.

'Fax for you,' he said.

He handed her the paper and removed his shorts, joining her on an adjacent chair.

Emma read it. The boat, being the property of Nic Lawson, was kitted out with hardware and could have functioned as an office. Emma had contacted Catherine and Chris, letting them know where she could be reached. Neither of them had bothered her too much. Emma read the message from Catherine. Things were going well at the Lomax Property Agency.

Just before her departure, she had told Catherine to keep the name. Lomax-Fox was ungainly and she wanted to be invisible to the business. Lomax-Fox had been a nice way of annoying Sonia Morgan.

Tony Wilson and Sonia Morgan had transferred the money they had stolen back into Lomax and then disappeared. Emma suspected more money was stashed somewhere, but the prospect of finding it did not excite her. Catherine was happy to be back in charge of the agency and Emma was happy to let her get on with things.

All of it had happened six weeks ago. Six weeks before that, she had still been at Morse Callahan on Wall Street, playing the game. Since leaving, she had heard from no one and was neither surprised nor upset by it. That was a self-enclosed world and once someone stepped outside it, they no longer existed. That world no longer existed for her either.

Six weeks earlier, she had told Matt she loved him. It was in a heated moment and they had not mentioned it since, but she had no regrets. What she had meant was, she loved him as much as it was wise to do so at that stage. Nothing had happened since then to change her mind – in fact, the feeling grew stronger the more time she spent with him. Emma was so close to him she had lost her sense of perspective with him and it pleased her.

Emma stood and went to retrieve something from her bag, something she had packed very consciously and then forgotten about completely.

Until that moment.

She stood on the deck of the boat, looking out into the clear water, the horizon almost indistinguishable as sky and sea melded into one. Emma looked at the Patek Philippe watch, her leaving present from Morse Callahan, rubbing her finger over the face of it, the glass smooth. She turned it over and looked at the inscription on the back of it.

'From your friends at MC.'

With a single fluid movement of her arm, Emma pitched the watch high and far over the side of the boat, seeing it travel in half speed through the air and then make a small splash as it hit the water.

'What was that?' asked Matt from behind her.

'Nothing,' she said, turning towards him.

BACK IN CHARGE
Mariah Greene

A woman in control. Sexy, successful, sure of herself and of what she wants, Andrea King is an ambitious account handler in a top advertising agency. Life seems sweet, as she heads for promotion and enjoys the attentions of her virile young boyfriend.

But strange things are afoot at the agency. A shake-up is ordered, with the key job of Creative Director in the balance. Andrea has her rivals for the post, but when the chance of winning a major new account presents itself, she will go to any lengths to please her client – and herself . . .

0 7515 1276 1

THE DISCIPLINE OF PEARLS
Susan Swann

A mysterious gift, handed to her by a dark and arrogant stranger. Who was he? How did he know so much about her? How did he know her life was crying out for something different? Something . . . exciting, erotic?

The pearl pendant, and the accompanying card bearing an unknown telephone number, propel Marika into a world of uninhibited sexuality, filled with the promise of a desire she had never thought possible. The Discipline of Pearls . . . an exclusive society that speaks to the very core of her sexual being, bringing with it calls to ecstasies she is powerless to ignore, unwilling to resist . . .

0 7515 1277 X

HOTEL APHRODISIA
Dorothy Starr

The luxury hotel of Bouvier Manor nestles near a spring whose mineral water is reputed to have powerful aphrodisiac qualities. Whether this is true or not, Dani Stratton, the hotel's feisty receptionist, finds concentrating on work rather tricky, particularly when the muscularly attractive Mitch is around.

And even as a mysterious consortium threatens to take over the Manor, staff and guests seem quite unable to control their insatiable thirsts . . .

0 7515 1287 7

AROUSING ANNA
Nina Sheridan

Anna had always assumed she was frigid. At least, that's what her husband Paul had always told her – in between telling her to keep still during their weekly fumblings under the covers and playing the field himself during his many business trips.

But one such trip provides the chance that Anna didn't even know she was yearning for. Agreeing to put up a lecturer who is visiting the university where she works, she expects to be host to a dry, elderly academic, and certainly isn't expecting a dashing young Frenchman who immediately speaks to her innermost desires. And, much to her delight and surprise, the vibrant Dominic proves himself able and willing to apply himself to the task of arousing Anna . . .

0 7515 1222 2

THE WOMEN'S CLUB
Vanessa Davies

Sybarites is a health club with a difference. Its owner, Julia Marquis, has introduced a full range of services to guarantee complete satisfaction. For after their saunas and facials the exclusively female members can enjoy an 'intimate' massage from one of the club's expert masseurs.

And now, with the arrival of Grant Delaney, it seems the privileged clientele of the women's club will be getting even better value for their money. This talented masseur can fulfil any woman's erotic dreams.

Except Julia's . . .

0 7515 1343 1

PLAYING THE GAME
Selina Seymour

Kate has had enough. No longer is she prepared to pander to the whims of lovers who don't love her; no longer will she cater for their desires while neglecting her own.

But in reaching this decision Kate makes a startling discovery: the potency of her sexual urge, now given free rein through her willingness to play men at their own game. And it is an urge that doesn't go unnoticed – whether at her chauvinistic City firm, at the château of a new French client, or in performing the duties of a high-class call girl . . .

0 7515 1189 7

A SLAVE TO HIS KISS
Anastasia Dubois

When her twin sister Cassie goes missing in the South
of France, Venetia Fellowes knows she must do
everything in her power to find her. But in the dusty
village of Valazur, where Cassie was last seen, a
strange aura of complicity connects those who knew
her, heightened by an atmosphere of unrestrained
sexuality.

As her fears for Cassie's safety mount, Venetia turns to
the one person who might be able to help: the
enigmatic Esteban, a study in sexual mystery whose
powerful spell demands the ultimate sacrifice . . .

0 7515 1344 X

SATURNALIA
Zara Devereux

Recently widowed, Heather Logan is concerned about
her sex-life. Even when married it was plainly
unsatisfactory, and now the prospects for sexual
fulfilment look decidedly thin.

After consulting a worldly friend, however, Heather
takes his advice and checks in to Tostavyn Grange, a
private hotel-cum-therapy centre for sexual inhibition.
Heather had been warned about their 'unconven-
tional' methods, but after the preliminary session, in
which she is brought to a thunderous climax – her first
– she is more than willing to complete the course . . .

0 7515 1342 3

DARES
Roxanne Morgan

It began over lunch. Three different women, best friends, decide to spice up their love-lives with a little extra-curricular sex. Shannon is first, accepting the dare of seducing a motorcycle despatch rider – while riding pillion through the streets of London.

The others follow, Nadia and Corey, hesitant at first but soon willing to risk all in the pursuit of new experiences and the heady thrill of trying to out-do each other's increasingly outrageous dares . . .

0 7515 1341 5

SHOPPING AROUND
Mariah Greene

For Karen Taylor, special promotions manager in an upmarket Chelsea department store, choice of product is a luxury she enjoys just as much as her customers.

Richard – virile and vain; Alan – mature and cabinet-minister-sexy; and Maxwell, the androgynous boy supermodel who's fronting her latest campaign. Sooner or later, Karen's going to have to decide between these and others. But when you're shopping around, sampling the goods is half the fun . . .

0 7515 1459 4

INSPIRATION
Stephanie Ash

They were both talented painters, but three years of struggling to make a living from art have taken the edge off Clare's relationship with her boyfriend. The temptation to add a few more colours to her palette seems increasingly attractive – and proves irresistible when she meets the enigmatic and charming Steve.

But their affair is complicated when Steve's beautiful wife asks Clare to paint his portrait as a birthday surprise. Clare is more than happy to suffer for her art – indulging in some passionate studies of her model *and* her client – but when a jealous friend gets involved the situation calls for more intimate inspiration . . .

0 7515 1489 6

DARK SECRET
Marina Anderson

Harriet Radcliffe was bored with her life. At twenty-three, her steady job and safe engagement suddenly seemed very dull. If she was to inject a little excitement into her life, she realised, now was the time to do it.

But the excitement that lay in store was beyond even her wildest ambitions. Answering a job advertisement to assist a world-famous actress, Harriet finds herself plunged into an intense, enclosed world of sexual obsession – playing an unwitting part in a very private drama, but discovering in the process more about her own desires than she had ever dreamed possible . . .

0 7515 1490 X

[ ]	Back in Charge	Mariah Greene	£4.99
[ ]	The Discipline of Pearls	Susan Swann	£4.99
[ ]	Hotel Aphrodisia	Dorothy Starr	£4.99
[ ]	Arousing Anna	Nina Sheridan	£4.99
[ ]	Playing the Game	Selina Seymour	£4.99
[ ]	The Women's Club	Vanessa Davies	£4.99
[ ]	A Slave to His Kiss	Anastasia Dubois	£4.99
[ ]	Saturnalia	Zara Devereux	£4.99
[ ]	Shopping Around	Mariah Greene	£4.99
[ ]	Dares	Roxanne Morgan	£4.99
[ ]	Dark Secret	Marina Anderson	£4.99
[ ]	Inspiration	Stephanie Ash	£4.99
[ ]	Rejuvenating Julia	Nina Sheridan	£4.99
[ ]	The Ritual of Pearls	Susan Swann	£4.99
[ ]	Midnight Starr	Dorothy Starr	£4.99
[ ]	The Pleasure Principle	Emma Allan	£4.99
[ ]	Velvet Touch	Zara Devereux	£4.99
[ ]	Acting it Out	Vanessa Davies	£4.99

X Libris offers an eXciting range of quality titles which can be ordered from the following address:

Little, Brown and Company (UK), P.O. Box 11, Falmouth, Cornwall TR10 9EN

Alternatively you may fax your order to the above address.
FAX No. 01326 317444.

Payments can be made as follows: cheque, postal order (payable to Little, Brown and Company) or by credit cards, Visa/Access. Do not send cash or currency. UK customers and B.F.P.O. please allow £1.00 for postage and packing for the first book, plus 50p for the second book, plus 30p for each additional book up to a maximum charge of £3.00 (7 books plus).

Overseas customers including Ireland please allow £2.00 for the first book plus £1.00 for the second book, plus 50p for each additional book.

NAME (Block Letters) _____

_____

ADDRESS _____

_____

_____

☐ I enclose my remittance for _____

☐ I wish to pay by Access/Visa card

Number _____ Card Expiry Date _____